THE WAR OF THE FAE

A CONTEMPORARY SCIENCE FANTASY

RETURN OF THE FAE
BOOK FOUR

MARTY C. LEE

Bookaholics Press

Book design, cover, and publication by Bookaholics Press LLC
Edited by Martha Rasmussen
Author photograph by Melissa C. Baxter

ISBN-13: 978-1-950230-45-7 (epub)
978-1-950230-46-4 (paperback)
978-1-950230-47-1 (large print)
978-1-950230-48-8 (hardcover)
978-1-950230-68-6 (audio)

Published by Bookaholics Press LLC
Provo, Utah bookaholicspress@gmail.com

Contact the author at MCLeeBooks.com

Dedicated to those who have been affected by wars and natural disasters around the world. Though I attribute fictional causes in this book, I yearn for real-life peace and safety for you as deeply as any of my imaginary characters do for themselves.

Contents

AUTHOR'S NOTE

While I have been meticulous to real life detail and science in some places, in others I could not find information, or changed things for the sake of the story or to protect real people, or simply made mistakes. Most of all, please remember this is a work of fiction. The characters are completely imaginary.

Academy Maps

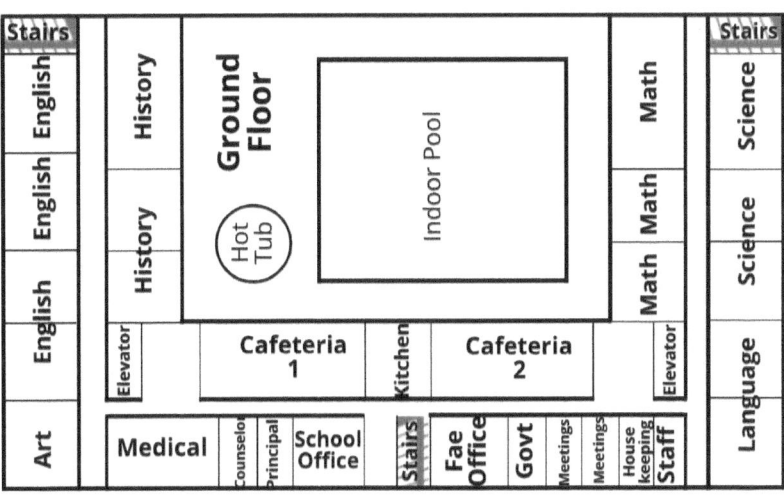

Ground Floor

		Ground Floor				
Stairs						Stairs
English	History	Ground Floor	Indoor Pool	Math	Science	
English				Math		
English	History	Hot Tub		Math	Science	
English	Elevator			Math	Science	
Art	Elevator	Cafeteria 1	Kitchen	Cafeteria 2	Elevator	Language
	Medical	Counselor	Principal	School Office	Stairs	Fae Office	Govt	Meetings	Meetings	House keeping	Staff

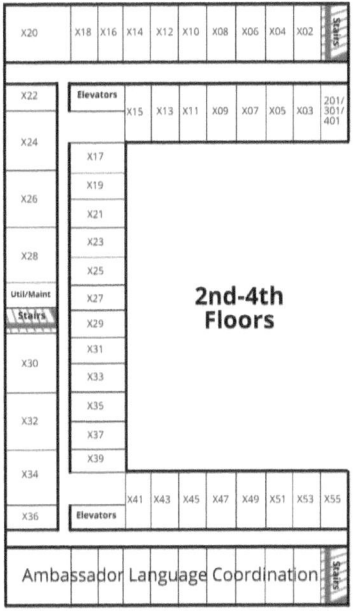

2nd-4th Floors

Rooms (top row, right to left): Stairs, X02, X04, X06, X08, X10, X12, X14, X16, X18

Left column: X20, X22, X24, X26, X28, Util/Maint, Stairs, X30, X32, X34, X36

Inner column: Elevators, X15, X13, X11, X09, X07, X05, X03, 201/301/401

Inner rooms: X17, X19, X21, X23, X25, X27, X29, X31, X33, X35, X37, X39

Bottom row: Elevators, X41, X43, X45, X47, X49, X51, X53, X55

Ambassador Language Coordination — Stairs

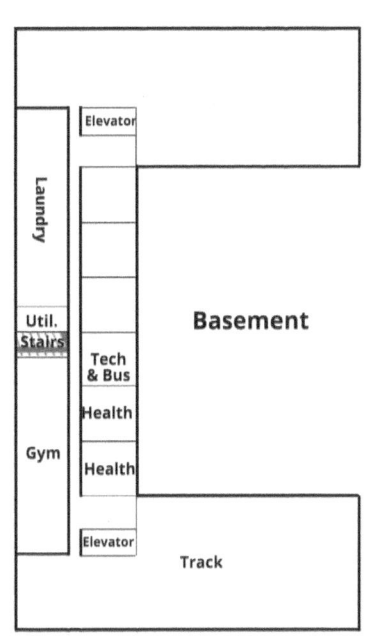

Basement

Laundry, Util., Stairs, Gym

Elevator

Tech & Bus, Health, Health

Elevator

Track

PROLOGUE

IN WHICH FATHER MOVES IN

JUNE 10, 2023
  Allentown, Pennsylvania, United States of America, Earth

ZAKITI PUSHED Father's wheelchair up the ramp and into the tall building. Light shone from every window, illuminating the night.

"This is my school, Father," she said. "Mostly, the students live here, but there are some family rooms on the staff floor. I already picked one for us."

Us. Father was back. For nearly an Earth year, they'd been separated while she learned about their new world and he navigated the rest of the Fae spaceships from the asteroid belt to Earth. Now the fleet was landing around the world, and they could live together again. The extra suites would be filled by adult fae moving in for language lessons.

"Mmm," Father mumbled, looking around him with wide eyes.

She couldn't blame him; when she had first arrived, she had been equally stunned. She grinned and headed for the elevator, hitting the button for the third floor. Once she got Father settled, she needed to move her few belongings from the second floor, which housed the girls like the fourth floor did the boys. Gaby would need a new roommate, since Freya and Jin had both graduated. Even with two-thirds of the students and families gone and four-person rooms becoming two-person, the school still wouldn't leave Gaby alone, since roommates improved the acquisition and practice of language.

The earliest fae to land on Earth had been the youngest fae on the ship. With the addition of human students, the first Fae-Earth school was established, cross-teaching languages and culture. Now the initial graduates were serving as interpreters and ambassadors around the world.

As the elevator bumped into motion, Father clutched the arms of the wheelchair.

"Don't worry," Zak said. "The human contrivances are very reliable."

At least as long as Freya wasn't touching them. That was a little unfair; her old roommate wasn't the only fae whose magic interfered with human technology, just the one who seemed to have the most dramatic mishaps.

"This is a contrivance?" Father asked. "Not magic?"

"The humans claim they don't have magic," she said, "though some of their contrivances seem like it."

His room would seem like magic to him, too. The elevator dinged, and the doors opened. She pushed the wheelchair down the hall to the assigned suite and explained how everything worked. The closet and dressers for clothes the humans would help him get. The private hygiene room with bathing facilities, running water, and no compost smell. Lights that weren't pixies and worked for anyone with a touch of a finger. The clear window that looked out at the city with its millions of non-magical lights.

The suite had two small bedrooms, each with a single bed, dresser, and desk. No longer would she have to share a room.

"Tomorrow," Zak said, "I'll show you the pool and physical therapy options, as well as the classroom where you'll learn English."

"I don't understand why we're staying here." Father kept his voice low, but his worry was clear.

"The newcomers' hotel is pretty full," Zak said, "and I assumed you wanted to be with me."

Had their separation ruined their loving familiarity? Or did he think she no longer needed him?

Father clutched her hand. "I do want to be with you. Why are you staying here?"

"I'll still be in school for a year or two," she said, "and I'm helping with the ambassadors when I'm not in classes or working on my contrivances. It's a lot more convenient to be on campus instead of needing a ride twice a day to and from another building."

Father sighed and tightened his grip on her fingers. "That's not what I meant. Now that I'm here, why are you staying around the humans? You are meddling in affairs that don't concern you. Why are you here in public instead of finding a safe retreat? And you are dressing like a girl where people can see you."

After a lifetime of fearing the highborn and sixteen years of hiding her gender to prevent her from being murdered like her grandmother, his concern was understandable. Reaching behind her to pull over a chair, Zak sat and patted his hand. "Things are different now, Father. We have new allies in the humans, and the lords will lose their power. On Earth, girls are as important as boys, and we can do any job we want. There are many female contrivers and female warriors."

Father snorted.

"I can introduce you to some," she offered.

The school principal was a professional warrior when she wasn't taking care of the school. Gaby's mother wasn't a contriver, but she was a scientist, which was close enough to hold interesting conversations. And Alex was both an impressive amateur warrior and a scientist-in-training who loved the stars.

Zak patted his hand again, then pulled free and rummaged through the dresser for some nightclothes. "I showed you how to use the shower, and there's already a chair and towels in there. Once you're clean, I have a snack for you, and then we can go to bed and talk more in the morning."

After nearly a year in a small barge with limited water, a bath was definitely the first thing he needed. She had been breathing through her mouth to avoid some of his overpowering stench, but she was reaching her limits of tolerance. Had she smelled this bad when she landed? Ugh!

And since food had been rationed on their spaceship for months before it reached Earth, and had surely been rationed on the barge while retrieving the rest of the fleet, a snack would soothe his stomach so he could sleep comfortably. Though he would eventually have to get used to the odd human food, she had selected only semi-familiar fruits for tonight.

Tomorrow, there would be a tour of the school, an introduction to the human leaders, and the first of many lessons in Earth language and culture and technology. Well, not quite the first lesson, since she had talked to him about many things while she worked on the contrivance. But they hadn't had a chance to discuss how much he had heard. She had so many things to show him!

"Oh, we definitely need to talk," Father said. "We need to make plans to leave here and find a safe place to live."

She took a deep breath and stepped into the bathroom to leave the pajamas on the counter. "I'm not leaving, Father. You helped with the journey here, which was the most important thing you could do to save our people. Now we must earn our home, and I can help with that. I want to make a difference in this world."

"You're a girl," Father said, "and a commoner. How can you make any difference?"

She flinched. "I *am* a girl. I thought that didn't matter to you."

He had trained her in navigation and contriving himself, and fought to have her accepted as an apprentice while she was still considered a child, regardless of being the fleet's second-best navigator.

"I didn't mean—" Father slumped in his chair.

Zak straightened her shoulders. "I want to help Gil and the others negotiate the treaty. I'm the closest thing to an expert for questions about technology — contrivances. I'm sure you can catch up in a few months — conjunctions."

She wasn't one of the chosen ambassadors due to her age, but she was the most expert on the similarities and differences between human and fae technology. The fae had very few contrivances or contrivers, and she was currently the only one who could use both technologies together. Father would soon be the second one, hopefully.

A year ago, she had never imagined English would be so natural that she would use Earth words instead of her native terms. A year ago, she talked to very few people and spent most of her time in isolation, hiding from possible encounters with the lords who would kill her for being a female contriver. A year ago, she was thinking of herself as a boy so even her thoughts wouldn't betray her.

So much had changed, and yet they still hadn't accomplished their goal. Though the young ambassadors had spread across Earth, the treaty was still to come. So close, and yet too far.

"We don't need to stay here for you to teach me the alien contrivances," Father said.

"Until the treaty is signed," Zak said, "we don't have permission to wander off and choose a home. And most of the humans just found out about us a few days ago. They aren't yet used to the idea, so random encounters are not safe."

In fact, their secret had come out a little early and a lot more dramatically than planned, thanks to a rebel.

"There must be some way," Father insisted. "If nothing else, we can hide from the humans as well as the lords."

Enough. She was done hiding. If he wouldn't help her, she would help herself.

Zak pushed the wheelchair to the bathroom doorway. "Go bathe, Father. I'm staying here. I want to learn more, and this is the best place for that. And I want to help with the treaty, and I enjoy being a girl. In fact, I think I will stay in Gaby's room."

Gaby was willing to teach Zak to speak Spanish and French and to help her with math and science.

"You can have this room to yourself," she continued, "or choose a new roommate. Or if you want to change buildings, I'll arrange it. If you stay here, I will see you every single day, and if you leave, I'll visit frequently. But I'm living here."

She draped her arms around his neck from behind the chair, then dropped a kiss on his cheek. "Your snack is on the desk. I'll see you in the morning."

"Zak!" Father struggled to move his chair, but it was stuck in the doorway.

"And that reminds me," Zak said, "I'm known as Zee here. I'll send someone to help you move your chair after your shower."

There were plenty of strong arms available, and he clearly needed a little time to adjust. But she wouldn't change her mind.

Marching out, she shut the door behind her. She wasn't the same person she had been on the spaceship, and she had no intention of hiding again. She had contrivances to create and achievements to reach. Father could help — she hoped he would — but with or without him, she had plans.

CHAPTER 1

REACTIONS

JUNE 12, 2023

AFTER CHECKING her phone for any text updates, Gabriela Ortiz clicked to the next social media post. Her family was coming to take her home for the summer, but they weren't to the school yet, so she might as well keep working. Several TVs on the basement wall broadcast news — or drama — about the fae, one television per channel, while human students helped interpret for their fae classmates. Replays of Saturday's landing ran almost constantly, with commentators analyzing every splash into the ocean and every emergence of the fae. More people monitored computers and tablets set on long tables. On Friday, the new ambassadors had departed for their posts in countries around the world. Those left behind were trying desperately to keep up with the flood of worldwide discussions.

Ever since Alex and U.N. Fitch and several of the fae had gone on TV last Thursday to announce the existence of the fae and the imminent landing of the fleet, the internet, radio, and television had been going crazy. More people had watched the broadcast of the fleet's beginning descent than had watched the Artemis launch. Apparently, aliens were more exciting than another moon mission.

Sadly, no amateur telescope was strong enough to see the silver fae spaceship that was permanently parked on the moon. Like the ships still being emptied, it could not survive a trip through the atmosphere. But *New Kunisu* had been the first to arrive a year ago, and the last of its passengers had already landed.

"Yeah, here's another group," Gaby said to the fae working with her. "This one is pro-fae, though there are some pretty funny ideas of what you can do."

"Like what?" Chantelle peered over her shoulder at the screen.

Unlike Freya, the siren could touch technology without frying it, but she wasn't very comfortable with computers. Or reading, since the elves kept that secret from the commoners to keep them in submission.

"Carry willing people to a perfect land where they will live forever." Gaby omitted the part about fae lovers, temporarily thankful for Chantelle's poor reading skills.

From the other side of the table, Tom snorted. "If we had a perfect land, why would we come here?"

The naga was practicing his fighting skills, or maybe just exercising, though his motions looked vaguely like martial arts moves to Gaby's inexperienced eyes.

"I like Earth," Gaby replied mildly.

He stopped exercising and bowed. "Apologies. I did not mean to slight your world. It is simply not what we are used to."

"I understand," Gaby said.

Curiosity burned about the worlds the fae had left behind in their dash for safety, but their mutual vocabulary still lacked a lot, especially in more technical areas or where there were no real equivalents. She would have to stay curious for now.

Gaby clicked on the next post. After reading it to herself, she moved on without repeating it aloud. She'd already learned the hard way that sharing the most antagonistic comments only upset the fae.

Now that the ships that could travel through the atmosphere had all landed, the world continued to watch the unloading of the few remaining in orbit, though little could be seen until the barges reached lower airspace. At that point, who could blame them? The sight of dragon-pulled barges flying through the sky was like a fairy tale, even before they landed and released fae of every legendary type.

Fae-identification had become a worldwide sport, with cultures competing to see who could first find mythological equivalents to the real fae. A few were surprisingly accurate, but most legends differed in at least one significant way. For instance, Chantelle was a siren with no mermaid tail who did not enthrall men or kill them. Her voice was mesmerizing, but her magic song helped others remember and learn. U.N.'s already rapid acquisition of Fae had doubled and tripled when Chantelle sang him vocabulary and grammar lessons. The fae healers were "vampires" who tasted blood to diagnose illness, not drank it by the pint. And the dragons didn't breathe fire or eat people, being solar-powered and normally living in space.

Some public responses were hugely supportive of the immigration — though not necessarily any more accurate than the one she'd just read to Chantelle — but others called for the equivalent of the Salem witch trials, with the fae at the stakes. Many countries had demonstrators marching for attention, frequently across the street from a group marching for the opposite viewpoint. "Send the fae back where they belong" faced "Fae lives matter" and "Pick me, I'm available."

Gaby wasn't the only one monitoring the situation, of course. Not only were many of the students helping the fae, but the U.S. government had an entire new task force to squelch the worst rumors and track threats. Periodically, the watchers left the basement screens to bring notes to those tabulating statistics and marking problems to pass on to the government or the fae ambassadors.

More quickly than the fae could read over her shoulder, Gaby clicked through the internet, scribbling her own notes to be passed on. Social media groups and blogs were as busy as the streets, with even more hypotheses flying around the world. Despite the broad coverage still going on, a fair number of people thought the fae were a hoax or a movie marketing stunt, and groups had already sprung up to try to discover filming locations and if extras were being hired.

Others voted for various conspiracies ranging from "they were always here but hidden" to "mad science gone wrong" to "wiped the

President's mind and will conquer the world." Since a psycho had tried to kill a fae last year and injured Alex in the process, everyone was taking the conspiracy theories seriously. The school security guards had stopped wearing civilian clothes and returned to their military dress to convince surprise visitors the campus was still off-limits. Only Ms. Maxwell, the military-assigned principal, maintained her frilly, feminine disguise to throw people off balance, including the patriarchal fae.

Gaby's phone buzzed, and a text popped up from Mamá.

Almost there.

"My family's here," Gaby said. She signed out and beckoned another student to take her place. Quickly, she forwarded the text to a preset group of her friends.

"Say hello to your mother for us," Chantelle said, and Tom nodded.

Mamá had been the earliest science advisor to the fae, though many scientists were now involved.

"Sure." Gaby stuffed her phone into her pocket and raced for the stairs.

Her bags were already packed and ready to go. Most of the other students going home for the summer had left last week, and she missed her family so much it hurt. They'd kept their promise to visit, but once a month was simply not enough. Those visits had all taken place off-campus, since the school was top secret until a few days ago. Ever since the announcement, she'd been fielding crazy texts from her big brothers. Now she could finally introduce all her brothers to her friends. Well, the ones who were still at school, anyway. Some had graduated and moved out.

By the time she reached the lobby, her friends were pelting down the hall from every direction. Alex and U.N. raced each other, laughing despite Alex's unfair height advantage. With Miknon flying above him, Gil bounced from the principal's office and grabbed the wall to swing himself around the corner. Even Zee hurried her usual sedate pace. They screeched to a halt at the front door and waited for Gaby to go first.

Gaby opened the door and peered through the rain until she saw the familiar van. Unable to wait longer, she dashed into the cool downpour, reaching the vehicle as it parked. Mamá jumped from the passenger side and squeezed Gaby hard enough to force the air from her lungs. The van doors all flew open to a loud chorus of greetings.

"Everyone inside." Mamá let go of Gaby with one hand so she could drag Ed toward the school.

Mark took Gaby's other hand, splashing through puddles as they hurried. Papá grabbed Bear and ran, ducking his head against the wet. The twins raced ahead of everyone and held open the doors. The whole family skidded inside, laughing and shaking out wet hair before burying Gaby in hugs.

"I missed you," Ed whispered, swinging Gaby's hand.

"I missed you more," Bear shouted. He wiggled under Gaby's arm and wrapped both arms around her waist.

"Eh, who needs sisters?" Andy teased, reaching over Ed to rub Gaby's head.

"Not me." Manny winked at Gaby.

"Oh!" Mark glanced sideways and froze.

Gaby turned to see what had caught his attention. Gil bounced on his toes and waved, smiling broadly enough to show his too-sharp teeth. So much for a subtle introduction.

"These are my friends." Gaby started with the easiest. "Alex will be a senior, like the twins." She turned and pointed to each one, though they were similar enough to be frequently confused. "Andy and Manny."

Andres, the drama star, had the more recent haircut, and Armando, the sports enthusiast, was a little more muscular. Fortunately, the decision of introducing with nicknames versus real names was easily decided by fae culture. Her big brothers squared their shoulders and stood taller, quickly brushing their dark hair farther from their dark eyes.

Alex grinned cheerfully and shook their hands. "Nice to meet you."

She was almost as tall as the twins, though considerably more slim, with light brown hair and hazel eyes. She moved like an athlete and had a black belt in judo.

"U.N. is her brother," Gaby continued. "He's fourteen, so right between me and Mark, but he's in my grade." She pushed Marquez gently forward.

Forehead wrinkled in thought, Mark shook hands with U.N. "Wait, how are you a sophomore?"

"They made me do it," U.N. said. "No worries." His long blond bangs covered one gray eye, and his left hand held a ring frisbee instead of the usual book. As skinny as Alex, he was even a little shorter than Mark.

"He's in charge of the language program," Gaby said.

"Who is?" Papá asked. "Watch your antecedents, please."

"U.N. is." Gaby raised her hands in a "what can you do?" gesture.

"Really," Mamá said. "He's the best Fae interpreter we have."

"Fae." Eduardo dragged out the word and stared at the other three in the hall. "Does that mean fairies?"

"Sort of," Gaby said. "Miknon is an actual fairy, or pixie. She'll be a senior, too."

From Gil's shoulder, Miknon waved, not offering to shake hands for the cultural reasons or because she was only a foot tall and handshakes could be dangerous. Pale blue skin and dark blue hair, eyes, and feathered wings contrasted with a pink blouse and pink and white flounced skirt.

"Fae refers to other mythological creatures, too." Gaby glanced at Zee and turned to Gil instead. Though a little scarier, he was a lot less patient and looked like he would explode with excitement at any moment. "Gil is a werewolf. No, he won't bite you."

Despite the normal fae reluctance to touch, Gil thrust out his hand, grinning broadly. "Nice to meet you."

His light blue eyes shone brightly in his absolutely black face, and his pointed ears wiggled through his straight black hair cut human-style. Along with the side-slit skirt that approximated a traditional fae kilt, he wore sandals and a t-shirt Alex must have picked, since it had an astronomy joke on it. Mamá, already familiar with him, shook his hand and admired his shirt. It took Papá another moment to gather courage, but he finally held out his hand.

Gil shook it gently. "You have raised your daughter well."

"Gracias," Papá muttered weakly.

"Me, too," Bear demanded.

Kneeling to be closer to the nine-year-old's height, Gil offered his hand again. "What's your name?"

"Bear." Bear giggled as he shook hands. "I mean, Bernardo. I'm not a real bear."

Gil nodded solemnly. "I see. That's good to know. Bears are bigger than wolves."

Bear covered his mouth with both hands and giggled again. Whenever he finally outgrew his silliness, Gaby would miss it.

While Gil stood, Gaby pulled Zee closer. "This is Zee. She's a gremlin and specializes in technology and how it works with magic."

"Good morning," Zee whispered.

Her green ears turned orange, and her hand shook as she extended it. Gil touched her softly on the back, as supportive as always.

"Are you my age?" Eduardo shook hands without prompting. "I'm eleven."

"I'm seventeen," Zee said, "a little older than Gil."

They had held her birthday party last week, the first she'd ever had, and Gaby had to explain everything as they went. Skeptically, Ed examined her from head to toe. They were about the same height, though Zee's features were more mature. Her green hair was braided around her head like Miknon's, and her pointed ears were still a distressed orange. Unlike Gil, her ears did not wiggle. She wore ordinary jeans and sneakers and a feminine t-shirt.

"So," U.N. said, "anyone for a game of frisbee?"

"In the rain?" Mamá protested.

"In the basement gym," U.N. explained.

Since the school was an old hotel, the amenities were surprisingly good.

"Yes!" The twins high-fived each other.

"I have things to do." Miknon waved and flew away. Hardly surprising, since a frisbee could knock her from the air and break every bone in her body.

"I want to talk for a while," Gaby said.

Zee narrowed her eyes at Gil. "Are you going to trample me this time?"

"No, I promise." The werewolf bowed, one hand over his heart.

Zee sniffed. "Okay."

She led the way to the stairs, with the Fitches and all of Gaby's brothers following. Gil ducked into a room and emerged a minute later as a huge black wolf with a silver chain around his neck, bounding after the others with toenails clicking on the floor.

"Wait," Papá said. Too late. The wolf was already gone.

"Don't worry." Mamá patted his arm. "He won't hurt them. The legends are all wrong."

Papá whined like a steam-kettle but followed Gaby and Mamá to a room where they could visit. All three crowded onto the couch to be as close as possible.

That was when Gaby finally realized one member of the family was missing. "Where's Grand-mère?

Mamá groaned. "She is not dealing well with the announcement of the fae."

"Either it is a hoax," Papá quoted, "and everyone is stupid, or it is real and Gabrielle is a traitor."

The French version of Gaby's name made the source immediately evident. Grand-mère thought she was a traitor? Gaby sucked in a breath and squeezed her eyes shut.

Mamá elbowed him. "You didn't have to say that."

"She deserves to know." Papá stuck out his chin. "And I'm afraid it is worse than that."

"Worse?" Gaby croaked. "How can it be worse?"

Putting her arm around Gaby, Mamá took a deep breath. "We don't think you should come home for the summer. Give Grand-mère a chance to calm down and get used to everything."

"Oh, no!" The tears could no longer be held back, and Gaby fumbled in her pocket for a clean tissue. She'd been waiting impatiently for months and frantically for the last week, and now she couldn't breathe.

"We hope she just needs some time," Papá said. "But now that the secret is out, the family will visit more often."

Gaby scrubbed at her face. "It's not the same."

"I know, cariña, I know." He pulled her close and hummed softly, like he used to do at bedtime. "Lo siento."

It was all Grand-mère's fault. Her fault Gaby had to go away to school in the first place, and now her fault she couldn't go home again. Why did Grand-mère have to be so mean?

Her parents let her cry until she stopped on her own, then asked for a tour. In the basement, they gathered the boys and dragged them upstairs for lunch in the cafeteria. Alex sat across from Gaby and divided her time between devouring her lasagna and watching Gaby pick at her food.

Mamá and Papá finished eating and left to talk to other adults and collect the boys. Gaby mashed her cake flat and wished it was Grand-mère.

Alex folded her arms on the table. "Okay, spill it. What's wrong?"

Gaby pressed her lips together to hold back more tears. "I have to stay here all summer."

Because Grand-mère thought she was worthless, or worse.

"Ah, I see. That's rough." Alex tilted her head sideways and narrowed her eyes. "Would it help if you had something to do?"

"I've been helping in the newsroom," Gaby said.

"Yes," Alex said, "but I have a special job for you, if you want. Since I'll begin the summer session of college in a couple of weeks, that gives us barely enough time to start training you."

Gaby abandoned her fork in her smashed cake and leaned forward. "Okay, now I'm intrigued."

Alex winked. "Knew you would be. I'm sure you heard we have a host of new experts dropping in all the time to question the fae."

"Yes, of course."

"That includes a new math and science expert." Alex raised her eyebrows as if that explained everything.

"Mamá has to go back to her real work tracking asteroids," Gaby defended.

"Yes, yes," Alex said. "She has done an excellent job, and nobody thinks less of her. But the new scientist doesn't speak any Fae and already tried to insist on shaking everyone's hand at the first meeting."

"Oh, no," Gaby said.

Since a touch and a real name gave fae thought-mages the ability to read minds, the fae habitually went by nicknames and avoided touch.

The commoners might settle for thinking the scientist rude, but the elves could take revenge in magical ways.

"Right," Alex agreed. "Bad news. So we really need someone appointed specifically to him. Our emphasis on languages so far has been on daily living, not math and hard science. Because you've been helping Zee, you know more math and tech words than any of us."

"Why don't you ask Zee to do it?" Gaby asked. "Obviously, she knows more Fae than I do."

"But she knows less English," Alex said, "and she doesn't know much about Earth science. I have no objection to you getting Zee's help, but you should be the main interpreter for this. Not only will you help the scientist, but we need someone to translate back into terms the fae can understand. What do you say?"

"I'm no astronomer like you and Mamá," Gaby said.

Alex waved her hand. "Not necessary. You'll be fine. You won't have time to be bored, though there's no such thing as too busy to miss your family. Sorry." Her lips turned down briefly before she smiled again. "So, will you do it?"

Gaby nodded. "You're right; it's better than being bored."

Alex reached across the table and collected Gaby's tray. "Since your cake is dead, how about reviewing vocabulary right now?"

"As soon as I say goodbye to my family." Papá was already beckoning her from across the room.

"I'll be in Maxwell's office." Alex headed to drop off the trays.

Gaby hurried toward her family with a lighter heart. Between more frequent visits and something important to do, maybe this summer wouldn't be miserable.

Chapter 2

In Which News is Mixed

July 3, 2023

Whistling cheerfully, Gil bounded up three flights of stairs and through the school halls. Humans waved at him, but most of the fae flinched as he passed. Fae music was magic, always and ever before, and thus suspicious no matter how many humans played it with no effect. But his older foster brother had taught him how to whistle, and Gil found it a perfect way to express his good mood. The ambassadors had been working on peace terms for three weeks, and more and more agreements were being reached. Success was around the corner, and then Gil could finally relax.

The almost fifteen years of space travel to reach their new home had required nothing of him but his assigned chores, leaving plenty of time to play with his friends. But everything changed when the king died and the prince was nearly assassinated. At first, Gil just helped the prince survive, but when lords tried to execute Gil's sister for spying, he had to save her. And as long as they were escaping to Earth, he was the fae's only chance to negotiate for a home instead of having to fight for one.

He'd spent three days traveling in a box barely larger than his body, two weeks struggling with vocabulary to establish basic safety and refugee status with aliens, and a year learning the language and culture necessary to make a treaty. Now almost all the fae had landed, and the responsibility wasn't all on his shoulders. Gil could stop worrying about the tentative peace breaking apart. He added an extra bounce to his step and trill to his whistle before sliding to a stop at one of the translation rooms.

Gil's friend Nash was perched on a low table in front of the desk, since no chair would fit the little hydra well. The human student acting as his secretary-translator sat before the computer, rapidly typing as Nash spoke in a mix of English, Fae, and the Russian he learned from a roommate last year. Sometimes all at once, because nine heads meant he could make corrections without pausing. Now one head bobbed at Gil while the others divided their attention between the paper on the desk and the human typing.

"Okay, that's all for now," Nash finished. "Come in, Gil."

Without being asked, the human tossed several fruits to Nash and poured water into a bowl on the desk. After nodding at Gil, he returned to the computer, reading emails and either replying or marking them to deal with later.

Gil flopped in a chair. "Everything okay here, Nate?"

Around humans, he always used the assigned nicknames as carefully as he stuck to use-names or titles among the fae. Names were power, and calling Nashuja by his full name in the presence of anyone else at all would destroy trustworthiness and friendship in a moment. Revealing a *highborn's* true name was usually a death sentence. With any luck, that would eventually change on Earth, either naturally or by law, but until then, old habits were wise.

But humans wanted names to use, so Shalla and Mak-swill had assigned names to most of the fae to avoid them freaking out about the scary humans knowing even their use-names.

"We're working on it," Nash said. "Two and Abe are reporting riots in Japan."

Touji Kihara was the human side of the ambassador team for Japan, and Ashur, known as Abe Brown, was the fae half.

"Everywhere is." Gil sighed. "I suspect it will take a while for the humans to get used to us."

Nash stuck out half his tongues.

"You're here to calm everyone," Gil said. "Tell them everything is okay."

"Oh, what a great idea." Nash had learned human sarcasm as well as he had English and Russian.

Gil laughed. "Okay, okay. Anything else you want me to report?"

"Abe thinks maybe mind-touching is being used," Nash said. "Humans are changing direction in the middle of a sentence and saying things they weren't saying before."

"What does Two think about that?"

Nash rippled a neck in his version of a shrug. "He says diplomacy makes humans rephrase sometimes."

"Hmm." Gil swung his feet. "I'll report it anyway. Anything else?"

"Not yet," Nash said ominously.

They chatted for a few more minutes, then Gil headed to the next support team. As of yet, there were no interpreters for Arabic, Hindi, or any of the African languages. Well, not exactly. They had someone who spoke Hausa but had decided sending a troll among the humans would be too alarming. Without him in the field, there was no point to having an office for backup. Africa must make do with English and French speakers.

Most of the ambassadors had nothing concrete to report, though they also felt nervous. The Mandarin team, however, had more bad news.

The human student of the pair, unfamiliar to Gil, said, "Jin says the highborn are talking to Freya about squashing the 'rebellions.' We're having trouble convincing them the humans are just talking."

"They aren't blindly accepting what the highborn say," Wes said. "You know how the lords feel about that."

In fact, Wes was one of the highborn who still hadn't entirely conquered that attitude. As support staff, Gil and the others could monitor him, but nobody was willing to send him into the field. Freya had adjusted a little better and was partnered with her prior roommate, Jinyuan Chung.

Wes's coworker folded her arms. "Compliance isn't really a human trait. Remember history class."

"It's a fae trait," Wes retorted.

"Okay, stop it." Gil forced his voice to remain calm despite his growing worry. "The humans are just expressing themselves. There's no war. We have to expect a few weeds in the garden, but it will work out. Keep trying. And please try to work together."

The girl pursed her lips and furrowed her brows but said nothing. Wes sneered. Gil sighed and moved down to the third floor.

The fae and human interpreters working on Portuguese, Spanish, French, and German were all fine and working hard, though they reported some of the newly landed highborn sending messages directly to them instead of going through the ambassadors. And some of the requests sounded a little suspicious.

"If they aren't going through the trained ambassadors," Gil explained, "I expect to run into cultural and communication barriers. Inform the ambassadors so they can deal with it on that end, please." He smiled as if not worried but added the problem to his mental list to report.

On his way back to the stairs, he ran across a servant mopping the floors, back turned toward Gil. The glimpse of familiar white hair hit him like a blow. Gil backed around the corner and leaned against the wall. He sucked in a desperate breath and held it for a moment before letting it go.

Gil no longer had a twin, and half his heart was missing. R— His bro — The traitor had been outcast, stricken from fae society for trying to incite war between humans and fae. Now a slave, he had no rights. His name was never to be mentioned, and he no longer belonged to any family.

Gil squeezed his eyes shut against the burn of tears and concentrated on slow breaths. The chatter of voices echoed down the hall, then jolted silent when they drew near. In a moment, two fae rounded the corner. After looking over their shoulders, they returned to their conversation, but in whispers.

Steeling himself, Gil peeled away from the wall and forced his feet to carry him around the corner. The pale-faced shifter was leaning on the

THE WAR OF THE FAE 21

mop, frowning and staring down the hall. A glowing thumbprint shone in the middle of his forehead, marking his banishment. Gil staggered past him, clenching his fists to avoid reaching out. The outcast flinched and turned his back, scrubbing at a spot on the floor. Unable to breathe, Gil kept walking until he entered the stairwell, then he collapsed on the steps and wept silent, hot tears, pressing his hands to his aching chest.

If only he had stopped his br— the traitor faster, they might still be a family.

The clatter of feet on the stairs made him jump up and scrub at his face. Head turned a little toward the wall, he hurried downward, passing the other people without looking at them.

On the third floor, the first three offices were empty. Not surprising. As the king's Companion, his chief warrior and bodyguard, Taras still spent much of his time either training or arranging for subtle protection for the disguised prince. The healer, Merodach, kept the fae healthy and helped them regain their strength after years in space. Mother, who had worked with the leaders starting when Grandsire was the king's Companion, mostly worked with Alexandria to help the new fae acclimate culturally to Earth.

Gil poked his head into the next office, which held Shalla, the king's housekeeper. On Earth, that apparently meant little more than cleaning, but she had run the king's entire household, managing servants, inventories, schedules, training, and more. Besides the king's secretary, she knew more about the king's business than anyone. Those five were the leaders of the common fae and responsible for day-to-day operations for all the fae, including the highborn. The lords certainly couldn't be bothered to do the hard work. Before the secretary landed, the other four had covered for Shar's supposed death and passed on his decisions when they weren't handling everything themselves.

Shalla's office whiteboard was blank, since her new reading skills were still rusty, but her memory was exemplary. With help to transcribe, she accomplished as much as anyone. And it seemed Gil's younger foster brother was helping today.

Ian looked up from his notebook and smiled. "Hey, Gil. What's up?"

Shalla looked at the ceiling, then shook her head with a grin at her misunderstanding.

"Just checking on everyone," Gil said.

"We're fine," Shalla said in her quiet, musical voice.

"Chantelle and I are just discussing a few things," Ian said.

"Then let me update you both at the same time." Gil shut the door and quickly rehearsed the problems the translators had reported.

Shalla closed her eyes and hummed softly while Ian typed the notes.

"I'll tell Nik," Gil said, "but Tom, Miles, and Mother are gone, so you'll want to talk later."

"Of course," Shalla said. "I'll let you know what we decide."

Ian checked his watch. "I'll wait to email the translators until you have a plan. I'd better get moving. I have a stack of curriculum notes to deal with."

He was in charge of the entire language program, though not the political issues, and he was always busy. They rarely got time for a long game of frisbee nowadays.

"Okay," Gil said. He scanned the room, noting the usual pitcher of water and basket of snacks. After a year of short rations on the king's spaceship — two years for the latecomers — the humans were being very careful to keep the fae well fed. Shalla had been on Earth for nearly a year and was no longer disturbingly thin. Fortunately, the rest of the fleet had avoided the disasters that caused starvation on *New Kunisu*, so most of the fae were landing in better condition, other than the unavoidable brittle bones and weak muscles.

"I'll see you at home, U.N." Gil ruffled Ian's hair, then headed to the next room, shutting the door as he entered.

"Hey, Nik, Shaun. How do you fare?" he asked.

This Nik was not human and not his foster brother. The duplicate short-name was a little confusing for everyone, but no one who knew his full name would dream of calling him Nikandros. In fact, most of the fae called him merely "the king's secretary" instead of risking disrespect.

The short pukel turned his wheelchair away from the wall-mounted whiteboard that was covered in Fae writing. "Greetings, Gil. We are almost ready to send our updates to the ambassadors."

"Excellent!" Gil said. "I'll send in a translator as soon as I find one."

Though the king himself had taught Nik to read Fae, he spoke very little English so far and could read even less.

Sharrukin raised a notebook. "I have the notes already translated. A typist will be sufficient."

"Even easier." Gil winked at the prince, hiding his amusement at the role reversal. If Shar weren't still in hiding, Nik would be *his* secretary. "But I'm afraid I have more work for you."

Yet again, he repeated what the translators upstairs had told him, adding that Shalla already knew and the other leaders were absent.

Shar made a note. "We'll talk to them. I don't think there's anything to worry about, but it's a good idea to be aware of problems early."

"Do you need anything else?" Gil checked for snacks and saw both a basket of fruit and a covered dish that smelled of cinnamon and baked apples.

Since Nik had only landed a few weeks ago, extra food was still vitally important. Every bone and angle showed through the pukel's skin, and all his movements were careful and slow. Earth's gravity would still be making him feel too heavy. The corner of the whiteboard listed appointments with the healer every other day.

Shar compared his page of notes to the board and nodded. "We're fine."

"You know," Gil said slowly, "this could be easier."

"What could be easier?" Nik asked. "How?"

Shar sighed. "Not this again."

Meeting his gaze, Gil shrugged but said nothing. He had been encouraging Shar to reveal himself for the past year.

"If necessary," Shar said, "I will claim my throne when I come of age. No one will accept me before then, so you might as well give democracy a chance first."

Gil rolled his eyes. "The lords aren't fond of the concept. I still think you should tell them to behave. The commoners would support you."

Gripping the arms of his wheelchair, Nik looked from one to the other. After double-checking that the door was closed, he spoke in a whisper. "Prince, you cannot reveal yourself now. It isn't safe yet."

Shar raised an eyebrow at Gil. Time after time, he had reminded Gil that until he became an adult, he wasn't actually in charge. Gil shrugged again. Since Shar had promised to keep his father's oaths, his reign still seemed like a better idea than leaving decisions to the lords.

"Earth wants our king to sign the treaty," Gil reminded them.

"The treaty isn't ready yet," Shar said, "And they want any leader to sign. Someone else will do until I am of age."

"Do we want someone else?" Gil asked.

"Perhaps the lords will see reason in time," Shar said, "and I won't have to force equality on them. I trust our people. Give them time to adjust to Earth, and maybe you won't need me."

Gil snorted. "I doubt it. But Mother wouldn't mind having no king. No offense intended, Sire, and she is always loyal. She merely favors no lords or rank at all."

"You say that as if I didn't know," Shar said. "Under the circumstances, I don't know how you think that's a surprise."

"What circumstances?" Gil asked.

Mother had always been discreet on the spaceship, watching her tongue until they reached the new world. Or had Grandsire betrayed her opinions to the king?

Crossing his arms, Shar raised an eyebrow again. "She didn't tell you? How strange."

"Tell me what?" Gil narrowed his eyes at the prince, then glared at Nik, who pressed his lips together and bowed his head.

"I assume she has her reasons for keeping her secret," Shar said. "As she has faithfully kept mine, I will protect hers."

"But—" Gil protested.

What kind of secret could Mother possibly have? They had been together every day on the spaceship, and he thought he knew everything about her. Except her life before they left the fae worlds. All he knew was that Father had been killed in the same incident that took Zak's grandmother and Miknon's parents. He had assumed that was why Mother didn't talk about that time, but now it seemed she was hiding something else.

The prince rose to his feet and opened the door. "If that is all, we must return to work."

The dismissal was clear. The discussion had ended. Gil bowed and returned to the hall. If he was seen, he would claim he had bowed to

Nik, who deserved the respect for his responsibilities despite his lack of rank. Maybe Mother had the right idea. Could Gil convince the ambassadors to push for total equality? Would the highborn agree to surrender their rank as a cost of their new home?

And what was Mother keeping secret from him?

The questions almost overwhelmed his nagging worries about the reports upstairs.

CHAPTER 3

TROUBLE

July 17, 2023

STILL CHEWING HIS LAST BITE, Ian dumped his breakfast tray. Since two-thirds of the students had either graduated or gone home permanently, the school was empty enough for all the kids to eat in the same meal shift, though most of the staff ate later with the few adult students. Mom and Nikos ate with Ian, as did Alexandria when she was around. For the last three weeks, though, Alexandria's college classes had kept her busy.

Ian waved at Mom and headed to his office. Fourteen years old, and he had his own office. Life was weird sometimes.

But if he didn't make some serious progress with his job over the summer, he'd be out of time once school started again. Ever since Mr. Abernathy had been fired — a memory that still brought joy and a lot fewer migraines — Ian had been in charge of the entire language program. Not the ambassadors, thank goodness, except for helping with the occasional translation. He did have to keep track of new vocabulary and assemble the dictionary and grammar for the Fae language. Currently he was focusing on Fae-English translations, but at some point he'd have to work on other Earth languages. Fortunately, he knew several already, but he couldn't possibly learn them all.

The hanging file on the wall inside his door was full of paper, both complete sheets and small scraps, even several sticky notes. Ian sat at the card table that served as his desk and sorted the papers. A few were tasks to do, but most were random bits of Fae vocabulary the interpreters had discovered. He opened his computer files and input the ones he could read, then arranged the others by who wrote them. Experience had made signing the notes a required step so Ian could identify the authors and request a translation of bad handwriting. Not that the signatures were any more readable, but at least they were predictable, since the fae had mostly chosen a symbol to sign their names. The humans tended to email. This time, only a few notes needed clarification. Maybe his constant requests to be more careful were working.

He repeated the process for the emails in his inbox, including a long list of science and math words from Gaby. After writing task reminders on his white board, he collected the indecipherable notes and a question and left. The first stop resulted in an impromptu spelling lesson for both the human and the fae on that team. The second was as quickly sorted out by the writer.

The third was Shaun, whose handwriting was peculiar but precise. "Need to discuss run," his note said. Ian found him in the office of the old king's secretary. Despite the king dying, the pukel had maintained his title, for some reason the fae hadn't disclosed, and he was important enough to rate having highborn Shaun as his personal translator and secretary.

Ian flopped into an extra chair. "Hey, Shaun. Nik, have you considered a nickname so we don't confuse you with my brother?" He spoke in Fae, except for "nickname."

The duplicate name was really distracting, and only Ian's brother being gone most of the time was keeping everyone from constant confusion.

"Nik *is* my name," the short fae said slowly, forehead wrinkled.

Shaun covered his mouth with his hand, but his eyes twinkled and his shoulders shook. Ian paused to replay his question in his mind, then burst into laughter. Apparently the pukel knew enough English to understand "name," but not enough to translate "nickname."

"Sorry," Ian said, "that was very confusing. A 'nickname' is an alternate name, like your short names, but sometimes not related to the original. Like my siblings call each other Shorty and Beanpole sometimes, which have nothing to do with their actual names, and U.N. is actually a joke about me. If you don't want to, that's fine. It's not that much of a problem."

"Use-name," Shaun explained.

"I don't mind." The pukel raised his eyebrows. "Do you have a suggestion?"

"We've been using the same initial, for ease of remembering. What about Ned?"

The pukel shrugged. "Okay."

Ian made a note. "Okay, great. So, what's the issue with run?"

"We need an explanation," Shaun said. The highborn turned a page in his notebook. "I thought run meant move your legs very fast. Like in gym class?"

"Correct," Ian said.

"And an office is a work room?" Shaun motioned at the walls.

"Yes."

"Then why are the humans asking us about our proposed laws for running for office?" Shaun asked. "Why do they care how fast we reach our rooms?"

"Oh!" Ian wrinkled his nose. "I'd better make a note for everybody. So, 'run for office' has nothing to do with actual running or rooms. Office also means a position you hold, like ambassador, and running for office means you apply for the position and try to get people to vote for you."

"Vote?" Nik asked.

Ian mentally practiced "Ned." "Yeah," he said. "People say they want you to be in the office or do the thing, and if more people want you than anybody else, then you win and get to do the job or whatever. Like when the cafeteria asked what desserts to have more often, and everybody said what they wanted. That was a vote."

Both fae stared at Ian without moving or speaking.

"Do I need to explain more words?" Ian asked. "I thought I got all those right."

"Humans vote on who gets jobs?" Shaun clarified.

"Sometimes. I mean, you guys all voted me into this job." Ian barely managed to not make that sound like a complaint. True, Mr. Abernathy had been a disaster, so he didn't blame anyone for wanting that jerk gone, but after experiencing how much paperwork was lumped in with the language parts, Ian was second-guessing his agreement to supervise.

"The lords appoint all positions among the fae," Ned said.

He didn't say "even yours," but Ian got the point. The fae had been pretty set on him being in charge.

"Well, the humans don't." Ian crossed his arms. "Sometimes, but not usually. We like more choice for ourselves and others."

"Hmm." Shaun frowned. "Human customs are strange."

"There could be advantages," Ned said quietly. "Less power *and* burden for the lords. More equality for the commoners. More selection by qualification."

His look at Shaun seemed to have a hidden message in it, but beyond the obvious call for democracy, Ian couldn't interpret it.

Shaun, however, nodded slowly. "I see. Yes, we must discuss the custom." He turned to Ian. "In the meantime, tell the interpreters to call it 'presenting for appointment.' That will be close enough for now."

Ian made a note. "Okay, anything else?"

After looking at Shaun, Ned shook his head. "We appreciate your efforts."

"You're welcome." Ian bowed to Ned.

As he left, he caught Ned giving a worried look to Shaun, who smiled and shrugged. Should Ian not have bowed? Because Ned wasn't highborn, or because being the king's secretary wasn't important enough? Shaun didn't seem upset about the break in protocol, even though he was highborn.

Ian returned to his office and emailed the update to all the translators and ambassadors, then worked his way through his list of things to do. By lunch time, he was desperate for a break.

He filled his tray but didn't see Mom. On his way to save her a seat, Gil and Miknon waved, so Ian joined them. "Hey, guys. How's it going?"

"Not well," Gil said.

The normally cheerful werewolf slumped in his seat and picked at his food. Miknon ate steadily, but her wings sagged.

"What's wrong?" Ian asked.

"The highborn diplomats are asking questions about human weaknesses," Gil said. "Where are they lacking?"

"I'm sure they're trying to learn more about potential allies and where they can offer benefits, right?" Ian drowned his fries in ketchup before picking up his hamburger.

"Perhaps," Gil said. "But what if they aren't?"

"What else do you think they mean?" Squashing his hamburger to make the tomato-stacked sandwich fit into his mouth, Ian took a huge bite.

"I'm worried the lords think diplomacy is too much bother," Gil said. "They favor conquest over negotiation. That's why I had to sneak away to offer peace before they landed."

Ian chewed rapidly and washed the hamburger down with chocolate milk. "But we already have the treaty in the works. We're discussing terms now. Why would they throw all that away on a fight they probably can't win?"

"Because they think they can win," Miknon said. "They always think they can. They've always won in the past. They do whatever they want, and none of us could ever stop them." She clenched her fists, face grim.

"Have you talked to the adults about this?" Ian asked.

"Of course," Gil said. "But we have no king keeping the lords in check now, and the lords do not listen to our commoner leaders." He grimaced and looked across the cafeteria.

Ian followed his gaze but couldn't tell what had caught his attention. All the students were eating lunch nicely, chatting and laughing.

"So what's the plan?" Ian asked before cramming more hamburger into his mouth.

"Watch and wait, I suppose." Gil sighed. "What choice do we have?"

"Mmm," Ian mumbled around his food. He wrinkled his nose and shrugged.

Gil forced a smile and changed the topic. "So, how's the dictionary going? Will you be done early enough tonight for a game of frisbee?"

Enthusiastically, Ian nodded. Between bites, they made plans for a game, and Gil promised to spread the word to the other students.

Mom never did join them before they finished eating, though Ian saw her coming in on his way out and stopped for a stealth hug before returning to his office. He lost himself in dictionary definitions, emerging only when someone knocked on his door.

"Yeah, come in." Gaze on his screen, he hit the save button and checked the time. Four-thirty, almost time to stop anyway. The door closed softly, and he looked up as Gil dropped into a chair. "Isn't our game after dinner?"

"The lords have stopped talking to the ambassadors and the humans," Gil said.

"What time zone?" Ian asked. "Is it bedtime already?"

"All of them," Gil said. "Every country. Several ambassadors report that thought-mages were summoned before the lords disappeared into their rooms and locked the doors. They must be talking to someone, but it's not to our people or yours. We fear they are conspiring together." He ran a shaking hand across his face.

"What do Ned and your other leaders say?" Ian asked.

"They are afraid, but what can they do?"

Ian shut down the computer and pushed back his chair. "Come on, let's go talk to Ms. Maxwell."

The principal was a military linguist in her real job, and the fastest way to reach human authorities. On the way downstairs, they gathered Tom, Ned, and Chantelle, with Shaun to take notes for the fae. Miles and Gil's mother, Meg, were still off campus, but Miknon took her usual spot on Gil's shoulder. The group found Ms. Maxwell in her office and piled in, shutting the door behind them.

Hands clasped on her desk, Ms. Maxwell listened seriously to Gil's quotes from every ambassador who had reported the problem.

"So what do you recommend?" he finished.

"I think it's premature to worry," Ms. Maxwell said in Fae, which she spoke almost as well as Mom, though not as well as Ian. "I'm sure they're just discussing terms before they return to talk to everyone else. Diplomacy can be very complicated sometimes."

"But this isn't normal," Gil insisted. "It's making all of us nervous. I don't think you understand what they can be like."

Ms. Maxwell sighed. "What do you want me to do?"

"Can't you get somebody to make them cooperate?" Ian asked.

The principal's eyebrows shot up her forehead. "I could fire Abernathy because I'm in charge of the humans involved with the school. I can report the bad behavior of other humans to my superiors. But the fae are only potential allies and not under my command. We reviewed this with the runaway, remember?"

Gil winced at the reminder of his traitor brother, and Ian sighed in sympathy.

"Other than basic discipline of students that is directly related to school matters," Ms. Maxwell continued, "there's nothing I can do to control any of the fae. None of my superiors, not even the President, have any authority over the fae until a treaty is reached with provisions for such. I thought the fae had their own leaders for this sort of thing?"

Ned, Tom, and Chantelle bowed their heads, hiding their faces. Shaun watched Ms. Maxwell with a thoughtful expression.

"I'm sorry I can't help," Ms. Maxwell said. "Now, I'm afraid I have things I need to do. I will pass on your concerns in case anyone has any ideas, okay?" She checked her watch. "If you hurry, you can still grab some dinner."

She stood and held open the door until everyone left, Tom pushing Ned's chair. The door closed, and Ian and the fae stood in the hall, staring at the floor. Gil's stomach growled, and Chantelle laughed.

"Go eat," she suggested. "If we can't do anything now, we might as well eat."

"Go," Shaun said. "Starving does no good."

Ian grabbed Gil's elbow and dragged him several feet. "Come on, I'm hungry, too."

The werewolf shrugged him off. "Okay, okay. I can beat you there."

Miknon wisely flew off his shoulder, and Gil ran down the hall. Ian raced after him, leaving the others behind.

But during dinner, Gil ate without looking at his food, and Ian's thoughts ran in circles. What if Gil was right about the lords? What if they had lost interest in the treaty and were reverting to Plan A:

Conquer Earth? While there was no guarantee their magic could win a war, there was also no guarantee human technology and numbers could triumph instead. If the fae had enough gorgons and basilisks, they could turn whole armies to stone.

The fae were now spread across the world, so any conflict couldn't be confined to one area. Visions of World War III burned across the inside of Ian's eyelids. How many people would die, human and fae, before one side won or both lost too many soldiers to continue?

And even if his friends all survived, which seemed unlikely, would they ever be the same? Dad went to Afghanistan and came back different. Angry, impatient, paranoid, even dangerous. He never liked Ian again after that, and he was so mean to everybody that Mom divorced him. Then he tried to make them stay anyway, and Nikos had to help them escape.

Sometimes Ian still had nightmares.

But just because Dad was right about the "asteroid" being an alien spaceship didn't mean he was right about the aliens being enemies.

Was he? What if Gil turned into a monster like Dad? A scary werewolf like the stories. Ian pushed his dessert away, stomach churning. They had to prevent that, somehow.

"Hey, Gil, can we talk?" he asked.

Gil abandoned his own dessert, a sure sign he was as disturbed as Ian, since he never ignored food. "Sure. Before or after frisbee?"

"Oh, yeah." Ian had forgotten about the game. "Instead of? Can we sneak a few people away without being noticed?"

"I can find people," Miknon offered. "Who do you want?"

"Who do you think sees the same problem?" Ian countered.

Together, they made a list.

Ian and Gil started a large frisbee game in the backyard while Miknon collected their hopeful allies. Once the game was too involved for anyone to notice their absence, the boys slipped inside and to the basement. Only one light was on in the distance, and the halls echoed as they walked softly around the corner. In the gym, their conspirators motioned to empty places saved for them between family members.

Sitting cross-legged, they met everyone's gazes. All five fae leaders had made it, as well as Miknon, Nate the hydra, Vince the troll, Zee, and

Shaun. The humans were represented by Alexandria, Nikos, and Gaby Ortiz. Mom was in a teacher meeting.

Ian took a deep breath. "Hey guys, welcome to the council of Elrond."

The humans chuckled, but most of the fae looked confused.

"Never mind," Ian said, "that was a joke. But we might have a serious problem on our hands. Gil?"

His friend yet again reviewed the reports from the ambassadors, which were not a surprise to more than half their group. "War Lady said not to worry," Gil said, "but I think we can't sit back and wait."

"Yeah," Ian said. "No way do we want a war on our hands."

"What do you want to do?" Alexandria asked.

Ian leaned against her shoulder and flashed her a tiny smile. His sister was always ready to plan.

"What *can* we do?" Gaby bit her lip and squeezed her fingers together.

"Spy." Miknon stuck out her tongue at her brother. "As much as I hate the idea, we need information before we can do anything. If we can get evidence of what they intend, maybe we can stop them."

"If we find proof," Meg said, "we have other options." Gil's mother raised her eyebrows and looked pointedly at Tom and Shaun.

Tom snorted. "Perhaps. But information is a good idea. Talk to the ambassadors and ask them to discover what they can. If we combine all the rumors, perhaps we can discover what the lords intend in time to stop any mischief."

"Okay," Ian said. "How will we do that?"

As people offered suggestions, Alexandria took notes and Ian translated the more obscure words. By the time Ian's phone rang with Mom's number, they had tentative assignments.

On the way upstairs, Alexandria draped her arm over Ian's shoulder. "Good job, shrimp."

"Maybe." Ian sighed. "I just don't like fighting, you know?"

She pulled him in for a tighter hug. "I know."

But that night, Ian's nightmares started again.

CHAPTER 4

IN WHICH REPORTS ARE ALARMING

JULY 29, 2023

SEVEN WEEKS AFTER FATHER LANDED, he and Zak had still not reached an agreement about her new life. After breakfast, Zak told him she was going upstairs to check on progress with the treaty.

"That is none of your affair," Father said. "You should concentrate on your contrivances. Better yet, let's find a safe place to wait out the conflict."

Zak took a deep breath and slowly exhaled. How could she make Father see that humans and the fae would never achieve peace without effort?

"Go practice your English, Father. I'll talk to you later." She embraced him and walked out, closing the door gently behind her.

Instead of taking the elevator, she climbed the stairs, using the time to calm herself. She couldn't blame him for being traumatized. Not only was he still recovering from learning the humans had seen their worlds already dead, but his mother had been murdered by the lords, and he had lived in fear for decades. As had she, but Zak wasn't surrendering her new life, especially when it was so precarious and nobody knew what would push it over the edge one direction or the other.

For the past two weeks, small bits of espionage had come from the ambassadors, some promising and some not. On her way to Shar's office — Ned's office, according to the sign on the door — she ran into Gil heading the same direction. He was scowling, but when she veered from the door to allow him to enter, he grabbed her elbow and knocked on the wall beside the open door.

"I have news," he said without a greeting. Then he pulled Zak into the room and shut the door. "Bad news, Sire."

Shar put down his pen, and Nik turned away from the notes on the whiteboard.

"Go ahead," Shar said.

"Today our ambassadors reached the negotiations for legal process-es," Gil said. "When the highborn discovered the same laws are expected to apply to everyone regardless of rank, they insisted that was unaccept-able. The ambassadors assured them it was required, and the humans agreed. So the highborn walked out and locked themselves in their rooms. When they didn't come back, the humans and translators ended the session for today."

Zak groaned. Would the highborn eventually agree, or was that the end of the treaty? Shar winced, and Nik rubbed his forehead.

"Okay," Shar said. "Let's not panic yet. Have all our teams contact their assigned ambassadors. Ask them to knock on doors and see if they can convince the highborn to come back to talk. They should report if it works, and anything the highborn say. Then ask our council to meet after lunch to discuss options."

"I'll help," Zak said. "If I deliver half the messages, we'll finish sooner."

Gil nodded. He bowed to Shar and ushered Zak from the room. She started on the fourth floor while Gil talked to the other leaders on the second, then they divided the third floor. At every office, she closed the door so the students living on that deck couldn't overhear. Though the news was disturbing, instigating a panic wouldn't improve the situation.

Once her messages were all delivered, she returned to her own room and emailed Freya and Jinyuan Chung. Her old roommates were now the ambassadors in China, and though Freya was a highborn, she had lost many of their typical attitudes after living with a commoner and two humans for nine months.

"How is everything over there?" Zak wrote. She typed and deleted several more questions, then finally left it at the vague request. Freya already knew their concerns, and though her magic tended to kill electronic devices, she could text with voice commands.

While she waited for a reply, Zak worked with Gaby on the latest list of science translations. They had nearly finished when her phone rang. Definitely not Freya, but Zak answered it anyway, putting it on speaker so Gaby could also hear.

"I can't find Freya," Jin said breathlessly, "and my door is locked." She grunted, and something thudded in the background. "I wasn't allowed into the meeting this morning, and Freya never came back. Now I can't leave my room."

"Bedroom doors don't lock from the outside," Gaby said.

Zak's stomach instantly cramped. "They could with magic. That means the fae are behind this."

"Is she trying to break out?" Gaby whispered. "That's the wrong way to do it." She raised her voice. "Jin, wait until they bring you food."

"But Freya—" Jin protested.

"If you can do nothing, then do nothing with cunning," Zak said.

"Have you called for help?" Gaby asked. "Besides us, I mean. The cleaning staff, or one of the Chinese officials?"

"Do you want me to say the fae are sabotaging the negotiation process," Jin asked, "or would you prefer the Chinese government think this is only a temporary pause? Besides, what are they supposed to do against magic?"

"Don't tell them," Zak blurted. They must preserve the chance for peace or all was lost.

Gaby winced, but her voice remained calm. "We will ask for help here. You look for another way."

Jin sighed. "Fine. I'll see what I can figure out. Freya can't even take her phone with her, you know, so I can't track her that way."

"We promise we'll call you back," Gaby said.

Zak touched the red button on the screen, then stared at her roommate. "What do we do now? *We* don't have a way to track Freya, either."

"Is anyone else missing?" Gaby asked.

The idea was terrifying. "I'll start asking," Zak said.

"I'll ask on the top floor," Gaby said.

She raced upstairs, and Zak ran to the other side of the deck and requested all teams to call their people.

"They were fine an hour ago," a human student protested.

"Call anyway." Zak glowered at him and ran to the next office.

She had barely finished her rounds when the halls began to fill with confused and upset people. Zak listened to as many as she could in the chaos. In another few minutes, those from the upper floors also streamed down, protesting loudly. Gil and most of the fae leaders emerged to investigate the noise, but by then, nobody could be heard above the clamor. Gaby shoved her way through the crowd, and with Zak's help, herded all twenty into Nik's office and shut the door. Never mind waiting until after lunch; this was now an emergency.

Several people had to crowd in behind the desk, and still Zak was crammed shoulder to shoulder with fae and humans. She hunched her shoulders, trying not to touch anyone, but it was impossible. Backing up only buckled her knees as she ran into the hydra's wagon, which he still used sometimes for speedier travel and safety in busy halls.

Nik motioned for quiet. "What's going on?"

"All the fae ambassadors have disappeared." Zak summarized the problem as quickly as possible.

"All of them?" Shar asked.

"Every one," Gaby confirmed. "Most in the last hour."

"What about their human partners?" Gil asked.

"Most of them are locked in their rooms," Zak said, "support teams and all. One or two also seem to be missing, although it's possible they were sleeping and didn't hear the phone ring." But she didn't feel much hope.

"Are the ones in their rooms well or injured?" Shar asked.

"Fine so far. They still have their phones, with access to email," Gaby said. "I don't understand why."

"Because most of the fae don't understand technology," Zak said. "They rely on magic for communication, and they know the humans don't have magic. They assume that leaves them helpless."

"Aren't they?" Gaby asked. "If we can't tell anyone local to them without endangering the treaty, how are they supposed to get help?"

"We must think of a way," Shar said. "Let's be organized. I will take notes in Fae. Who can do the same in English?"

Gaby wiggled closer and put her notebook on the desk. "I will."

"Who wants to report first?" Nik asked.

Nate waved a head. "My wagon takes a lot of space. If I leave, everyone will be more comfortable."

"Agreed," Shar said. "Proceed." He and Gaby made notes as Nate recited what Two had told him.

Touji and Ash had gone into a meeting with the Japanese humans and the highborn assigned to the delegation. Before they finished the discussion, the highborn had left, taking Ash with them. As a mere dryad, he couldn't argue with the ruling class.

Two had tried to stall, reviewing options with the Japanese, as well as ways they could phrase things for fae sensibilities, but eventually he ran out of things to say, and the meeting trailed to an end.

Then Two went looking for Ash but couldn't find him anywhere, and Ash didn't answer his phone. After using his private bathroom, Two discovered the door to his suite was locked from the outside. And that was all Two knew.

With Nate's report finished, several people went into the hall to give him room to exit. Once they were back in and the door was shut again, the reports continued. As the room slowly emptied, the scope of the problem mounted until Zak could hardly breathe despite fewer people using the air.

Some human translators had been allowed into the meetings, like Two, and some had been kept out, like Jin. But in every case, their fae partners disappeared, never came back, and couldn't be found. Those that could use human technology didn't answer their phone or email.

Finally, the room was half empty, and Zak sat on the floor, knees drawn up to save space. Gaby and Shar remained at the desk to take notes, and Nik stayed in his wheelchair. Alex, free of school for the day, squished next to her brother on the floor with Zak. All the commoner fae leaders looked distressed. Zak couldn't blame them, since dealing with the highborn was always difficult, particularly for the commoners.

"I don't understand," U.N. said. "What are the highborn doing with the fae translators? And why did they only lock the humans in their rooms?"

"They don't dare kill the human hostages," Gil said, "but their own commoners are inconsequential."

"Hostages?" Gaby squeaked. "Kill?"

Zak nodded. Whatever the highborn were plotting, it couldn't be good. Perhaps they only wanted to stall the negotiations, but this might also be the first strike in the war. Remove the ambassadors, and peace dies. After that, war was only a formality. Freya and the few highborn working as ambassadors might survive and be released eventually, but the rest— She pressed a hand to her churning stomach. The commoners had always been disposable.

She turned her face away from Gil and accidentally read Gaby's text to her parents, advising they didn't visit for a while.

"They *are* important," Alex protested. "Everybody's important."

Reaching to touch her elbow for a second, Zak explained, "You know they are, but the highborn have never thought so."

"Even when they're helping your people?" Gaby asked.

"I think we have reached the point that definitions of 'help' have diverged," Nik said grimly. "If peace is no longer desired, then peace negotiators are no longer needed."

"So let's go talk to Maxwell again," U.N. urged.

"There's nothing she can do about it," Shar said. "Whether to pursue diplomacy or withdraw ambassadors is an internal fae matter."

"Then tell the highborn to release the ambassadors." U.N. looked at Nik and Shalla, flinging his hands wide in frustration.

Zak put her head on her knees. Perhaps Father was right about staying away. If the lords discovered she was plotting against them — as they would surely see it — she would suffer her grandmother's doom.

"I have no power for matters of that magnitude," Nik said. "My authority is limited to the daily running of the king's household. The lords don't care if I overstep my bounds to deal with the commoners, but they won't listen to my opinion on state matters."

"Nor I," Shalla said. "Nor Miles, Meg, or Tom. We all have our duties, but none of us can tell the highborn what to do without a higher authority backing us. Without a treaty to change politics, that leaves the lords in power, followed by the highborn."

"What about the ambassadors?" Gaby asked. "Don't they have authority to deal with things?"

"Yes and no." Gil cleared his throat. "Their negotiations still have to be approved by the highborn."

"We're a bunch of kids and commoners," Zak mumbled against her knees. "We're nobody. No magic, no political power, no rights."

No one replied, and a depressed silence smothered the room. All their hopes of equality on the new world were ending. Despite King Arishaka's promises, the highborn would continue to trample the commoners underfoot on this world as they had on the old.

About twenty-five years ago, to use the Earth reckoning, the fae had discovered their seven worlds were being destroyed by their own sun. Their magic was inadequate to save them, and their spaceships were built only to travel to their neighboring worlds, as close to each other as Earth and its moon.

In their time of despair, Zak's grandmother had announced her recent invention of a new navigation contrivance that would allow them to travel between the stars, though she knew no safe destination. Her only price was a promise that when they landed, all fae would be equal. With no alternative save death, the highborn agreed.

When the mapmaker found the mural showing the way the Starry Lovers fled millennia ago, the fae finally had a destination. But she, too, required a promise that the supremacy of the lords would end. Her identity had never been revealed, which was a good idea, considering Zak's grandmother had been murdered either for blackmailing the lords or for being a commoner female with influence.

Those two commoners had provided the way for the fae to escape, and it was the combined efforts of highborn and commoners that built a fleet, trained crews, and gathered supplies in time to evacuate one-tenth of the fae population. Since Father had never mentioned Mother, Zak assumed she had not been lucky in the final lottery. Or perhaps had died in childbirth, like the queen.

Those who grew up on the spaceships, like Zak and Gil and the rest of the fae students, had been reared with the dream of a new world with freedom and equality. Their parents remained skeptical, especially when the king died in an accident and assassins hunted his son.

Without the king's rule and his magic, it seemed the adults had been correct. Despite Gil's tireless efforts to bring peace, and all their attempts to help, the highborn would never surrender power, regardless of their promises. Now it was only a matter of time before they attacked the humans to conquer Earth and take their new home by force. And if they won, they would restore the old ways and oppress the humans as well as the commoners.

If Zak took Father and ran now, they might escape. But probably not. She didn't know where to go or how to travel or gather food. Father was still crippled by the long journey in lesser gravity, and it would take months for his muscles and bones to recover. The human sentiments toward the fae were still radically uneven, so she couldn't risk asking for help.

But if she stayed to fight, they would surely die. True, no war had yet begun, but if the lords had stopped negotiating for peace, then conflict was coming soon. Did she even have time to try running with Father?

"Enough." Shar broke the long minutes of silence.

Zak jumped at the sound of his voice and raised her head to look at him. His mouth was set in a firm line, and his silver-blue eyes glittered with anger. The light around him sparkled with energy from his magic.

"It is time," Shar continued. "I have waited long enough."

"Yes," Gil hissed in triumph.

"No," Taras groaned.

"Time for what?" U.N. asked.

Shar pushed back his chair and stood, shoulders thrown back. "Time to claim my birthright."

Zak stared at him in shock. No wonder Taras was so upset. After the king died, someone tried to poison Shar to get rid of the heir. Gil saved him, and Shar went into hiding. Ever since then, he had been pretending to be an ordinary highborn. Taras had followed Shar around subtly all year, protecting him without revealing his identity. Once the prince was out in the open, his task would only be harder. Shar wouldn't be safe if the lords knew he was alive.

If he *could* be king, he would keep his father's promises of an equal society, but the lords still wanted to kill him. They would never accept his rule.

CHAPTER 5

PRINCE

July 29, 2023

"Your birthright?" Gaby stared at Shaun in confusion. "What do you mean?"

She knew Shaun was highborn, but so was Freya, who had never mentioned anything like a birthright. Unless he meant the right to butt in line and boss the commoners around. It had taken months to break Freya of those habits. If Shaun was suffering from the same attitude, she'd recruit Gil to squash it. There was no room for that ego. It was as bad as Grand-mère thinking French was better than any other language.

Though even when the other highborn had been cutting in line, Gaby hadn't noticed Shaun doing so. In fact, she rarely noticed him at all. He was quiet and hard-working and unremarkable.

"I am the king," Shaun said, not in a bragging voice, but like he was commenting on the weather.

The king? Gaby didn't know the fae had one anymore, though the lords had frequently been mentioned. Standing behind the desk, Shaun looked like the secretary he had said he was. He wore a plain button-up shirt and jeans, unlike a lot of the highborn who wore the fanciest clothing they could get. His long bangs flopped across half his face, and he wore no jewelry. The other humans in the room seemed as confused as she felt, but none of the fae showed surprise.

U.N. frowned at Gil. "You said you spoke for the king, but you never said who he was, and everybody else said the king died on the ship."

Gil shrugged. "They told the truth as they knew it."

Now Gaby was more confused. She'd assumed all the fae were in on the secret, but how many actually knew? Half of them? Those crowded here in this room?

Gil unfastened the silver chain around his neck and removed the gold signet ring, rising from the floor to stretch toward Shaun. "Here, Sire. Take back your father's ring."

Shaun slid the ring onto his finger. While he examined it in silence, Gil put the chain and remaining silver tag back on his neck.

"I don't understand," Gaby said. "If you are the king, why didn't you announce yourself before?"

"He was hiding," Zee said, "like me."

"Not quite," Shaun said.

Gil snickered, and Shaun elbowed him. Gil covered his mouth, but his shoulders still shook. Gaby looked from one to the other. What was the joke?

Shaun continued. "When my father died from an accident—"

"Maybe," Miles interrupted. "He should have healed." The fae healer looked offended at the failure.

"When my father died," Shaun amended, "he left the crown to me. Shortly after, someone poisoned my breakfast. One of my guards died instead, and I went into hiding."

Gil shook harder with silent laughter, but he said nothing. Shaun scowled at him. Gaby furrowed her brow. It didn't sound like a humorous situation. She updated her notes with "Shaun is king, hid after poisoning."

"Once we landed," Shaun said, "my advisors deemed it wiser for me to stay anonymous until we were sure it was safe."

"Which it still isn't," Tom said.

"But it is time." Shaun pushed back his bangs and met Tom's gaze.

"The lords are not adjusting to Earth and aren't cooperating. They had their chance and didn't take it. Now they must obey me."

It would be nice if they would obey somebody, but Gaby doubted they would.

"They won't obey you," Ned said. "You can't rule until you become an adult."

"That's at two hundred conjunctions," Gil informed the humans. "For Shaun, almost nineteen more."

"Twenty months," Zee translated before Gaby could calculate.

"Father left the crown to me without a regency," Shaun said, "so he thought I am adult enough already."

"But the lords won't," Meg said. Gil's mother had hardly spoken a word before now, and she sat with her hands clasped tightly in her lap and her expressive ears drooping. She looked remarkably like her younger son, though her black hair was long and tightly braided to her head. "They never do anything they don't want to do, and they never accept anyone else's opinion. They will use every technicality to keep you from the crown, and your age is the easiest, since you can't change it except with time."

Gaby ran the math through her head. Two hundred conjunctions was 19.7 years. Odd for humans, but two hundred was a nice round number. Wait...

"Now that you live on Earth, can you claim adulthood by our customs?" Gaby asked. "In the United States, that's eighteen years, or ... about 182 conjunctions."

Gil whistled. "That's brilliant, Gaby. Shaun, you would only have to wait one more conjunction, wouldn't you? In fact, you could announce yourself now but wait to be crowned then."

"Yes," Shaun said, "that would work."

He finally sat again, but now his mild-mannered Clark Kent demeanor was gone. Despite his ordinary clothes, he looked confident and powerful, and Gaby believed he was king. Prince, for another month.

Tom put his face in his hands and groaned, but the other four leaders nodded. Gaby added the plan to her notes with a guess at Shaun's birthday. Sometime in early September? She could ask later for the exact day, since the highborn — uh, king — might not have calculated the Earth date yet. If not, Zee could.

The lunch bell rang. Even though the class bells had been silenced for the summer, meals were still on a schedule to make life easier for the kitchen staff.

"I suggest waiting until after lunch to finish our discussion," Alex said. "People will pay more attention if they aren't hungry."

As if to emphasize her words, Gil's stomach growled. Gaby bit her lip to keep from giggling.

"Hang on a minute," U.N. said. "We have to wait longer than just after lunch."

"We just discussed all this," Gil said. "Shaun will announce himself now, then wait a month to be crowned."

"Yeah, yeah." U.N. raised his hands. "But I meant we still have to wait for the announcement. You forgot about the hostages. We have to free them first, so the lords can't retaliate by killing them."

"Oh, dear," Shalla said. "They might do that."

Gaby winced. The more she heard about the lords, the less she liked them. The fae were lucky to have a good king this time.

"We're here and the ambassadors are all over the world," Tom said. "They can't ask for help where they are, so how are we supposed to rescue any of them, much less all of them?"

"Help them discover how to rescue themselves," Ned suggested.

"Since residential doors don't lock from the outside," U.N. said, "there must be magic holding them closed. Most of the translators are humans and commoners who have little to no magic. How are they supposed to deal with magic locks?"

Gaby thought of all the fairy tales she'd read as a kid. Too bad there weren't really seven-league boots to carry them around the world in a flash, or fairy godmothers to zap obstacles. Real magic was turning out very different than the stories.

Meg sighed. "We can think about it during lunch."

U.N.'s stomach growled, followed by Shaun's and Gil's.

Gaby giggled. "Teenage boys are always hungry."

Her stomach joined the chorus, as did Zee's and Alex's. Okay, teenage girls also wanted food. The adults laughed and hopped up from the floor.

Meg opened the door and swept her arm outward as she bowed. "Go eat. We'll meet after."

The teenagers stampeded out, and when the boys and Alex ran past, Gaby slowed to merely a fast walk. She couldn't beat them anyway, so she might as well not try. Being late didn't matter, since the kitchen always made enough food for everybody. Zee looked back and slowed to walk with Gaby.

"King, huh?" Gaby asked.

Zee shrugged. "Yes."

"So all you fae were hiding him from us for a whole year?"

"His survival was a closely guarded secret," Zee said, "even among us."

"That makes sense." Gaby pursed her lips. "You hid your surprise well."

"I knew," Zee said. "On the ship, he hid in my room, dressed as a girl."

Gaby nodded. "Since everybody else slept in the dorms all together, right? I guess the emergency meant it didn't matter he was staying with a girl."

Zee's green ears turned orange. "He didn't know I was a girl."

Gaby stopped walking and stared at her. "Hang on. *Nobody* knew? Not even the prince?"

"Only Father and Gil," Zee said, "and I didn't know about Gil."

She hunched her shoulders and kept walking, ears burning an even brighter orange. Apparently the topic of her lifelong disguise was still sensitive, though Zee now seemed comfortable in her feminine clothes.

Gaby stayed quiet until they reached the cafeteria and collected their food, but her brain kept recycling the story. Zee, a girl disguised as a boy, had shared a room with Shaun, a boy dressed as a girl. And Shaun didn't know the other half of the secret. Suddenly, Gil's amusement made sense.

Once seated, Gaby changed the subject. "Any ideas how to break the magic on the locks? Or should we concentrate on windows in hopes they missed those?"

"Can Jin get out her window?" Zee asked.

"That's an excellent question." Gaby pulled out her phone and dialed Jin. The call immediately went to voicemail. After finishing her burrito, Gaby tried again.

This time, Jin sent a text.

Call you back soon.

That was odd. Gaby ate her dessert and emptied her tray, but Jin still hadn't called back by the time everyone reconvened in the basement, which had more room than the office of the king's secretary.

Huh. Gaby had assumed he was only the secretary of the dead king, but in fact, Ned and Shaun had been working together ever since the pukel finally landed. Though they told everyone Shaun was helping Ned as well as translating for him, Gaby now wondered how much service had gone the other direction. Sneaky fae.

After the door closed, the fae bowed to Shaun before taking seats. Someone had brought folding chairs downstairs so nobody had to sit on the floor.

Gaby opened her notebook and prepared to continue her notes. At the desk, Shaun did the same. Interesting. Though he was now acknowledged as king, he was still taking his own notes. Was that because Ned didn't write English or for some other reason?

Shaun clicked his pen and held it above the paper. "Does anyone have any ideas about rescuing our people?"

Gaby tentatively raised her hand. "What about going out the windows?"

"That might work for some," Gil said, "but others are too high to get down safely."

"Okay, do we know who's low enough to try?" Shaun asked.

"We can find out," U.N. said. "I'll send all the humans a text. Give me a minute."

He was still typing when Gaby's phone rang. She winced and reached to turn it off, but paused when she saw the caller.

"It's Jin." Her finger hovered above the screen, then tapped. After all, this meeting was to discuss the hostages, so they needed all the information they could get, as soon as possible.

"Hi, Gaby," Jin panted. "Whew! I thought we'd never find somewhere to hide."

"We?" Gaby asked. "Hide? In your room?"

Jin grunted, then sighed. "No, we escaped."

"We?" Gaby repeated, putting the phone on speaker. "And how?"

"Hello," Freya chirped, her voice much softer, as if she were farther away.

"Yeah, Freya rescued me," Jin said.

Everyone except U.N. jerked to attention. U.N. kept typing, but he leaned toward Gaby's phone. Gaby held the phone toward Shaun, but he motioned for her to continue.

"That's great," Gaby said. "We've been trying to find a way to free everyone. Please tell us how you did it."

Freya laughed. "By breaking things."

Ned groaned. "Be more specific."

"Well, Jin says she told you about the meeting, right, and how they wouldn't let her come? As soon as we got there, Lord Fancypants walked out and made the rest of us go with him."

Ned whispered to Shaun, who made a note, possibly of who Fancypants actually was. Gaby wrote down the alias, just in case.

"I didn't have a choice," Freya protested. "They grabbed my arms and marched me out. Ooh! But once we reached their rooms, I batted my eyelashes and said I was glad the boring meeting was over — true — and asked when we got to have some fun. Then I fussed with my clothes and demanded a fancy meal. After that, I took a nap with a pillow over my head. That messed up my hair, so clearly I had to spend a couple of hours brushing and braiding."

Meg coughed back a chuckle, and Gil elbowed his mother, though his own grin was broad. Gaby didn't bother hiding her own smile. Freya had sometimes been late to class because she spent too long fiddling with her clothes or hair. Who knew it was actually a useful talent?

"They got bored watching me primp," Freya continued, "and they eventually left me alone."

"Because clearly she's a harmless idiot," Jin said.

"Right!" Freya laughed. "So then I opened the door, made sure nobody saw me creeping down the hall, and freed Jin. Then we both snuck downstairs and outside."

"I think we're missing something," Shalla said. "Even if they didn't bother magicking your door again, how did you unlock Jin?"

"Oh, they locked both," Freya said, "but you're forgetting what magic I have."

U.N. put down his phone and laughed. "Does that work on magic as well as tech?"

"Sure does," Freya said triumphantly.

Shaun raised an eyebrow. "I'm still lost."

"She fried the lock magic with electricity," U.N. said, "which is why she can't use a phone."

"Lightning magic," Chantelle clarified.

"Oh." Shaun's eyebrow rose even higher. "That's generally considered a war magic, good for nothing but killing enemies."

"Yes, and killing is not nice," Jin said, "but I'm all for zapping nasty spells. So here we are, under a bush a couple of blocks away. We packed a few essentials, but we couldn't bring everything."

"We left all my pretty clothes," Freya complained.

Jin snorted. "Please tell us you have a plan to evacuate us."

"We thought we still needed a plan to get you out of your room," Ned said, "but we will arrange an escape rapidly. Please text your current location to Gaby, and we will be in touch."

"Thank you so much," Jin said. "I'm putting my phone on silent, but I'll keep checking it."

The call ended, and Gaby lowered the phone. "Well, we have alternatives for the humans now. Try the windows if they're low enough, or electrocute the door." She bit her lip. "We'd better research exact methods so nobody fries themselves."

"On it." Alex tapped frantically on her phone while U.N. finished his texts.

"If the humans can escape," Shaun said, "are they willing to rescue their partners?"

"Of course they are," Gaby said. "Why wouldn't they be?"

Gil's phone rang, and when he answered it instead of silencing the call, everyone stopped talking.

"Hello, Two," Gil said, tapping the speaker button. "Thanks for calling. We're trying to learn who has a window low enough to climb out, or if they need to electrocute their door to kill the lock."

"Thanks for asking," Touji said, "but you're a little too late." His voice was high and choked.

"Hi, Gil," someone else cheerfully said.

"Abe?" Gil asked. "I thought you were still a prisoner."

"We're both free now," Two said. "Where do you want us to go?" He sucked in a breath and exhaled noisily.

"What's wrong?" Gil asked.

Touji gasped for breath again. "I don't particularly like scaling down twenty stories, thank you very much."

"How—" Gaby blurted.

"They didn't lock the window," Abe said.

"Because it's twenty stories high!" Two said. "You didn't tell me my partner is crazy! Come on, let's get out of here."

Pounding footsteps echoed through the phone line. Gil put the phone on the desk and waited. After a few minutes, the voices returned.

"Okay, we're out of sight," Two continued. "Imagine, if you please, me sitting nicely in my room, waiting for a proper plan like an intelligent person."

"Imagine me making my own plan," Abe said. "Also intelligent."

"Now imagine a tap on my window," Two said. "I look over, and there's a leaf knocking on the glass."

"The wind in the trees?" Gaby asked.

"So I thought," Two said. "But no, it keeps knocking and waving at me. So I open the window, and it climbs inside."

At this point, Gil covered his mouth with his hand, not very subtly. Gaby squinted at him, trying to decipher what clue he had caught.

"It's a vine," Two said, "that stretches to the closest tree. Quite a long way down to the closest tree, mind you. And in that tree, there's a redheaded crazy person waving at me."

"Hello!" Abe chirped. "Not crazy."

"And the vine kept crawling on my floor until it found the bed frame," Two said, "and then it wrapped around the legs. And then the leaves waved toward the window. Are you imagining this for me, hmm?" His voice was very indignant and occasionally cracked.

Gil's shoulders shook. Gaby stared at the phone. Did he actually mean…

"I had to climb my own vine with no anchor point outside," Abe said. "Much trickier, even with the tree's help. Only easy part was them thinking I'm too stupid to need a guard and too useless without real magic. It was easier for Two."

Gaby shook her head. Neither stupid nor useless, but crazy might be possible.

"Easier?" Two wailed. "I had to climb twenty stories down the outside of a building!" He squeaked. "I think I want a transfer."

"How did nobody see you?" U.N. asked. "You're right in the middle of the city."

"Not stupid," Abe said. "Grew more vines to cover him. Who notices vines?"

"You are the second-fastest to escape," Shaun said. "Well done."

"I bet the fastest didn't have to scale twenty stories," Two complained.

Gaby made a note to remind Jin not to gloat about her escape, either the speed or the method.

Gil burst out laughing. "You are correct. Please text your exact location, and we will send someone to get you."

"I'm not climbing any more buildings." The phone clicked off.

U.N. waved his phone. "I don't think we should actually pass on that method. Maybe just the low windows or electrocuting the locks? Or sneaking out, if they can?"

"Agreed," Shaun said, and the others nodded.

"Okay," U.N. said, "I'm updating everyone else on the possibilities. Is someone making arrangements to get the four who are free?"

Shaun turned to his computer and typed. "As soon as the locations come through, let me know."

"I have Jin and Freya's already." Gaby moved to the desk to show him the address her roommates had sent her.

"Excellent." Shaun typed faster.

When he was finished, Gaby put her phone back into her pocket. Two teams almost safe, about thirty to go. Could they free them all before the lords used the hostages as convenient leverage to get what they wanted?

Chapter 6

In Which an Announcement is Made

July 31, 2023

Two days later, all the translators had rescued themselves and each other. Gil cheered when the last escapee was marked off the list in Nik's office. Whatever the lords were doing, it was apparently occupying too much of their attention. Or they were too sure of themselves to keep proper guard over their prisoners. Perhaps it wasn't surprising, since the commoners had been too afraid of the highborn to rebel. The humans had convinced them to try.

Now that the hostages were safe, it was time for the next move on their side. Finally, more than a year and a half after King Arishaka's death, Sharrukin must take his place as the new king and relieve Gil of responsibility.

Partly because Shar had been in hiding, and partly because Gil was the first fae on Earth, Gil had taken the lead for a long time to prevent war and protect humans and fae alike. Being friends was better than fighting, but the lords had favored conquest. Someone had to make allies before everything was ruined, and he was the only one who was willing.

Gil didn't mind helping, but he had thought he would only be in charge for a few weeks. Instead, the wearying responsibility had gone on and on for an eternity. Over a year! He would rather have fun than sit through endless meetings and be responsible for decisions that would impact everyone he knew. Honestly, he didn't know how Mother endured it. Shar had at least been trained for it his whole life and ought to be used to it by now.

But finally the misery was almost over for Gil. One more month, and then he could do whatever he wanted to do. If he survived this meeting with the king's council first.

"Gil." Shar's raised eyebrow suggested perhaps it wasn't the first time he had called him.

"I'm listening," Gil lied.

"Great. And the answer?"

Gil's text beeped.

> When can you double-check my translation of his announcement for the humans?

"We'll get the translation done during lunch," Gil promised. *Thanks,* he texted back to Ian for the prompt.

His best friend grinned without looking up from his phone. Gil sat straighter and focused on the prince. He could pay attention for a little longer, even if he had to pinch himself.

Shar rolled his eyes in a very unroyal manner and continued. "Gaby has arranged the technology with all locations and will handle the call on this end. All the support teams have arranged for locations where our ambassadors can meet with the fae in each country, including human divers for the water fae. Is there anything else we need to do?"

Murmurs of "no" ran around the room.

"Then we will announce my survival to the fae right after lunch," Shar said.

Gaby raised her hand. "What about the humans?"

"I'd like to get responses from our own people before we plan an announcement for our allies," Shar said, "but I promise it won't be long." He looked around the room. "That will be all."

As everyone stood to leave, Shar said, "Gil, please stay."

Ian widened his eyes and shook his head at Gil. "Trouble," he mouthed.

But Gil hadn't done anything. He stayed seated while everyone else left. Shar stood, arms folded, watching Gil silently. Maybe Ian was right about trouble. Was the prince that upset about Gil's daydreaming? He would have to try harder to pay attention for a few more weeks.

Once the room was empty except for the two of them, Shar sighed. "I want to apologize."

"No worries, Sire," Gil said. "I should have been listening better." He leaned forward in a slight bow.

"No," Shar said. "I apologize for ignoring your advice and under-valuing your hard work and friendship. If I had listened to you much earlier, we might have been able to avoid our current predicament. And I apologize for slapping you last year."

"I—" No highborn ever apologized, much less their leaders. Certainly never to a commoner. Gil swallowed hard and tried again, addressing his friend instead of his prince. "I accept your apology, Shar, though I must point out that the lords have always been difficult. There might have been no difference."

"Nonetheless, I regret disappointing your expectations." To Gil's shock, Shar offered his hand.

Even among friends, the fae rarely touched each other. The last time Shar had touched him was when Gil was leaving the spaceship to approach a world of unknown enemies with a reasonably small chance of survival, let alone success. As the last time they might see each other, it had made sense then.

Gil stood and extended his own hand. When Shar stepped forward, Gil boldly threw his arms around the prince instead. Knowing Shar's mind-touching would definitely work at that range, he filled his thoughts with the joy Shar's friendship had always brought him. He held the embrace for only a second, then stepped back and bowed low.

"I look forward to your reign, Sire. Your father would be proud of you."

"Thank you," Shar whispered.

Thanks, too, was unusual for the fae, and perhaps something he had learned from the humans. Whether he meant it for the comment or the thoughts was unclear. As Gil straightened, he thought he saw a quiver of Shar's lip, but it was gone before he could be sure.

He left the room with a spring in his steps and a merry wave at Taras, who lurked in the hall with a glower. At least the king's Companion had trusted Gil enough to let him talk to Shar privately. When Gil's grandsire was the Companion, he never would have left the king completely alone, either.

During lunch, Gil kept his promise and checked Ian's perfectly adequate translation. They modified a couple of words, but it would still have been understandable if they hadn't.

After everyone ate, they again gathered in the basement. Gaby — and Alexandria between college classes — had bossed the decorating committee all day, and one corner of the usually drab room had been converted to a throne room, more or less.

"Nice." Gil admired the satin wall hangings (sheets, Gaby said) and the gold-painted chair on a dais made of wooden crates supporting painted flat wood.

Gaby wiped her sleeve across her forehead, keeping her paint-splattered hand away from her face. A smudge of gold on her nose indicated she hadn't always been successful. "It should be good enough for the camera, anyway."

"How long will it take the paint to dry?" Gil asked.

"About an hour before we can touch it," Gaby said. "That will give enough time to practice the speech and dress up Shaun." She turned to Zee. "Are we doing makeup?"

"The news only did the powder for shine," Zee said.

Gil nodded. When they had gone on television to announce the arrival of the fae fleet, most of them had been given minimal makeup. If that was good enough for professionals, it should be good enough now.

"Okay, we can do that after he's dressed." Gaby grimaced at her hands. "I'll go wash."

Gil rubbed his nose as a hint, and she sighed and scrubbed her nose with her sleeve. It didn't help.

Hiding a grin, Gil headed upstairs to Shar's room. In the past, the king and prince had many servants, ranging from the secretary and the housekeeper that kept their household in order, to the Companions that protected them, to cleaners and dressers and cooks and gardeners and more. Shar had none of the lesser servants because he had been in hiding for over a year. Since he had also been dressing in ordinary human clothes, that hadn't been a problem. Until now. Ever since Shar's roommates left, he had lived alone, which meant he had no one to help him dress for more important events.

Though Taras was again standing in the hallway, the Companion wouldn't dream of abandoning his post or being familiar with his charge. When Gil knocked on the door and announced himself, Shar pulled him inside.

"What do I do with my hair?" the prince asked.

The hair in question was rumpled oddly, as if Shar had been pulling on it. The typical highborn on the old world wore their hair long and intricately styled. On the spaceship, they usually settled for some kind of braided approach to keep their hair under control when the gravity turned off.

Shar, like most of the commoners, had cut his hair when he landed on Earth. He had chosen a medium-length cut that hid some of his face, similar to the way Ian looked. Gil's was cut nearly the same, but he pushed it back to cover only his pointed ears, which were much longer than those of gremlins or highborn and attracted too much attention from humans.

Gil stepped back and examined the prince. Instead of the usual buttoned shirt and blue jeans, Shar wore one of his father's old silk tunics, embroidered with gold and silver and edged with ribbon. His belt held a jeweled dagger, and his father's gold signet ring was on his right hand. Instead of his usual human sneakers, he wore soft leather boots. Everything looked in order, though the shoulders of the tunic were a bit tight.

Gil nodded and walked around Shar to grab a brush. "I think if we braid the front and let the back hang loose, you'll look enough like normal. Sit, Sire."

"Shar," the prince corrected as he settled into a chair. "We are still friends, aren't we?"

Dragging the brush through Shar's hair, Gil smiled. "I certainly hope so, Shar."

Once the mess was smooth, Gil carefully braided a narrow plait on either side of Shar's face and tied them with a handy Earth elastic instead of struggling with ribbons. "There, what do you think?"

Shar leaned toward the mirror and squinted intently. "Yes, well done." He stood, smoothed his tunic, adjusted his belt, and took a deep breath. "Are we ready?"

"Almost, I think. If we head down now, the camera crew can fix your microphone and run their checks." Gil opened the door and motioned for Shar to precede him.

The prince squared his shoulders and marched out. Poor Shar. Though his mother died in childbirth, he should have had decades or centuries of his father's tutelage before he had to reign. Even Gil had one parent, and for most of his life had benefitted from a grandsire as close as a father. Well, Shar wasn't alone, whatever he thought, though Gil didn't know anything about being a king.

Gil closed the bedroom door and followed Shar, and Taras fell in behind. In the basement, everyone was frantically rushing through the last of the preparations. As Shar entered, the fae bowed automatically. The humans awkwardly copied them a moment later.

"We're ready for the sound check," Ian said.

Unlike the television studio, there were no fancy cameras or microphones here, but Gil hooked a small microphone to Shar's collar while Mama Helen and Gaby arranged a laptop computer and camera. Shalla and Mother moved lamps inch by inch until they were satisfied with the lighting. Alexandria, back from classes for the day, talked Shar through the technical aspects and how to make a good impression.

Finally, everything was arranged perfectly. Shar took his place on the fake throne and nodded. When Mama Helen nodded back, Shar looked directly at the camera, as instructed.

"Greetings, fae of Kunisu and its neighbors. I am Shar, son of Arishaka, and his heir." He paused as recommended, to allow his watchers to express surprise without missing any of his words. Saying his true name, even the shortest version, was a risk, but if he didn't, none of the fae would trust his word.

Next to Gil, Alexandria squinted at Shar and tightened her lips. His magic command to forget his name had been weakened during the fight a few weeks ago, and Gil doubted it would hold at all after this. He touched her elbow to keep her silent as Shar spoke again.

"You were told I died in an accidental poisoning after my father's death. In truth, the poisoning was not accidental, and one of my faithful guards died instead of me. To save my life, I went into hiding on the ship and stayed in disguise after we reached Earth. Though I regret you have not heard from me in a dozen conjunctions, I am indeed alive."

He paused again, unplanned, and touched his thumb to his father's ring. Gil wrapped his hand around the silver family crest on the chain around his neck. Grandsire had died from the same accident that eventually killed the king, and he hadn't had time to say farewell. He was sure the prince felt the loss of his father equally.

"My father led everyone to this world to save our lives," Shar continued, "but that's not enough. We can do better than mere survival. We can thrive on this new world with our new allies, though some changes are necessary and desirable. As my father promised, I intend to shape our society with peace and equality for everyone. No longer will anyone be exempt from the laws because of race or rank. Working together, we can all succeed, as we did when the navigator and the mapmaker gave us the way to escape our destruction."

Yet again, curiosity burned Gil. The navigator was Zak's grandmother, who had died on Kunisu, but who was the mapmaker? No story told what had happened to her. It seemed unfair that she, too, might have failed to escape.

Shar sat straighter. "In a conjunction, I will reach the age of adulthood by the standards of my host country. At that time, I will officially become king. As such, I ask you to return to peace negotiations with the humans. Cooperate in good faith and seek solutions to help all of us on both sides." He glanced at Alexandria as if debating her choice of words, then stuck to the planned speech. "If any of you have questions or concerns for me, please tell your local ambassadors, who will pass on your message."

Gil let himself grin. The fae kings weren't in the habit of getting feedback from their subjects in general, but it would be good practice for Shar.

Alexandria waved at Mama Helen, who tapped at the computer and nodded.

"Okay, we're off the air," Alexandria said. "Well done, everyone. You may return to your regularly scheduled plans for the day." She looked at Shar, who was resting his head in one hand, and whispered to Gil. "Does he need help? Also, *he's* Shar? From the fight? And… from Halloween? How did I forget that?" She glowered at the prince, suspicion all over her face.

Yep, the magic had dissipated. "At the time, his secret was vital to keep," Gil explained. "I'm sorry."

"Oh, we'll talk about this," Alexandria threatened, "but not until he looks less terrible. Go get him water and a snack or something." Back rigid, she stalked off.

Gil collected Shar and took him to his room with the suggested food. "We will take care of everything for an hour or two," Gil said, "if you would like some time to yourself."

Time to mourn, perhaps, or to gird himself for the lifelong tasks ahead. Though Shar had never seemed to mind the endless duties as much as Gil did.

Shar merely nodded and threw himself onto his bed. Gil shut the door and waved at Taras, then ran downstairs to burn energy in a vigorous game of frisbee with Ian and Alexandria.

Reports began to pour in from around the world. The commoners were thrilled and ready to return to work, and a few of the highborn agreed. Even Wes, who had spent the day wandering around the school and telling everyone he couldn't believe Shar was alive, had finally decided the treaty was a good idea because the prince said so. He still sneered at the humans and commoners, though he kept his opinions of them to himself.

But most of the highborn had yet to express an opinion, and the highborn advisors were still absent. Until they agreed to obey the prince, Gil wasn't ready to relax his worries.

A couple of hours later, a reply video was emailed to the school and every fae outpost. At the school, the inner council of fae and humans gathered together to watch it. Since Mak-swill had declared herself only in charge of the school, they didn't invite her, though Mama Helen came with her three children.

On screen, Lord Kishar looked composed and regal. He was dressed in blue silk but wore no jewels or embroidery. Though Shar's hair was golden like his father's had been, Kishar's was silver, tied behind his neck with a gold ribbon.

Miknon made a choking sound and tightened her grip on Gil's ear until he flinched. Kishar had tried to kill Miknon on the spaceship and might have been involved in the death of her parents and Gil's father as well as Zak's grandmother. Lord Zaidu certainly had been responsible, and the two were the closest of allies.

"I speak for the highborn," Kishar said, "and we categorically deny the claim of this imposter. Illusion is powerful and can show anything." His image flickered and then steadied into an imitation of Shar.

In Shar's voice, Kishar continued. "The real prince would have the crown to prove his identity. This fake does not." He flickered back to himself. "Prince Shar died on the ship, and as his heir, designated by King Arishaka himself, I am the true king. I am the king's cousin, the last of his bloodline. I call on the fae to follow me. We will take this world for ourselves and restore our proper society."

The video ended, and Gil pulled his ear free of Miknon's fingers.

In the stunned silence, Alexandria said, "Well, this is not good."

Gaby stared at her. "That's a little mild, don't you think? He said they want to conquer Earth!"

Chaos erupted in the room. Gil put his fingers to his lips and blew a piercing whistle, holding it until everyone stopped talking. Then he bowed to Shar and sat on the ground, looking significantly at Ian, who sighed and pulled Alexandria to the floor. One at a time, everyone followed their example.

Back in his human clothes, Shar still looked like the prince he was. He folded his arms and met each gaze. "This is bad news, but I think the common fae will believe me despite Kishar."

"We would rather have you," Miknon said.

Shar bowed his head in acknowledgment. "So we merely need to convince the lords. This is not particularly surprising, though trying the easy way first was a good idea."

"What about the crown?" Gaby asked. "Can you use it? Where is it?"

"If I had it," Shar said, "it would certainly prove my identity, but it disappeared between my father's death and his funeral. Kishar's announcement did settle one question, though. He doesn't have the crown, or he would certainly have used it by now."

"Then how can you make the lords see the truth?" Gil asked.

Shar frowned. "I'm afraid I'll have to parley face to face."

With a shout, Taras jumped to his feet. For once, Gil agreed with him. Going anywhere near the lords was a stupid idea.

CHAPTER 7

PARLEY

July 31, 2023

Ian ducked back against the people behind him, pulling his feet out of the way as Tom lunged forward, shouting at Shaun. Shar. Whatever the king's name was. This would take some time to get used to, and they needed to decide what name to use in the future. Also, prince or king? If he hadn't been crowned yet, what was the protocol?

"If you go to the lords," Tom bellowed, his snake fangs bared in a snarl, "you might conveniently disappear. And then Kishar *will* be the heir, and the rest of us are lost. As your guard, I strenuously protest."

"I agree," Ned said, and the other fae leaders nodded.

Shaun-Shar frowned harder. "But if I don't convince the lords that I am who I am, then they won't obey me. Our quest for peace is in danger."

"Losing you still won't improve our chances," Meg said softly.

"I'll go with him," Alexandria said. "Nik can help."

"You will not," Ian said. "Mom, tell her no."

"No, Alex," Mom said. "Thanks, U.N., but I already thought of that myself."

His sister glared at him, but Nikos, on her other side, leaned against her shoulder until she nearly fell. Having her get injured once was more than enough, and that hadn't even been a situation they knew would be dangerous. No way would her brothers let her walk into trouble on purpose.

"Can we get the military to protect him?" Gaby asked. "The humans, I mean?"

"We can ask," Ian said. "Ms. Maxwell might know, or she can pass on the request."

"They can't deal with the magic." Gil shook his head. "No, we need the lords to come to our ground."

"Okay, fine," Alexandria growled. "Let's invite them to come here. Kishar is still in Pennsylvania, right? Easy."

Eyebrows raised, Gaby made a note in her book, as she had for everything. Did all girls love lists, or was it just her and Alexandria?

Ian elbowed his sister instead of making his own note. "Oh, yeah? How will we do that, exactly? I don't think they text or email, and would they take a letter seriously?"

"Important messages are always delivered in person," Gil said. "We would have to send someone to invite them to parley. I'll go."

"No," Meg cried. "They'll kill you. By now, those who landed early have certainly reported that you're the one who told Earth about us." She grasped her son's arm, lip quivering.

"My life is no more important than anyone else's." Despite the harsh words, Gil spoke softly and put his arm around his mother. "And less important than Shar's."

Ian clutched his pen harder as he wrote the name usage for future reference. Gil was important to *him*. But he didn't want anyone else to die, either. "Isn't there anyone the lords would trust? What about one of the other highborn? Wes, maybe?"

Wes hadn't been invited to the meeting because he hadn't quite kicked his attitude problems, but he wasn't a bad guy, just a little too entitled and snobby.

"Wes has shield magic to help protect him," Zee said.

Chantelle tilted her head to one side in thought. "Kishar and Zaidu are the lords still in the vicinity. Zaidu has water magic, including scrying. As long as Wes stayed on high ground, he would be safe from drowning."

"Only from the outside," Miles warned. "Not necessarily from Zaidu pulling all the water in his body into his lungs."

"Ew," Ian said.

The healer grimaced. "Is Wes strong enough to block all magic, even the subtle?"

"Probably not," Ned said. "He's better at the quick and obvious."

"Zaidu is also expert at moving the smallest objects at exactly the right time," Meg said. "A stick rolling under a foot, or a sprinkle of powder into food — he knows how to make the most use of his lesser magic."

Most of the fae in the room looked either sick or angry, as if the examples were personal. Why did Ian feel like he was missing half the conversation?

"It doesn't matter," Shar said. "Even if Wes shields against Zaidu, he can't protect himself from Kishar. My cousin's mind-touching is weak, but it complements his command voice perfectly, and his power in that was second only to my father's. If we send someone Kishar doesn't already know and trust, the message will never even be delivered."

"Oh, great," Ian said. "Who does that leave?"

Gil straightened slowly. "I know someone."

"Bad idea," Miknon said.

"But—" Gil protested.

Miknon shrugged, rippling her wings. "I feel the same way, but no."

"No," Zee said. "We can't trust him."

"Who?" Ian asked.

"Sire," Chantelle said, "I agree with Zee and Miknon."

"Oh." Meg blinked rapidly. "But — If he would — Could he redeem himself?" She gazed at Shar, hands clasped together.

"Who?" Ian asked again.

Alexandria elbowed him and tipped her head toward Gil, eyes wide and lips clamped shut.

"The lords would let him talk to them, at least," Gil said. "He's the only one who has a chance."

Just before he asked again, Ian realized who. Gil's brother, Rafe, that's who. The one who already tried to betray them once. Okay, sure, the *lords* might trust him, but Shar couldn't be that crazy, could he? He opened his mouth, and Alexandria jabbed him again. He glared, and she shook her head.

Shar knelt in front of Meg and took her hands, pulling gently at her fingers until they were untangled. "He is not your fault," he said. "Nothing you did was wrong. You are a good mother, and you are not responsible for his choices. I regret all the pain he caused you."

Tears ran down Meg's face.

"I understand why you want to give him another chance," Shar said, "but I don't see how we can trust him to deliver the message and nothing else. If he chooses to betray us again, he knows a lot about the school and our allies and plans."

"We could send someone else with him," Gil said, "to witness what he actually says and keep him from deserting."

"And sacrifice the witness if he betrays us again?" Chantelle asked.

Gil rubbed his face with one hand. "If we could think of someone likely to survive? And command R— the slave to keep certain matters private, forbid him to speak of them. You have enough power for that, Sire."

His hair was pushed behind his ears, which now flattened to his head like a sad dog's. Ian forced himself not to watch, no matter how fascinating they were. As his family had said so many annoying times, Gil wasn't a dog. Though he looked like a dog when he wanted to, and played a mean game of frisbee on four legs. But really, Ian ought to be paying more attention to finding a solution.

"What about Vince?" he asked.

The troll had graduated in June like most of the fae, but hadn't been sent out as a translator because he was too big and scary for delicate negotiations with humans raised on Earth legends. And it was impossible to buy formal clothes in his size, and tunics made of sheets were a little too distracting.

"Zaidu can't drown Vince," Tom agreed. "And he's too big to shove around and extremely hard to kill. He's as likely to be caught by illusion magic as anyone else, though."

"But illusion magic is less likely to be harmful," Shar said thoughtfully. "It can't kill anyone directly, though it's a good idea to be careful of environmental hazards that might have been concealed. And Vince knows how to play dumb to be underestimated."

Gil said nothing, but his ears twitched.

Letting go of Meg's hands, Shar settled down cross-legged. "A suggestion has been made. The fae are all aware of the inherent problems, but few of you humans know the whole story."

"Do any of us?" Alexandria whispered in Ian's ear.

He shrugged her off. He'd arrived late to her fight with Rafe, long after it began. Though she filled him in as much as she could, there were still suspicious gaps in the story.

"Two months ago," Shar continued, "just before the rest of the fleet landed, one of the students here decided the imminent arrival of the lords meant it was time to rouse support for them. With the news of the fleet's proximity still secret, he ran to betray us. If Alex hadn't stopped him, he would have destroyed the peace between us and the humans."

"Maybe it was a mistake?" Gaby suggested.

Shar shook his head. "It could have been for someone who believed the story of my death, but this one knew I was alive and here in the school. While still on the spaceship, he had joined the army to conquer Earth, fully convinced that was the proper strategy. He supported Lord Kishar's claim to the throne, and continued to do so after he discovered my survival."

"Halloween," Alexandria muttered. "I knew something was odd."

Ian gave her a puzzled look. He remembered nothing besides touring the town for a while. She mouthed "later" and looked back at the prince. Ian did the same, though his mind kept racing. Come to think of it, hadn't Gil and Rafe talked about some prince after the fight? But nobody would ever say who that was. So much was making more sense now.

Shar kept talking. "Since he recognized me, even in disguise, and made a deliberate choice to support the lords instead of me, his decision must be considered a betrayal rather than merely a poor decision. Though we spared his life for the sake of his family, he was stripped of his name and rights in our society."

"Ooh," Gaby breathed.

"Since then," Shar said, "he has served at the school rather than learn."

Zee mumbled, "Didn't learn the right lessons anyway." When Gil sent her a disappointed look, her ears turned faintly orange.

"Gil is right about one thing, though," Shar said. "Because he was trusted by the lords before, they would probably at least listen to a message through him. Whether or not they comply is a problem we can't control. So, let's discuss how to reduce the risks and increase the chance of success, and weigh the two against each other. Tom, would you like to speak first?"

Unsurprisingly, Tom was heavily concerned with the risks. Now that Shar was publicly royalty and Tom admitted to being his guard, it made more sense why the snake-man was so often in Shar's classes. It must be hard to bodyguard somebody on the sly.

Ian listened for a few minutes, then scanned the crowd, wondering who else had already known about Shar. Who had a secret role besides Ned and Tom? How often had the fae leaders talked to the humans and then left to privately consult with their real leader?

When Tom finished, Shar gave a turn to each of the other leaders. Meg, predictably, was the most in favor of giving Rafe another chance. The others were somewhere between, skeptical but desperate.

To Ian's surprise, Shar then asked the opinion of every fae in the room, regardless of job or rank. Most of them were also conflicted, though Zee bit her lip and hunched away from Gil when she voted no. Gil, like his mother, begged for hope. Miknon was still against the idea, though Rafe was as much her brother as Gil was.

Then Shar turned to the humans, starting with Mom as the oldest. Ian sat straighter and gawked. He wanted *their* opinions? Why? They weren't fae and had nothing to do with their internal politics.

Mom, Nikos, and Alexandria voted against sending Rafe, and all referenced the fight in June as a reason. Because a traitor couldn't be trusted, Mom said. Because he didn't care who he hurt, Nikos said, looking at Alexandria. Because he tried to kill his brother and his ruler, Alexandria said. Gaby voted to send Rafe because the treaty was worth the risk.

Shar turned to Ian. "What do you say?"

"Well," Ian said, "if you want to be logical, we have to have the treaty, right?"

Shar nodded gravely.

"And we have to parley to get the lords to cooperate," Ian said. "Which means we have to send somebody. So I think the first question is if anybody else has a chance to be heard?"

The crowd murmured but didn't suggest anyone.

"The second question," Ian continued, "comes down to what will happen if we send Rafe and things go wrong. If Rafe doesn't ask the lords to parley, are we worse off?"

"Not if he can't reveal anything else," Gil said.

"And if they kill the messenger, who would we rather lose? Rafe, or someone else?" Ian winced at how callous that sounded, but the question had to be asked.

Gil whined but said nothing.

"All of you have good points," Shar said. "I appreciate your honesty. While I agree a risk is worth the gain, I think we are missing one more source of input before I make a decision. Tom, please bring the outcast here."

Tom jumped to his feet, beckoned two more fae with a crook of his finger, and stalked out. Shar rose and slowly paced the room, frowning thoughtfully. Gil and Miknon huddled with their mother, heads bowed.

Within a few minutes, Tom was back, marching Rafe in front of him. The three guards forced Rafe to his knees in front of Shar.

"Greetings," Shar said.

Rafe said nothing, and he kept his gaze on the floor. The thumbprint on his forehead still glowed brightly, despite his white bangs combed over it. Ian yet again noticed how Gil and Meg were ink black but Rafe was white as could be. Only their blue eyes matched. "Like Father," Gil had said, but how did the genetics actually work?

"Are you enjoying your new status?" Shar asked. "Was your loyalty to my enemies worth your punishment?"

For only an instant, Rafe glared at Shar. Before Ian could be sure of his expression, he was again staring at the floor.

Shar folded his arms. "I would rather begin my reign with mercy. We have an opportunity for you to regain your citizenship and freedom, if you are willing to realign your allegiance."

Rafe twitched but did not look up.

"We wish to parley with Lords Kishar and Zaidu," Shar said. "We need a messenger that will be trusted by them, and you are our best option. Not our only option. Nonetheless, if you will carry our message there and their reply back, without any more trouble, we will reconsider your case."

"Say yes," Gil whispered, so softly that only his proximity to Ian let him hear.

"You will let me go alone?" Rafe raised his head partway to look at the prince.

"No," Shar said. "Vince will go with you." Over Rafe's head, he twitched a finger at Tom, who sent one of his warriors from the room. "And I will bind your tongue so you can betray no more of our secrets."

"Keep your magic away from me," Rafe growled.

"Then stay as you are," Shar said. "I care not."

Gil hunched his shoulders, and Miknon folded her wings around herself. Their mother shrank behind Nikos, hiding her face, shoulders shaking.

Ian wrinkled his nose. Rafe was such a punk. They should be glad he had been kicked out of the family, like Mom divorced Dad.

Bowing his head again, Rafe stayed silent for a long minute. Ian fidgeted until Alexandria nudged him, but everyone else stayed as motionless as if a gorgon had turned them to stone.

"I will take your message." Rafe kept his gaze on the floor.

"Return him to his room," Shar said to Tom. "We will finish our plans before the binding. Make sure he communicates with no one."

Tom nodded and yanked Rafe to his feet. With a warrior on each side of the outcast, they marched out.

Gil leaned forward and touched Ian's shoulder. "Thank you for your questions," he whispered. "I think they were what convinced Shar."

"You're welcome," Ian said doubtfully.

Gil seemed to only be looking at the hopeful side of the equation and not the possibility of disaster. Would he still be grateful if the lords killed Rafe for impertinence? Had Ian set in motion the end of his friendship? And yet, the fate of Earth was more important. He closed his eyes against the future emotional pain and the suddenly very current headache.

CHAPTER 8

IN WHICH THE MESSENGER IS SENT

JULY 31, 2023

ZAK WATCHED Gil's brother until the door closed behind him. With his head so low, it was hard to tell, but had he been smiling?

The council returned to their plans. Zak listened and made suggestions and occasionally corrected Gaby's notes, but she kept thinking about the white wolf. That smile was the first hint he actually cared about his family. If he could be restored to citizenship, Gil, Miknon, and Maia would be so much happier. And if he quit being a pain, everyone *else* would be happy.

"Okay, I think that's everything," Shar said. "Unless anyone has any last suggestions?"

Nobody volunteered any. Zak looked over Gaby's shoulders to double-check her notes, but everything seemed to be there. How they planned to make the lords obey. What they would ask for and concede to in negotiations. The future of fae society. Gaby was very comprehensive.

Shar checked the clock on the wall. "It's almost dinner time. I'll head upstairs for the binding, then we can all eat before we take Vince and the messenger to the other building."

Most of the fae had spread out recently, but another old hotel was still being used in the area.

"I can drive them," the human Nik offered. "My truck has enough room for Vince in the back, and you can send a couple of guys to keep the other one under control until we arrive."

If Rafe actually convinced the lords to parley, everyone could use his name again. Zak glanced at Gil quickly. Her father was also being a pain, but not to the same extent. At least she could still talk to him and be with him.

"I was going to ask you." Shar flashed a smile at Nik. "Since none of us can drive."

Nik nodded. "Exactly." He winked at Shar and held the door open for Alex. "See you after dinner."

As everyone filed out, Shar looked at the ceiling and winced. Zak stopped, blocking Gaby's exit. Above, the messenger waited for the king's magic to bind his tongue and block his mind. Shar's identity was no longer a secret, but who knew what other secrets he might have discovered. If nothing else, he knew the real names of many of the humans, and the fae could not afford to have their allies bent into enemies with the power of their names.

The messenger was the brother of the king's friend. Possibly his best friend. And the prince was sending him into danger. If he died, would it ruin the friendship between Shar and Gil?

"Do you want company?" Zak asked before she thought about it. She cringed and headed for the door again. "Never mind. You don't need me."

"I accept," Shar said.

Zak froze. "You do?"

Shar waved a courtly arm toward the door. "You think I want to go alone? And I won't take Gil. Bring Gaby, if you like, to witness for the humans."

"Oh, I don't know about this," Gaby muttered. She clutched her notebook to her chest and ducked her chin.

Ignoring her protests, Zak dragged her through the hallway into the elevator. With Taras, the three rode silently to the fourth floor. The king's Companion led them to the correct room and checked for danger. After letting them in, he stood with his back to the door and daggers in his hands. While Shar approached the bed where the messenger lay, arm across his eyes, Zak and Gaby shuffled awkwardly against the wall between the dresser and the closet.

"Sit up and face me," Shar said quietly.

He grabbed the closest chair and turned it around backwards before sitting, leaning his arms on the back. Slowly, the shifter uncovered his eyes and rolled to sit on the edge of the bed.

Shar took a deep breath. When he spoke, his voice echoed with power. "You will confirm my identity to the lords."

"Yes," Gil's brother said.

"You will tell them I want to talk to them and invite them to the school."

"Yes."

Zak watched carefully, but the messenger seemed to have no problems with the restrictions. Maybe the magic was an unnecessary precaution.

"You will give them no information about the humans."

The shifter's reply was slower this time. "No."

"You will say nothing of our plans for the future."

"Nooo." The word dragged from the shifter's mouth like it hurt.

Had he been planning to tell the lords something to give them an advantage in negotiating? Why was he so convinced the old ways were better?

Gaby shuffled her feet and put her notebook on the dresser before clasping her hands together tightly. Zak had to struggle to avoid a similar reaction. With a chance to save himself, why was the messenger being so difficult?

"You will obey Vince until you return," Shar said.

"Yes." The shifter's nose flared with disgust, but he didn't fight the command.

After a pause, Shar glanced at Zak. She shrugged reluctantly. If they were missing something, she didn't know what it was.

"We will send you after dinner," Shar said. "Your meal will be brought to you here."

Head bowed, the messenger nodded. Taras sheathed one dagger and yanked open the door, still watching the shifter. Shar led the girls out, and the naga closed the door again.

"I'm not hungry," Gaby murmured in the elevator.

"Me, neither," Zak admitted, "but starving isn't better."

Gaby flushed pink all over, not just her ears. "Sorry."

"Save me a place, okay?" Zak said. "I'll bring Father." Before she could ask, Shar punched the button for the third floor as well as the first.

"I appreciate your company," the prince said.

"Sure," Gaby said.

"Yes, Sire," Zak said.

Taras merely grunted.

Zak got off alone on the third floor and hurried to Father's room. He was already in his wheelchair, ready to go.

"I thought you weren't coming," he said.

"Of course I'm coming," Zak said. "I just had to help Shar first."

"We aren't on the ship anymore," Father said. "You are no longer a navigator. The prince doesn't need you interfering in his affairs."

"He asked." Zak kept her reply as short as possible and concentrated on not bumping the doorway with the wheelchair.

Father frowned. "He wouldn't feel compelled to ask if you would stay away and concentrate on your own problems."

Zak held her breath all the way to the elevator, then stabbed the down button. "Which problems are those?"

"We have had this conversation before," Father said.

"Yes, we have, and my answer is the same." Zak rolled the wheelchair into the elevator and pushed the button for the first floor. "I am staying here. I will help the prince. I will learn Earth technology. I wish you would find a place where you feel comfortable, but that will come with time."

The elevator doors opened, and Zak pulled him out and spun the chair. "I noticed you've been putting on some muscle lately, so let's make sure you get some protein in your dinner. Do you prefer chicken or fish?"

Food odors drifted through the hallway, tantalizing them, and students streamed toward the dining hall. The adults newest to Earth were easy to identify by their wheelchairs, since they hadn't been on the surface long enough yet to rebuild their bones and muscles after sixteen years in space.

"I forbid you to meddle with affairs that don't concern you," Father said.

"Okay." Zak deliberately used the English word to remind Father things were different now. "When I'm told by those involved that they don't concern me, I won't meddle. Here's your tray. Looks like they have apple cobbler for dessert."

"I don't eat shoes," Father complained. "Or shoemakers."

Zak shrugged. "English is a strange language, but there are no shoes in the food. So, chicken or fish?"

Through the rest of the meal, she ignored Father's attempts to return the conversation to his opinions about her life. He spent so much time arguing that the meal took twice as long as usual and she had time for extra dessert.

Once she took him back to his room, she checked her phone battery and headed upstairs to Ned's office. Shar was already there with the commoner fae leaders, as were Gil, U.N., and Gaby.

According to U.N., his sister was setting up her telescope to show everybody at school the super moon, which was an extra close full moon. Tonight was the second of three nights and therefore "absolutely perfect." U.N. mimicked his sister's excitement flawlessly. Miknon and some of the other fae were waiting to view the moon.

"Nik left already," U.N. said. "He wanted to get there before dark so Vince would have time to look around."

"I'm sorry I'm late," Zak said.

"They haven't called yet," Gaby said. "You're fine. How's your dad?"

With a shrug, Zak took an empty seat. How could she explain Father's stubborn opinions when she didn't understand them herself? "How close is Nik going to try to get to the rebel camp?"

"Moderately close, whatever that means," U.N. said. "Close enough to walk the rest of the way, not close enough for the truck to be seen."

Shar suddenly laughed. "Who are the rebels here? The lords are actually trying to maintain traditional fae society, and we're the ones changing everything."

"But you are the king," Nik said. "Your word is final."

The other fae murmured agreement. Zak yet again wondered why Father was still not adjusting. He didn't like traditional fae rules, so why didn't he want to help change them? Was he so sure they had no chance to succeed?

Gil's phone rang, and he answered it, putting it on speaker.

"Hey, Gil," Nik. "I just let out my passengers. They've still got a mile to walk across the park, but we figured that way would have the fewest observers. Anything else you want me to do while I'm here? Should I wait for them?"

"No, come back now, since we don't know how long it will take. Thanks." Gil hung up and looked around the room. "And now we wait."

Shar conversed quietly with the other leaders. Gil and U.N. chatted about frisbee and word definitions. Gaby traded places with Shalla to let her be closer to Shar's desk, then leaned toward Zak.

"I want to keep taking notes," Gaby said, "but I can't find my notebook. I thought I took it back to my room before dinner, but it's not on my desk or my bed. I've looked everywhere."

"U.N. can take notes tonight," Zak said. "I'll help you look later. It probably fell behind something."

"But what if we need an old note?" Gaby fretted.

"We'll make do," Zak assured her. "Somebody will probably remember."

"If you say so." Gaby bit her lip but leaned back in her chair.

Zak half-listened to the conversations on either side of her while she thought about Father. How could she make him see that what she was doing was important and worth the risk?

She hadn't found a solution by the time Nik walked in twenty minutes later.

"Any word yet?" Nik asked.

"None." U.N. patted the empty chair next to him.

Nik settled by his brother and joined the conversation with Gil. Gaby asked a question, and when Gil couldn't translate all the words, U.N. asked for Zak's help for the scientific and technical jargon.

Outside the window, the light gradually faded. The translators almost had the vocabulary chosen by the time Gil's phone rang.

"Greetings," Gil said. "It's Vince," he mouthed as he turned on the speaker.

"I'm worried," the troll rumbled in Fae. His attempt at a whisper sounded like distant thunder. "He left me here and went to scout a path where I wouldn't be seen. But he's been gone a long time. Should I go after him?"

"Why did you let him go alone?" Gil asked.

"We saw a couple of humans," Vince said. "He said I was too big and slow and we would get caught."

Gil covered his eyes with one hand, but his voice was calm when he replied. "Okay, never mind. It's dark now, so go look for him."

"Oh, never mind," Vince said. "Here he comes. And —" His rumble dropped even quieter. "The lords are here."

Something tapped several times, then the sound became muffled, as if the phone went into a pocket. Probably Vince's belt pouch, since his tunics didn't have pockets.

"I guess he missed the hang-up button," Gil whispered.

"Big fingers," Gaby suggested. "Should we hang up?"

"Shh," Shar commanded.

"Vince, where are you?" the messenger called softly.

"Here," Vince said. "I didn't expect the lords to come with you. If they are going with us now, we need to call our ride."

"Take him!" the messenger commanded.

The sounds of a struggle echoed through the phone.

Gil slapped his free hand over his mouth, and tears sprang into his eyes. U.N. put a hand on his shoulder, and Gaby hit the mute button on Gil's phone. With their silence now guaranteed, Zak let out the sigh she had been holding in.

Poor Vince. While it was true they sent him because he had the best chance to survive if anything went wrong, they had all hoped it was a needless precaution.

"Now," the traitor said, "ask him your questions. I can't answer, as I told you, but he can. Ask him to read the notes I gave you."

Gaby sat straighter. "My notes?" She winced. "Oh, no. I think I left them in his room. I'm so sorry."

Shar waved off her apology and held a finger to his lips. Everyone quieted to listen to the phone, and Zak almost held her breath.

"Everyone knows commoners can't read," Vince said.

"True," a smooth voice said in the background. Lord Kishar.

"Yes, he can," the traitor protested.

"Everyone knows trolls are stupid," Vince said.

"Also true," the other voice said.

Shalla's lips quivered, and tears ran down her face. "Everyone is wrong," she whispered. "Be careful, Vince."

"He can read," the traitor insisted. "Make him read it."

"Why would you do this?" Vince asked.

"Because I know how to be loyal," Gil's brother said. "I'm not a rebel."

Vince sighed. "Aren't you?"

"The wolf knows little," Kishar said, "but you must know more." His voice grew harder, and even through the phone, his command magic vibrated. "Tell us the rebel plans."

Vince gasped in pain, and Gil bowed his head. Zak reached toward him, then pulled back her hand. There was no comfort to give. His brother was still a traitor and would always be a traitor. An execution after his first betrayal would have been better than this.

"The king plans to make the commoners equal to the lords." Vince's voice cracked.

"We know that, idiot! Tell us something useful," another voice said. "Maybe this will persuade you."

Zak looked at Shar for identification.

"Zaidu," the prince said. "I'm not surprised he's involved."

Maia stifled a sob, and Gil looked ready to hit someone.

"The... humans... like... us." Vince groaned every word.

"Don't break him," Kishar said. "He's the only link we have since the wolf turned out to be useless."

"I'm not," Zaidu complained. "But we need the information, and he's just a measly troll. Come on, troll, tell us what we need to know, or I'll dissolve more than your finger."

Gaby's mouth opened in a shocked O, and U.N. flinched. Merodach looked ready to disembowel a handy lord to use his guts for sutures. Everyone in the room was clearly sick or angry or both. Gil dropped the phone onto the desk, where it gleamed like a beacon of disaster.

Zak clutched her suddenly churning stomach. "Should we turn off the phone?"

Eyes blazing, Shar shook his head. "We will listen to witness his bravery."

"Where is the prince hiding?" Kishar demanded.

Vince's groans rose to a roar.

"Can't we go rescue him?" U.N. asked.

"It takes twenty minutes to drive to the edge of the park," Nik said, "and we don't know how far they walked after that or where they stopped." Despite his discouraging words, he pulled out his keys and leaned forward.

"Can he survive that long?" Zak asked. The troll already sounded in mortal agony.

"What if he gives in and tells them everything?" Gil asked. "Nobody can withstand torture forever."

"Then we will listen to know what the lords learn," Shar said. His lips were pressed into a flat line, and his hands were clasped so tightly his knuckles had turned white.

Bile rose in Zak's throat, and she gulped hard to keep it down. Poor Vince. They couldn't even rescue him, and the only thing to hope for was that he died quickly.

"I'm sorry," Gaby blurted. "It's my fault. If they get someone to read my notes, they'll know everything." She covered her mouth and ran from the room, though she shut the door quietly behind her.

"Can't you make him talk?" Zaidu asked. "Or give up, and we'll begin the war anyway. They can't withstand us, whether or not we know their measly plans."

"I'm trying," Kishar growled. "No commoner should have been able to resist this long. If I just—"

Vince's roar turned into a scream, then abruptly stopped. The phone disconnected.

Nobody spoke. Nobody moved. Zak wasn't sure anyone was breathing. She certainly couldn't get air to move through her own lungs.

Vince was dead.

The messenger was still a traitor.

The lords would not listen to the prince.

There would be no parley, only war.

The commoners and humans must face the highborn magic, against which the commoners had never won.

The dark night outside matched the darkness in Zak's heart.

U.N.'s phone rang, and everyone jumped.

"Hello," U.N. croaked.

"Get outside and see this," Alex said.

"I don't think anyone's in the mood to watch the moon," U.N. said wearily. "I've got bad news."

"Get out here right now. Bring the others." The phone clicked off.

"What?" U.N. stared at his phone. "What's going on?"

Rising, his brother opened the door. "Only one way to find out."

"Let us know if it's important," the king's secretary said. "I'll wait here."

Merodach and Shalla leaned toward him for a quiet, intense conversation. Taras followed Shar as he led the others downstairs and outside. In the courtyard, Alex leaned over her telescope. Beside her, Nate, Miknon, and Gaby were at the front of a small crowd of fae looking upward. As Zak and the others approached, Alex straightened and pointed.

"Look," she said.

"Without the telescope?" U.N. asked.

Turning, Zak looked up. Across the huge, bright moon stretched the many-headed shadow of a hydra.

"Magic," Gil said.

"But what does it mean?" Alex asked.

"It's a declaration of war," Shar said. "The moon is visible from everywhere on Earth, sooner or later. They can reach all their armies with a single signal."

Yet again, Zak's breath stalled in her lungs. Already? They were starting the war tonight?

"Why a hydra?" Nate asked. "We're not an army."

U.N. winced. "If they were humans, I'd say it was a proclamation they couldn't be stopped. If we cut off one head, they will grow another one."

"How rude," Nate said. The little hydra stuck out most of his tongues at the moon.

Alex looked pointedly at U.N. "Maybe you aren't the only one who has poor judgment about what movies to show the fae."

"But how will we stop them?" Zak asked.

Chapter 9

Military

How WOULD they stop the fae armies? Gaby reached for her pen, then remembered her notebook was gone. Not just gone, but in the hands of the enemy. Grand-mère had called her a traitor to Earth, which was unfair — but had Gaby accidentally betrayed the fae and the humans to the fae lords and proved Grand-mère correct?

The shadow on the moon hovered, the necks stretched as if the hydra would dive to bite Gaby, punishing her for her indiscretion. Maybe it was good the promised visits with her family hadn't worked out yet.

She pushed aside the worry. "What do we do now?"

Next to the telescope, Alex crossed her arms. "We talk to the adults. That's what they're for. Somebody go get Mom and Ms. Maxwell."

"And Chantelle, Tom, and Miles." Shar ticked off the other three fae leaders on his fingers.

"Do you think they'll leave the signal up until the whole world sees it?" Alex asked. "Or will they take it down and replay it when the moon circles to the other side of Earth?"

"Magic is tiring," Shar said. "They'll probably end it."

Alex nodded and bent to her telescope. "I'll take pictures of the moon for proof."

"Who is going for the adults?" Shar asked.

Gaby, U.N., Zee, and Gil ran for the door.

"I'll find Mother," Gil said.

Zee nodded. "The other fae are together, so I can tell them all at once."

"I'll get Mom and Ms. Maxwell," U.N. said.

Gaby screeched to a halt. That was everyone they needed who was already on campus, so her running around was a waste of time.

"I'll text Mamá." She pulled out her phone and flopped onto the stairs.

> The shadow on the moon is the fae lords declaring war. We need a good astronomical cover story. And please text Riggs, Farrell, and Anthony.

She dithered about what else to add, but what else did they know at this point? She certainly didn't want to tell them she might have already revealed all their plans to fight back.

Returning to Alex, she and Nik ran interference to keep people back far enough so the amateur astronomer could get the photos she needed. Imagine if jostling the telescope ruined the all-important evidence!

"Got it." Alex moved back from the telescope and pointed her camera phone at the moon directly.

The school door slammed, and people streamed out. Gil pushed Ned's wheelchair like an Olympic sprinter.

The shadow on the moon vanished.

Alex straightened. "You were right, Shar; they didn't leave it up."

"What is going on out here?" Ms. Maxwell barked as soon as she reached the courtyard.

"Where is the signal?" Chantelle twisted to look at the moon behind her.

"It's gone now," Gaby said, "but Alex took pictures."

"Here." Alex waved her phone. "Is everyone ready?"

"We won't all fit around the phone," Ms. Ellison said. "Show the fae first, and then we'll take a turn." Alex's mother put a calming hand on Ms. Maxwell's arm.

Obediently, Alex handed the phone to Chantelle, who crouched between Ned and Miles on one side and Meg on the other. Tom remained where he was, gazing at the moon with narrowed eyes. After a minute, Chantelle passed the cell to the two human women, who rapidly flipped through all the photos.

"At least you were watching at the right time," Ms. Ellison said. "I wonder what made them lose patience tonight. Up until now, they've been difficult, but they didn't neglect negotiations entirely."

"We invited them to parley," Gil said. "This was their response."

Ms. Maxwell sucked in a breath and held it. When she finally exhaled, her voice was frigid. "You did what exactly?"

"We sent messengers to invite them to parley," Shar said.

"They tortured Vince," Gaby blurted, "and we think he's dead."

"What?" Alex shouted. "You didn't tell me that."

"Dead?" Nate's heads wove in a distressed pattern.

Ms. Maxwell scanned the crowded courtyard and growled. "Everyone inside! Now! If this discussion has nothing to do with you, then go to your room!"

Alex reached for her telescope, but Nik scooped it up and marched for the door as if it weighed nothing. Behind him, a stream of fae and humans headed in, splitting at the door to either go to their rooms or follow Ms. Maxwell into the school office.

Finally, the king's secret council and the adult administrators were behind a locked door. Gaby's phone buzzed with a text from Mamá.

> Oh, dear. Keep me informed. The others should contact Ms. Maxwell soon.

Ms. Maxwell's phone buzzed. She glanced at the screen, raised her eyebrows at Gaby, and shoved the phone into her back pocket. "I'll deal with them when I know what to say."

Gaby felt her cheeks heat. Maybe she had texted too early, but she hoped the government officials could be useful in the emergency.

"And to help me with that," Ms. Maxwell continued, "somebody had better tell me what you lot have been doing." She folded her arms and glared at each of them in turn. "How dare you children send Vince — and who else? — into trouble, without permission or safeguards or — I don't know what to say here."

Gaby's cheeks burned hotter, if that was possible. U.N. ducked behind his bangs, but Alex folded her arms and glared back at the principal until Nik bumped her shoulder with his.

Pulling himself to his full height and wrapping power almost visibly around him, Shar stepped in front of the others. "I sent them, by my own authority. Vince *was* the safeguard for... Rafe." His eye twitched when he said the forbidden name. "Vince is a graduated ambassador, though he did not have a post, and his strength is nearly unmatched."

Meg cleared her throat. "The council agreed with the prince. It was a joint decision after you said the humans could do nothing. And though we involved the children for their skills, the plan was approved by the adults. You can't blame us for the lords being cruel. We warned you about their odd behavior and the likelihood of their rebellion."

Ms. Maxwell rubbed her hands across her face. "Okay, this has bypassed my paygrade. Everyone find a seat. I need to call the major general."

Already in the corner, Gaby huddled with her knees to her chest, mostly hidden behind Ned's wheelchair.

The principal waited until everyone was settled on chairs or the floor, then dialed her cell. "Anthony, we have a situation. Did you see the moon tonight? Oh, they did text, did they?" She scowled at Gaby again, unerringly finding her despite her hiding place. "Yes, it's true. I have everyone here now. Yes, sir. Yes, sir. No, sir."

She hung up and dropped her phone onto her desk. "It's too far for him to get here tonight, so he'll come tomorrow morning. Everyone go to bed, and if you step one toe out of this school before the general gets here, I will cut off your foot. Get out of my sight."

Zee yanked open the door and ran from the office. The others followed as quickly as possible, though Gaby's position in the corner meant she had to wait until most of the people were gone and Tom could push Ned's wheelchair.

Once free, Gaby stumbled to her room, numb with guilt. With the moonlight streaming through the window, she could barely see Zee already in bed, covers pulled to her eyes. Gaby changed into her pajamas and climbed into her own bed, but she lay awake for a long time, wondering how many people would die because she had lost track of her notebook.

IN THE MORNING, Gaby ate breakfast slowly, struggling to choke down granola that tasted like sawdust. Washing it down with juice didn't help, since the bitterness in her mouth turned the sweet orange to cough syrup. Watching the room, it was easy to tell gossip had spread about last night. Everyone was quieter than usual, picking at their food and staring out the windows, though nothing was in view but the pool and the courtyard.

She barely finished eating by the time the principal arrived to collect Shar from the cafeteria. When the prince stood, his fae council immediately followed, stacking their trays as they exited. Ms. Ellison and Ms. Maxwell hurried after them. At a gesture from Gil, U.N. and Nik tagged along.

Alex scowled and thumped her college textbooks into a stack. From their study sessions, Gaby knew Alex had finals coming soon, and papers and projects due before then. No way did she have time for anything but school.

Gaby ducked her head and piled her silverware and dishes onto her tray, devoting all her attention to lining everything up perfectly. Someone nudged her shoulder.

"What?" Gaby protested.

"Hurry," Zee whispered. "Everyone's waiting."

"For me?" Gaby dropped her spoon with a clatter.

But she had let the plans slip into the enemy's hands. Why would they want her around anymore? Unless they wanted to punish her.

"Come on," Zee whispered frantically.

At the door, U.N. beckoned wildly. Gaby stumbled to her feet and rushed to dump her tray and follow the line of people across the hall to the nurse's office, which was the biggest private room available.

Chairs had already been set in rows, leaving access to the cots for more seating. Blushing hotly, Gaby followed Zee to the farthest cot and squeezed next to U.N.

At the other end of the room, Ms. Maxwell stood next to Major General Anthony, who wore his official uniform and a stern expression. Shadows under his eyes hinted at a long night. An aide of some kind hovered a few steps away with a stack of paperwork.

"Thank you for calling me," Anthony said. "My first question is if you are sure that shadow was meant to summon war? We've gotten no declaration of war through official channels."

"The fae don't work that way," Tom said. "The first attack will be the declaration. We're very lucky the circumstances of this world made it more difficult for the lords to use their usual methods, or we would have gotten no warning at all."

Gaby's memory of language sessions with Zee immediately supplied the scientific reasons. Their old worlds had been habitable on only one side, reducing the distance they needed to span. Their population had been smaller than Earth's, and they had more magic-users of various types before the exile. With all those factors simplified, communication was as easy and fast as technology allowed for the humans. But the lords didn't use technology, so they had to adapt on Earth.

Anthony's mouth tightened. "Well, we can't hit them first, because with no proof or declaration, we would be the instigators. All we can do is try to prepare. I'm hoping you can help me with that."

"We will tell you anything we can," Shar said.

"Second question, then," Anthony said. "How much time do we have?"

Ms. Maxwell cleared her throat. "I called the other building last night, after I talked to you. Nobody answered the phone or the radio. I think our guards are now out of the picture. I can only hope they've been captured rather than killed. Without your advice about magic, I didn't know what else to try."

Gil shrugged. "There is nothing you can do. Fortunately, most of the fae are still unaccustomed to Earth's gravity. Their mages might attack early, but they will have to wait to build an army."

Anthony nodded. "A small blessing. Should we recall the ambassadors? Maxwell tells me they are targets, though temporarily safe. I'd prefer to have them permanently safe."

So would Gaby. She knew most of them personally and counted many of them as friends.

"You can't afford to lose them," Chantelle said in her musical voice. "The ambassadors are the only ones who speak both Fae and Earth languages. Without them, you can't communicate with the three hundred thousand fae around the world, which will leave them at the mercy of whatever the lords tell them. And most of the fae are not your enemies; don't put yourself at that disadvantage."

"A valid point." Anthony didn't sigh, exactly, but Gaby suspected only discipline kept his long breath calm. "Then how can we prepare for war?"

"I don't see why we're worried," the aide interrupted. "They have no guns, no tanks, no planes, and we outnumber them. The fae would be foolish to attack because we'll mow them down in less than an hour." He sneered as he pretended to sweep a machine gun across the room.

Anthony covered his eyes with one hand. "Hays, be quiet."

Gil stood. "I tried to explain when we first met but didn't have enough language. Let me try again. There is no way you can win against fae magic. Now, maybe they can't win either and it would be mutual destruction, but there is no easy victory in view. The best option we have is to avoid the fight in the first place."

Like everyone else, Gaby nodded. Nobody smart wanted the war.

"Well, I still say—" the aide tried.

Tom smiled at him, his snake fangs showing, and the aide stumbled to a halt. The naga stood, lean and even taller than Gil, with piercing yellow eyes.

With a grin, Gil sat on the other side of U.N. again, pulling his feet onto the bed to sit cross-legged. "This will be good," he whispered.

"I've been a warrior for fifteen hundred conjunctions," Tom said.

"About one hundred and fifty-two years," Zee calculated aloud, a second earlier than Gaby's mental math.

Wow, a hundred and fifty years? And he looked a healthy middle age at most. Was that natural to the fae or the result of their healers? Gaby's fingers itched to write a note to remind herself to ask.

"And I've fought in many wars in that time," Tom continued. "Before I joined the king's Companions, I was a soldier for the lord of my city. As a warrior, I trained daily to strengthen my body and increase my skills. By the time the king's Chief Companion died, I was the best at weapons work and strategy."

On the other side of U.N., Gil frowned. Gaby almost leaned around to pat his shoulder. Poor Gil, losing his grandfather when he already had no father.

Tom kept talking. "Despite my prowess, a bit of bad luck will still let me fall to any of the shapeshifters that have teeth and claws. Stonegazers don't even need a mistake on my part to defeat me."

"Gorgons and basilisks," U.N. supplied. "We have a few at the school, if you want to meet one." His stare at the aide was defiant enough that his mother raised her eyebrows at him.

Tom ignored him. "Trolls and giants can smash me with a single blow. If I were foolish enough to venture into the water, any of the water fae could drown me. Fire fae can burn me, ice fae can freeze me, earth fae can open a pit to catch my feet, dryads can tangle me in greenery until I am easy prey. All of those have only their innate magic, specific to their form."

The aide was opening and closing his mouth like a fish. Gaby turned her face a little to hide her amusement and met Zee's equally amused gaze. The war wasn't at all funny, but watching the aide sputter relieved some of her stress.

Tom kept talking. "Then you have the fae with real magic. Some can pull away your guns or spin you to fire on your own soldiers or trip you in a charge. Some can make you hear the wrong command or see an enemy instead of a companion." He shrugged. "That is all minor magic."

He grinned again, narrowing his yellow eyes. "The lords have more magic than you can imagine. They can divert entire rivers to drown your company, open chasms to swallow your war wagons, leach air from the lungs of your whole army, burn the area to cinders, create illusions for every soldier at once."

"They can't possibly—" the aide tried.

Tom laughed. "In my youth, my lord sank an entire city that opposed him. A few lords can, under the right circumstances, take over a mind completely and make a commander give the wrong orders or betray his own men. They can control their own troops absolutely, sending them into battles no matter the odds. No fae would dare betray their lords."

"If the commands are magically set," Miles said grimly, "they *can't* betray them."

Anthony did sigh this time. "So we can't count on help from the rest of your people, either. Is there any way to at least avoid the mind control?"

"Don't touch a fae or give your whole name to them," Ned advised.

Anthony mouthed a swear word. "I will discover who has already given their names and replace them with someone else. I will also give orders for our officers to stop meeting with anyone other than your ambassadors or those you have cleared. Will that be sufficient?"

Shar shrugged. "I believe it is the best we can do."

"Okay." Anthony glanced at the clock. "If that is all for now, then I need to consult with the President. Please keep me informed of any new updates." He put his cap on his head and straightened his shoulders. "At least the enemy fae won't know what to expect from us anymore than we do from them."

Gaby nearly cried as she raised a trembling hand. "Actually, sir... They have my notebook with notes from everything we talked about previously. I'm sorry, sir." Her voice croaked into silence.

"You careless little—" Hays choked to a stop as the general grabbed the back of his collar.

"We'll talk later," Anthony promised, yanking his aide toward the door.

The two men marched out, and the council slowly followed.

Gaby stayed behind on the cot and gave way to tears. Grand-mère would never believe Gaby hadn't betrayed Earth on purpose. She would never let Gaby go home again.

CHAPTER 10

IN WHICH THE ARMIES ARE GROWING

AUGUST 4-8, 2023

THREE DAYS LATER, Gil was working on emails with Shar and his secretary when Mak-swill walked into Shar's office, still on the phone.

"Thanks, Anthony. I'll keep you updated." She tapped off the phone and slid it into her pocket. "Good morning, Your Majesty."

"Sire." Gil murmured the correction. Not that the prince would be upset, but the humans might as well get used to protocol.

"That was the general," Mak-swill said, with a nod at Gil. "He says the President won't attack first, Sire. We have to wait for the lords to make their move and prove they intend war. And you already said it will take time to build their army."

"They already declared war," Nik said.

"Yes, well, the President doesn't think a shadow on the moon is definitive." Mak-swill grimaced. "We have to wait for an actual attack by real soldiers."

Shar raised his eyebrows. "We will be sure to tell him when such an event occurs, if he is still alive then."

Gil pursed his lips in a silent whistle. The warning sounded almost like a threat.

Mak-swill scowled. "I'm sorry we can't get people to take your word for it. Keep me informed, okay?"

"Okay," Gil said.

The three fae waited until Mak-swill left, closing the door behind her, before they returned to their work.

"Jin says the same as the other ambassadors," Gil read from the email. "She and Freya talked to all the lesser fae they could find. They assured them we're still willing to negotiate with the highborn and asked how they felt about your survival and announcement. Like the fae in other places, those in China are happy you lived but worried about the war."

"Does she say if they are seeing preparations there?" Nik asked.

Shar scanned the computer over Gil's shoulder. "The early Kunisu refugees are already being pulled into training and drills."

"Probably because we're walking," Gil said. "We've been on Earth long enough to get used to the gravity, unlike those in the later landings, who are still rebuilding bone and muscle." He read further and scowled. "But Jin says there are fewer fae in wheelchairs than expected, and more are walking around. And not just the shifters, who heal a little every time they change form."

"Maybe Earth is good for them?" Nik asked.

Gil patted Nik's wheelchair. "You know that's not how it works."

"Then how are they recovering so fast?" Nik asked.

"That's an excellent question," Shar said. "Does Jin say anything more?"

Scrolling down, Gil read again. "They're having to sneak around the highborn, so it's hard to get information. That's all anyone has for now, but I will ask them to talk to the healers and see if they have any ideas how people are improving so quickly."

"Do the same for all the ambassadors," Shar said, "and tell Freya to stay out of sight. Her lightning magic is perfect for war work, and we would prefer to keep her on our side."

Gil winked. "She's also good at frying locks."

Shar laughed. "She's finding new uses all the time."

"Earth has been good for many of us," Gil agreed.

Despite Freya being more capable of defending herself than most of the fae, Gil obediently added the warning to the request to question the healers. He copied most of the message and sent it to all the ambassadors. The more eyes and ears looking for answers, the better.

THE NEXT DAY, replies started coming in. So many emails came that Shar asked the humans to help sort the information. Even Alexandria and Nikos, out of school for the weekend, grabbed a computer and helped the fae council read and sort data. By late afternoon, the picture was chilling.

The ambassadors had done well questioning the fae and had discovered alarming details. The shapeshifters were being forced to shift several times a day to increase their strength and recover bone density faster. Other commoners were summoned to see the healers every few days, and their strength also increased at a suspicious rate. Furthermore, as soon as any of them recovered enough to run without aid, they disappeared and were not seen again, leaving behind empty wheelchairs and homes. The larger or more formidable the fae, the more likely they were to be taken. Only the smallest, weakest fae races were left untouched.

"The lords are building their physical armies with healing and magic," Gil said numbly, staring at the numbers on the wall. "They aren't waiting until the fae recover naturally. We have much less time than we thought. Mere weeks, at most."

"What do the healers say about this?" Shar looked at each person for answers.

"None of our ambassadors can find a healer," Gil said. "They *hear* about others taken to see them, but nobody knows where they are."

"Brilliant," Shar said. "Absolutely brilliant. The lords have cut us off and increased their own resources in the same move."

Eyebrows raised, Gil stared at him. "You approve?"

The rest of the commoners and humans looked as shocked as he felt.

"Don't be ridiculous," Shar said. "When we win, I'll make the lords pay for kidnapping my people. But it *is* brilliant. I only wish they were on our side."

If they won, Gil mentally amended. But they had to win.

"Finding the healers just became a top priority," Taras said. "Please ask the ambassadors to gather as much help as possible to look for them."

"Sure." Gil started typing. "But in the big cities, there are too many buildings to search, and we don't have any seers."

"Ask the pixies and other small fae to help," Miknon said. "We make good spies."

Surprised, Gil stared at her. It had been more than a year since he persuaded her to spy on the lords on board the spaceship, and she was still mad at him. As his elder sister, she might hold that grudge for a hundred years. Considering they had to flee the spaceship to save her life when the adventure went wrong, he understood, though her espionage had saved the commoners from the lords' mischief. Silently, he added the suggestion to the latest email, even as the old worry for her safety roared to life. He couldn't protect her from risks she chose for herself.

"What else can we do?" Gil asked.

"Can the ambassadors help anyone else find places to hide for refuge?" Shalla asked.

"Probably not, but I'll ask." Gil added the request.

"The good part of this," Shar said thoughtfully, "is that it will still take the healers time to rehabilitate enough fae to fight the humans. And if spending the blood of commoners is their main plan, rather than exerting their own magic, it gives us precious weeks to plan our defense and coordinate with the military."

"That's a rather small positive," Gil said, "but I'm grateful we get any chance at all."

After all his efforts to win them a peaceful home, the past month had been extremely frustrating. If there was any way to still get a treaty, he *would* find it.

The group discussed the war for another hour without finding any more solutions. Gil copied the email and sent it to all the ambassadors before the meeting ended in time for dinner.

THE NEXT DAY WAS SUNDAY, a rest day for many of the humans. Some of them attended religious services of one kind or another, worshiping a supreme being they had never seen, which was an odd concept for the common fae. It was even odder for the highborn, who thought themselves the ultimate power. Gil hadn't ever minded going with Ian's family, but now that his people were on Earth, he preferred spending the time with them.

After breakfast and a rowdy game of frisbee, he joined Shar and the commoner leaders to read more emails and consider more plans. The day passed slowly until a chat arrived from Okoro Dambe in Nigeria.

"We took a trip to the countryside," Okoro said, "to see if we could spot anything suspicious. It's savannah here, which means mostly grass and a few trees, so we can see a far distance, unlike in the city. The important point is that as we were ready to come back, we saw many people walking around in the middle of the grasslands, which is unusual. We snuck closer and discovered rather a lot of fae marching and drilling combat skills. I think we've found our missing people, or at least some of them."

"Well done," Shar dictated as Gil typed back. "I wish all the locations could do the same. Can you rescue anyone or disrupt the training?"

"We went closer," Okoro said, "but when we reached the spot where we'd seen them, they were gone. On our way out, we stumbled across a vampire lying under a tree. Fortunately, the shade protected her a bit, though she's terribly sunburned. I thought the sun was lethal to vampires?"

"Don't call them vampires," Gil typed. "The bloodworkers don't like the association with the Earth legends. And no, they don't vanish in a puff of smoke; the myths get a lot of things wrong. Where is the healer now?"

"We brought her back with us," Okoro said. "We're treating her the best we can, but she isn't doing well."

"And of course you can't find another healer to help." Shar sighed. "Keep trying. If you discover anything else, let us know immediately."

"I will." Okoro ended the chat.

"Good news and bad," Gil said. "If they're building armies in Nigeria, then they're doing it everywhere, but at least we saved one healer."

"Yes," Shar agreed. "I imagine they were planning to come back for that healer when the area was clear again. Now they'll have to make do without her. How unfortunate we can't steal all the healers to delay the progress of the army."

"That's an idea, actually," Taras said. "Could we manage that?"

"Not unless we can find where they are hiding the armies," Gil said. "But at least they are continuing to build their troops before they attack."

BUT THE NEXT DAY, the weather across the eastern and southeast states moved from seasonally severe to more than seven hundred severe thunderstorms in a single day, including a tornado less than three hundred miles from the school. Yet again, everyone assembled to discuss the implications.

"This is magic." Shalla's face was pale under the flickering fluorescent lights of the basement. "It must be."

"I agree," Ian said. "I checked the records, and that's the most of any day this year. And the tornado was too severe to be normal."

"Then the lords are moving already." Gil rubbed his aching forehead. "It's probably a response to being discovered yesterday. But why aren't they hitting here? The prince is here."

"Kishar is only a town away," Nik said. "He likes his comfort, so I suspect he will save this area for his final blow."

"You are probably right," Shar said. "How long will we have before they increase their attacks? And where will they hit next?"

The answer came just after midnight. A hurricane on the other side of the world swung close to islands instead of passing them, and a brush fire caught the winds and burned for miles. By early morning, the wind was strong enough to blow down power lines, which hit dry brush and ignited more fires. Everyone at the school celebrated when the humans extinguished the fires by late morning.

They rejoiced too soon.

By mid-afternoon, the fire mysteriously reignited, forcing several evacuations, and within an hour, a strong wind blew fire and smoke across the area. Some witnesses claimed they had heard explosions.

"I'm sure they did," Taras muttered. "Someone is having too much fun making trouble."

Gil slumped in his chair, wondering if a fire mage was at fault or if someone had tormented a phoenix until it lost control. Not that it would matter to the humans being chased from their homes.

"Why would they do this?" Gaby asked, wringing her hands.

"War," Gil snapped.

"But we didn't do anything," Ian protested.

"You sided with the commoners," Gil said.

Ian spluttered into silence, and Gaby bit her lip.

The flames increased in area and intensity until evening, eventually growing so terrible that people jumped into the ocean to escape the fire. At the school, everyone watched the news on the television with muttered curses against the lords. By attacking potential allies first, they were destroying any help that might come when they moved against their own people, and burning the goodwill that Gil and the ambassadors had worked so hard to build.

And nobody could stop them.

Major General Anthony came and watched with them, but he remained skeptical. "Our scientists say it's climate change," he said. "The El Niño current is causing drought conditions."

"Enough for your country's deadliest wildfire in more than a hundred years?" Gil asked quietly. "Perhaps. But what if it isn't?"

"You said the same about the storms on the east coast," the general protested. "There's no way I can convince the President it isn't just bad weather."

Shar rose to his feet and faced Anthony. "You are being attacked, and more than a hundred of your people have died. Will you do nothing?"

"Even if you're right," the general said, "and if I could convince the

President, there's nothing we can do against bad weather." He rose and donned his hat. "Let me know if an army arrives." He bowed and left.

"Argh!" Ian yanked on his hair until it stood on end.

"This won't be the end of it," Gil said.

Shar sat again, his back stiff. "I know."

Nik leafed through a notebook he had copied from his old records, listing all the fae and their magical talents. "I wish we knew for certain who was on our side. I dare not ask for help until loyalties are clear among the highborn, and none of the lesser fae have enough power to match the lords."

"I know," Shar repeated.

He watched the television, lips white with strain. Sliding his chair closer, Gil reached for his friend's shoulder but pulled back before touching him.

On the screen, the Coast Guard was rescuing people from the ocean, hauling them one at a time into a small boat or lifting them into a helicopter. The news cameras were distant enough that little could be seen, just dots for bodies among the rolling waves. Despite the lack of details, everyone ignored the final bell of the day and stayed by the basement television for more than an hour to watch the entire rescue.

Once the shivering people reached the shore, the newscasters surrounded them, shoving microphones in their faces and shouting overlapping questions.

Most of the people merely said they were glad to be alive, pulling blankets tightly around their shoulders and wiping faces clear of salt water.

One young girl blurted, "The mermaids saved us," before her father shushed her.

A reporter asked her to repeat herself, but the grateful, weeping family surrounded the girl and her father and dragged them to safety. None of the others rescued from the ocean would discuss the idea of mermaids, though several of them watched the ocean with an odd mix of skepticism, curiosity, and wonder.

"Ha!" Gil said. "It looks like some of the water fae are still on our side, Sire. If they kept those people afloat until the other humans could rescue them, then they are still voting for peace and still willing to work for a treaty. Just as importantly, they aren't supporting the lords."

"There's not much they can do to help us on land," Shar said.

"Perhaps not, but having one less battlefield is still useful," Taras said.

"But is it enough?" Ian asked.

"If we can't win any of the battles," Gaby asked, "what chance do we have?"

And Gil had no answer for either of them.

Chapter 11

Letter

August 11, 2023

With his stomach tying itself in knots, Ian leaned against the cafeteria wall. Though the last three days since the Hawaii fires had been stressful, he'd held it together until the mail arrived this morning.

The light streaming through the doorway was just enough to read the letter a second time.

Ian. No "dear," unsurprisingly.

I saw you on television in June. When will you get a haircut? Never. The paper shook in his hands.

I had to call every school in ten states around the area covered by the television station that first aired your announcement. Nobody would tell me if you and Alex were students, but I finally found your mother listed as faculty. Without my name!

Ian mentally swore in Russian, Dad's second language. They should have listed Mom under an alias instead of using her maiden name. As for her keeping Fitch, that was out of the question. Erasing Dad from their lives was best for everyone. If only Ian could change his own name! Maybe he still could, though it was too late to be helpful except to prove a point.

Now that you've had more than a year to cool down, I'd like to talk. Your mother was unreasonable about hiding my children, and Alex was just as bad. Since she forbade me from contacting her until she was eighteen but said you could make your own choices, I'm writing to you.

Yeah, Alexandria said Ian could make his own choices. As in, decide to *never* talk to Dad instead of listening when he turned eighteen. Never sounded about right.

You should come back to live with me. I can protect you from the aliens. I was right about them, and I'm right about this. Come home, whether or not your mother and sister are smart enough to obey. I'll get you enrolled in a military academy immediately, so you can learn to protect yourself.

Sparks danced in front of Ian's eyes, and nausea rolled through him. Great, all he needed was a migraine to make this day perfect. Which was another reminder that living with Dad was a terrible idea. Dad thought Ian's migraines were proof of weakness, and if Mom stopped coddling him, they would disappear. But dealing with Dad frequently caused the headaches, so there was no winning.

As for the aliens, if they could stop the lords, nobody would need to protect him. Gil was his best friend and brother, and most of the fae were equally nice. And Mom and Alexandria were ten times smarter than Dad.

Signed, Troy. He wasn't even calling himself Dad. Fine with Ian. He was a lousy father.

P.S. You left your junk at my house. It took me all day to clear it out. Ian would have taken all his "junk" if Dad hadn't forbidden them from keeping anything he ever paid for, which was almost everything they owned. Ian still missed his books.

With shaking hands, he crumpled the paper and tossed it toward the garbage. It missed, but he closed his eyes and pressed his hands over them. If he moved right now, he might vomit on the floor. His medicine was with Mom, and the nurse's office was across the brightly lit hall. At least the cafeteria was dark between meals, now that everyone spent most of their time in the translators' offices or watching the news in the basement. The cooks must already be working on dinner, since the smell of chicken and apple pie was drifting through the air. If he stayed here for a while, maybe the migraine would ease enough for him to make it to the office.

"Ian, are you okay?"

Ian jerked at the sound, and warm hands gently clutched his elbows to steady him for a second.

"Hey, Gil. Can you walk me to the nurse and tell Mom I need my meds?"

"Yup. Keep your eyes closed." Instead of taking his elbow, Gil pulled Ian's arms forward and up. Ian bumped into Gil's back, and the taller boy stood, taking Ian with him in a modified piggy-back ride.

Ian buried his face against Gil's neck and let himself dangle. While the position would have gotten uncomfortable in a few minutes, the short trip across the hall was no trouble.

"Do you want Miles?" Gil asked.

Ian groaned. "Let's give my meds a try first. Miles has enough on his mind."

The school's healer had been emailing Okoro every few hours with ideas for treating the drained healer found on the savannah. So far, none of them had worked.

"Okay." Gil shut the door behind him as he left, leaving Ian in the dark.

The heavy blinds in the nurse's office were deliberately left closed most of the time for exactly this reason. With his arm across his eyes to block the hall light when someone came back, Ian stewed over Dad's letter. How could Dad possibly think he would ever go back to live with him again? Ian didn't even want to talk to him for two minutes. The only question in his mind was whether to tell Mom and Alexandria about the letter or let the two of them live in ignorant peace.

Put that way, the choice was easy. With the letter in the trash, Ian would forget he ever got it.

The door creaked open, closing again so quickly it must have been only cracked enough for someone to slip through.

"Here you go," Gil whispered. "Water." He touched the glass to Ian's arm for spatial reference. "And your pill." This he pressed into Ian's other hand.

When Ian struggled to sit, Gil slipped an arm under his back and lifted, all without spilling the water. Once the pill was swallowed, Gil lowered Ian and took the empty glass. Instead of leaving, he sat and put his feet on the bed.

"You don't have to stay," Ian said. "I'll be okay."

"I want to talk to you," Gil said softly, "if you feel able."

"About translating," Ian asked, "or is there another emergency with the lords?"

"Neither." Gil pulled something from his pocket and pressed it smooth against his leg, but it was too dark to see what it was. "I found the paper you dropped."

"It's trash," Ian said. "Toss it." Or burn it.

"Mmm. I read it," Gil said thoughtfully.

Ian groaned and yanked the pillow over his head. "It's trash," he mumbled through the barrier.

The pillow disappeared, and Gil leaned forward, waving the letter. "Isn't this from your father? You should answer him."

"No way." Ian turned and stared at the wall.

"I would love to have a father." Gil's voice was wistful.

"You don't understand how a bad relationship can be worse than nothing," Ian protested.

Gil laughed bitterly. "Oh, don't I?"

Right. His twin had betrayed them all. Ian bit his tongue and squeezed his eyes shut. "Sorry. Of course you do."

"But I still love my brother," Gil continued. "I only wish I knew why he believes the lies."

"Well, I don't love Dad," Ian said. "And he doesn't love me."

Paper crinkled. "Are you sure?"

"I won't answer the letter," Ian said, "and don't you dare tell anyone about it. It's garbage, like I told you." He pressed on his head again as the pain flared.

"Okay," Gil whispered. Paper crackled, then bounced softly into the garbage bin.

"If you're staying," Ian said, "you might as well tell me the latest news."

"The hail and thunderstorms in Minnesota are getting worse," Gil said. "The hail is now the size of golf balls. What's a golf ball?"

"A ball this size." Ian made a circle with thumb and finger. "Golf is a game where the players hit the ball on the ground to knock it into a hole with bent sticks."

"Instead of hitting a ball already in the air. Got it," Gil said.

Ian chuckled. Explaining the details sometimes highlighted the oddities of human life. "Never mind. The point is that the hail is big enough to cause a lot of damage."

"Roofs and cars," Gil agreed. "And the wind is snapping trees and power lines. Which are?"

"The tall posts that hold the electrical wires," Ian said. "No magic."

"Thank you for the clarification." Gil's claws clicked on his phone. "We think this is definitely fae magic. Will the President do something now?"

"Did you tell Anthony?" Ian asked.

"Yes."

Ian shrugged. "That's all we can do."

"But when will they listen?"

Ian sighed. "I don't know."

The door cracked open, and a tall figure slipped inside.

"Hi, Gil," Alexandria whispered. "How's he doing?"

"Fine," Ian said. "How did finals go?"

"Pretty sure I passed." His sister pulled another chair to the foot of the bed. "I've got ten days of vacation before fall semester starts. What can I do to help around here?"

"We're kind of stuck," Ian said, "until we get more data or the President changes his mind."

"More data," Alexandria mused. "Or a new look at old data? I think I'll have a chat with the secretary about what magical talents are available."

"They aren't powerful enough to stop the weather-working," Gil said.

"Maybe not," Alexandria said, "but you guys never thought of using Freya's magic like she's doing, either. New eyes might be helpful. You never know."

"Okay," Gil said. "I'll ask Shar to translate the list for you."

"The prince? Shouldn't you assign the work to someone else?"

Gil laughed. "He won't mind."

Ian's siblings kept strategizing quietly while he waited for his migraine to settle. When the dinner bell rang, it was almost gone. Alexandria stayed with Ian while Gil ran off, returning in a few minutes with Miles. The fae healer touched Ian on the head and the back of the neck, and the last remnants of the headache faded. Too bad they couldn't bottle that, or Miles could earn enough money to support him for life.

They made the end of the dinner line and sat with the rest of their family. Someone had brought a television in on a library cart, and they watched the latest updates of the thunderstorms. At least five storms were pounding the Buffalo Lake and Twin Cities areas, with hail getting as large as baseballs. ("Why do they always measure it in ball sizes?" Zee asked.) The skies were so dark, despite the lightning, that streetlights came on long before nightfall. As the wind crossed the Mississippi River, it intensified to almost seventy miles per hour. ("As fast as a car on the freeway," Ian explained to the fae.) More storms hit southern Minnesota, spreading the damage across a wide area.

Yet again, the council tried talking to the general, who yet again said the President was still considering the bad weather a natural phenomenon. Ian hung up the phone more dramatically than necessary.

"They'll never listen," Ian said. Dad, Mr. Abernathy, the President, and the fae lords were all of the opinion they were right and it was their way or the highway. He knew how it worked.

"We need better plans," Alexandria said. No surprise; she loved plans. But she was right.

Gaby ducked her head. "The President might be a bad idea, anyway."

"Why do you say that?" Shar asked.

"Because if he did decide the threat is real, his answer to war would be more war," Gaby said. "We need to *stop* the fighting, not meet it with greater force. Neither side can be sure of winning, and really, we don't want either side to *lose*. We don't want to fight at all."

"But the military would fight," Ian said, "if they were called in. Like Dad, wanting to shoot all the aliens."

"Right," Nikos agreed. "We need to end it fast, without the military, or we'll end up in another world war."

"That means if the humans can't do anything," Ian said, "it's up to the fae."

Gil tapped a clawed finger on his knee. "I still think you should make the lords obey, Sire."

"We already talked about this," Shar said. "The parley failed. I won't send anyone else into danger. I can't possibly use command voice on them if I can't get close enough. Even if I could get within range, my magic is still immature and much less powerful than Kishar's." His face was calm, but his voice cracked.

He ran his fingers through his hair, messing it up even more and uncovering one slightly pointed ear. "I'm sorry, but there's nothing I can do."

"There has to be something someone can do," Alexandria protested.

"When you think of it," Shar snapped, "let me know." He rose and stalked out.

Gil raised his eyebrows at Ian and followed his prince. The rest of the fae said quiet farewells and left. For a while, the humans sat in silence.

Finally, Alexandria jumped to her feet. "Sitting here won't make us think of ideas any faster. Go to bed, everybody. We'll think better on a good night's sleep." But she clutched her notebook like a security blanket.

The humans wandered out, heads bowed. Gaby had chewed on her lip so much that it was painfully red.

Ian texted Gil.

> We're ready to go home. Are you staying here tonight?

I'm coming, his foster brother replied.

Ian, Alexandria, and Nikos hunted down Mom. By the time she finished her conversation with another teacher, Gil arrived with Miknon. He looked exhausted, and his usually cheerful face was drawn.

"Is Shar okay?" Alexandria asked in a low voice, casting a side glance at Mom.

Gil shrugged. "It's hard for him to not be able to fix this. His heart yearns to protect our people and yours."

"If he can't do anything," Ian asked, "and the fae have no magic strong enough to match the lords, is the military our only hope? Against magic that can kill them all or turn them against us? Do we have any chance?"

Gil shrugged again. "I hope we think of another way."

"Okay, kids," Mom said. "Let's go home."

Nikos pulled his keys from his pocket. Gil winked at Ian and ran, leaving Miknon fluttering behind. Ian laughed and chased after him, with Nikos in hot pursuit. But Alexandria's long legs passed them all, and she won the race to the truck by a hand-length, slapping the blue door with a triumphant laugh. Though they climbed into their seats quickly, all four of them had to wait for Mom and Miknon to catch up.

The ride home gave time for the laughter to die and the reality of their situation to return. How could they possibly win?

Once home, half of them showered and everyone changed into pajamas. Since it was still a bit early, most of them retreated to their beds for a little quiet reading. Miknon and Gil hung out on the werewolf's top bunk, talking in a barely audible murmur.

With all the current events flooding his brain, Ian found it hard to concentrate on his Japanese novel. If the military was the only way to stop the lords from conquering Earth, was war inevitable? And even if they could convince the armies to move fast enough, how could they have a chance against the fae magic?

Would Dad eventually fight aliens after all? How odd his paranoia might have a basis in fact. But even if he was right about that, he was still wrong to treat his family like he had. He deserved to be alone.

But did he deserve to die alone?

Why did the thought of Dad dying bother Ian? It wasn't like he had many fond memories from recent years. Dad didn't even like him.

Ian slammed his book shut and buried his face in his pillow. Why couldn't he forget about Dad?

CHAPTER 12

IN WHICH THEY MAKE A PLAN

THREE DAYS after the hailstorms in Minnesota, the news told of similar storms in the Czech Republic. Torrential rains and hail pounded the area, and Zak emailed her friend Kirill to ask if he was well.

"I'm fine," Kirill emailed back. "I'm eight hundred kilometers away. Most of Poland is between me and those storms."

Zak looked up distance comparisons and blushed. True, the storms were in the same neighborhood of the world as Kirill, but that was all. She should have checked a map first.

"I've been talking to Yuri," Kirill's email continued, "and monitoring all the countries in our area. It's hard to say what are regular natural disasters and what are caused by fae magic, but it's a terrible year for disasters. Is that really coincidence or do the fae have mages in all those places?"

"There are not that many powerful mages who can manipulate the weather," Zak typed, "but if the pilots can shove a fleet of spaceships across galaxies, they can certainly transport mages to where they are wanted."

A few minutes later, Kirill's reply arrived. "I wish I could do something. I miss you. Keep up the good work, and keep writing."

Reluctantly, Zak turned off the computer and hunted down Shar for the latest update. She found him in his office, scouring the list of magical talents with his secretary and Gaby. When Zak walked in, the prince tossed the list on the desk and scowled.

"There has to be an answer somewhere," he said. "Zee, please gather everyone who is available. Bring them to the basement."

"Yes, Sire." Zak immediately turned around and headed down the hall toward the other commoner leaders. As she walked, she texted the humans, Gil, and the other non-leaders who had been helping. "Council meeting in the basement now, if you are available."

The fae would be available, no matter what else they had been doing. When the prince calls, his subjects answer. The humans had other responsibilities, but most of them would probably come.

She poked her head into Shalla's office. "Shar has called for a meeting in the basement now."

The king's housekeeper immediately stopped dictating to her human assistant. "I'll be there as soon as I arrange for food and water."

Her assistant nodded and grabbed his phone, thumbs flashing rapidly. Zak moved on, giving the same message to Merodach, Maia, and Taras. They all agreed to come, though Merodach had to first send an email regarding the injured healer in Nigeria.

By the time she finished, her texts were full of thumbs-ups, "sure," and a random picture from Nate that probably meant acceptance. Though he could read English, it was hard for him to accurately type with his tongues, and his tail was even more awkward. If his little wagon hadn't given him a way to transport the phone, he wouldn't have access to text at all.

On her way, Zak stopped by Father's room and collected him despite his protests.

"It's time you see what we're doing," she said. "If you don't want to help, that's your choice, but you should at least hear the issues. You were chief navigator on the ship, and I'm sure the prince would still welcome your guidance."

He said nothing more, though he looked thoughtful. In the basement, Zak wheeled Father out of the way, then took empty pitchers from Shalla and filled them with water, placing them on a folding table as the last of the council arrived. With everyone's help, the food and dishes were arranged in minutes, and chairs were set up in rows.

Instead of taking a seat and waiting to be served like the old king or any of the lords, Shar grabbed a plate and served himself, stacking fruit and vegetables and supplementing with a bag of chips. Shalla shook her head but filled her own plate.

Shrugging, Zak got her own food. What did they expect? First Shar had to hide for months to save his life. Then he had to pretend to be an ordinary student for more than a year. If he slipped at any time, he would have been exposed. And just because he had now announced himself didn't mean he would lose the hard-practiced habits, especially since he planned to fulfill his father's promises of equality for the fae. Among his trusted allies, he didn't even have a food-taster, though Taras surely had plans for that if Shar ate among strangers.

Once everyone was ready, Shar washed down his mouthful with a long drink of water. "I know we have talked about this before," he said, "so let's move fast. I've read all the updates and have been sorting the responses. My survival is creating factions, unfortunately. Some fae don't like the humans and think the lords have the better idea about conquering Earth." He kept his face neutral, though most of his audience groaned or made a face. "Most prefer my father's promises and hate the army impressment."

As they should. Taught by Father to be suspicious, Zak had never trusted the lords, but this only proved they would never change. The fae were lucky Shar had somehow learned better, either from his father, his friendship with Gil, or his experiences hiding from the lords or studying with humans. Or some combination of all of them. Whatever the reason, his attitude was highly unusual for the highborn. Even his father had been blackmailed by her grandmother and Gil's grandfather into promising equality, though he seemed to believe in the ideal eventually.

"The lords are already fighting against the humans," Shar continued, "whether or not their attacks are recognized. And we know they are building their armies, though we don't know where they are. We need a plan. Does anyone have any ideas at all?"

"I do," Miknon said.

Gil jerked his head sideways to look at his sister on his shoulder. "You do? How?"

She beat her wings and fluttered into the air. "I've been thinking about this for a long time, Sire, but since our last meeting, I've talked to a lot of lesser fae, especially the smallest ones. We're tired of being slaves, and we want it to end."

"You aren't a slave," Gil protested.

"Nearly," Miknon insisted, flying in circles over Gil's head. "But no longer. Either you lead us in rebellion, Sire, or we will fight alone."

Zak held her breath, anxious to hear the plan. Though the shapeshifters were commoners, they were formidable enough to avoid some of the oppression suffered by the smallest fae. Even gremlins, three-quarters the size of the highborn, were subject to derision and force. The pixies were considered nothing more than light bulbs. But what could they do against the lords?

"As we reorganize our society," Shar said gently, "all will gain rights, but you are not warriors. I do not wish to see you slaughtered."

"We're losing anyway." Miknon hovered to face him, folding her arms. "We'd rather go down fighting. Will you lead us or not? If we fight alone, we will no longer need a king."

Zak gasped, as did most of the fae. Across the circle, Taras clenched his fists and narrowed his eyes, but he kept his gaze on the prince.

"The common fae have never won against the lords," Shalla protested. "Even if we can get the humans to help—"

"We'll help," U.N. blurted. "Somehow," he muttered.

"And since so far they haven't," Shalla said, though the glance she shot U.N. was sympathetic, "we have no chance."

"I believe we do." Miknon fluttered to the ground and put her fists on her hips. "I have a plan."

Shar stroked his chin. "I'm intrigued. Tell me what you propose."

"We have conditions," Miknon said. "If you don't agree, we will simply disappear. We are small enough to find hiding places and leave you to battle the lords on your own. We don't need you to survive anymore."

Gil cleared his throat. Maia winced, reaching a hand toward her adopted daughter. Zak ducked her head to hide her shock. Nobody talked to the prince that way!

Shar's eyebrows shot up his forehead, and his mouth twitched. "What conditions?"

"Besides the old promise of equality," Miknon said, "you must try the lords for murder, as the laws of Earth allow. They shouldn't be allowed to do whatever they want with no consequences."

A murmur ran around the room, and Zak's heart pounded. Did Miknon mean—?

"They killed my parents," Miknon said, "and Gil's father, and Zee's grandmother. Possibly your father. And Vince." Her voice choked on the last word.

Zak blinked back tears. Most of those she mentioned had died when she and Gil and Miknon had been infants, so the pain, though real, was for people they only wished they knew. But Vince had been their friend.

"Any—" Father choked, then continued. "Any justice would be appreciated."

Of course he would feel that way, since his mother was no mere name to him. She put a hand on his knee, and he clutched it, trembling.

Miknon stared at Shar, fists still on her hips. Though her face was brave, her wings trembled. She said nothing more, merely waited.

"I will try the lords for murder whether or not your plan succeeds," Shar said, "if I myself survive."

"You can't do that," Taras objected.

"Why not?" Shar asked. "Do you think the lords should get away with killing people?"

"No, but your lords will never stand for these changes."

Shar shrugged. "It's true my father preferred a more gradual change, but I am not my father. He did not know this world was already occupied, and I think beginning our lives here is a good time to make sweeping changes."

Taras sighed, and Shar looked back at Miknon. "But I will not send you into a battle you cannot possibly win. Convince me you have a chance."

If he didn't survive, Zak didn't expect Earth to emerge in a recognizable state. Lord Kishar would rule a ruined world, with fae and humans mere fragments of their former populations. What could Miknon possibly think could work against the magic of the lords?

Miknon nodded sharply. "Everybody underestimates us," she said. "Yes, I mean the commoners with little magic, but especially we small ones. They think we are a burden, or at best a convenience. We are given jobs that could be done by a lamp or a cleaning brush. Just because we are small doesn't mean we can do nothing important."

She took a deep breath. "From a suggestion of Alex's, I've been reading stories of human fighters and the damage they can do in small ways. Unseen, we can poison the food or water, ruin supplies, and set traps. Even at our size, we can hit small targets like eyes and ears, or low ones like hamstrings."

She suddenly lunged sideways and slashed her arm under Taras's knee. "If I had used a knife, he would be crippled now."

"That is not how the fae fight," Taras protested. "We meet our enemies face to face."

"Not all of us," Zak said. All eyes turned to her, and she clenched her fists in her lap to keep her hands from shaking. "The lords hide behind the commoners and make us take the risks. Only their magic goes onto the battlefield."

"We wish to change everything else," Maia said. "Why must we maintain the old ways of fighting? Is it not better to end the battle quickly, with as many survivors as possible?" She smiled at her adopted daughter, though her lips trembled.

Taras nodded. "True, Sire. And since we prefer to keep our people alive, crippling is a good strategy. The healers can mend them when the war is over."

Zak winced. If thousands of fae were injured to keep them out of the war, it would take the healers months, if not longer, to heal them. But that was still better than death.

"There are already small fae in almost every refugee camp," Miknon continued. "Where there are not, a pilot or dragon can transport dozens of us at once. We can hide in small places and wait for an opportunity to damage the enemy." She inclined her head at Taras. "We would appreciate tactical advice from those more experienced in war." She bowed to Shar. "And we are happy to have the king's approval."

"I'm curious," Shar said. "Why are you so sure you can get the other small fae to go along with this dangerous plan?"

"We've been talking," Miknon said. "Human technology doesn't interfere with *our* magic."

She raised her eyebrows and smirked but didn't offer more details. To Zak's surprise, Shar laughed at her impertinence.

"Very well," he said, "but this plan will take some time to arrange." He ticked off points on his fingers. "We must research what poisons will debilitate without killing. We must gather weapons and supplies for sabotage. We must train our combatants to be both safe and effective. We must coordinate our efforts to hit all at once, so the lords don't have time to find a defense. We must decide how to do the most damage where it is needed and the least where it isn't." He smiled at Miknon. "We aren't like the lords to destroy everyone in our way."

Human technology didn't interfere with their magic. The words echoed in Zak's mind. The lords always discounted the commoners because their magic was so much less powerful, but what if that could be changed, even a little? Her grandmother had once thought the same. Before Zak fretted too long, she raised her hand for attention.

"Yes, Zee?" Shar asked.

"The circlets combine talents," she reminded him. "Grandmother invented them to allow minor mages to work together, giving the fleet enough power to move all the ships, and boosting mind-touching to reach all decks regardless of the original strength of the thought-mage. She tuned them only to specific talents, but perhaps we can adjust them to work with other magics than originally intended, or use Earth technology to boost their effectiveness."

Beside her, Father sucked in a breath. "Yes, Sire. If the secretary would make a list of talents that would be useful if they were stronger, I would be happy to assist my daughter." He inclined his head at Nik and smiled at Zak.

Tears prickled the back of her eyelids. *He* would assist *her*. Not only was it the first time he had shown an interest in helping, he was acknowledging her as the lead contriver. She reached over and clasped his hand, and he squeezed her fingers.

"An excellent idea," Shar said.

"Would that work for you also, Sire?" Gil asked. "Since your magic has not yet reached its adult strength, could we use one of the circlets to boost your power enough to force the lords to obey?"

Shar shook his head. "We can try, but I doubt it. The circlets combine powers, not enhance one alone."

Gil sighed. "Too bad. It was a good idea."

"I will cooperate with any experiments Zee wishes to run," Shar assured him. "All right, we have the beginnings of a plan. Let's divide the preparations and get moving. Tom, you will handle physical training and determination of targets."

At Taras's nod, Shar continued. "Miles, find me poisons that will spare as many as possible. Chantelle, you are in charge of gathering and tracking supplies. Ned, ask who we have where and decide on troop relocations. Zee and Ike already have their assignment. Meg, I need to know every detail you know or can discover about any lord's involvement in any crime."

Maia bared her teeth at him through her tears. Gil put a hand on his mother's shoulder.

"What about us?" U.N. asked, waving a hand between him and Gaby. "What can we do?"

"Please help research sources of supplies we need," Shar suggested, "translate as usual, and since you read and write faster than we do, would you continue to scribe? You may postpone your other tasks for a while."

The research was an honest request, considering their unfamiliarity with Earth, but Zak knew Shar was nearly as literate in English and much more so in Fae. But it was true his commoner council was not, and perhaps he anticipated being too busy to help with such mundane tasks.

Gaby nodded, and U.N. pulled out his phone to make notes.

For a while longer, they discussed details, until everyone was sure they knew their responsibilities. Since Zak had to show Father the school tech room that held her tools and supplies, she left the others to clean up and pushed him down the hall.

Once they were in private, she asked the question that had been burning at her since Father had volunteered to help.

"Why did you change your mind, Father? I'm glad you did, but why?"

He sighed. "You were right about everyone being needed. We must have every advantage we can get. Our magic is weak, and compared to the humans, our contrivances are pitiful. Your idea to combine the two is brilliant, but humans know nothing about magic. With my knowledge of Mother's work and your experience with Earth tech, we're the only chance to give the commoners enough strength to face the lords."

If they could somehow combine magic and tech. But if they didn't, then Miknon's plan might not be enough. If only they had a team of contrivers, like their team of ambassadors. But they didn't, so the two of them would have to do the best they could alone.

Zak opened the tech room door and turned on the light. "Let me show you what I already know, and then we can discuss what to try next."

CHAPTER 13

FIRE

THE NEXT DAY, Gaby woke with one thought in her brain. Somehow, she had to protect her family from the fae war. Magic-created storms had already hit the United States, and if they moved closer, her family could be in their path.

If she couldn't stop the storms, then she had to warn her family and protect them. Somehow. Mamá and Papá and the boys believed in the fae, even if Grand-mère didn't. Surely they would listen to Gaby instead of Grand-mère's claims of her being a traitor.

The accusation still stung. She had spent a year separated from her beloved family, originally because sharing a room with Grand-mère was intolerable. But Gaby had stayed for the chance to help and learn, to build allies, not to betray Earth. And now the alliance was in as much danger as her family, and she didn't know how to help anyone.

Even if her parents forced Grand-mère to evacuate, what good would it do? Where could her family go that would be safe? Attacks were already landing around the world, and with fae magic at the helm, anywhere could be a battlefield. The only way to really protect them was to end the war soon.

Gaby scoffed and rolled out of bed. How were they supposed to do that? They had neither an army nor enough magic. She could only hope Miknon's plan and Zak's technology would find an advantage somewhere. And that Grand-mère would come to her senses.

Gaby arrived for breakfast in time to hear an announcement of new P.E. lessons, despite the summer break. The teacher enthusiastically talked about the strength and flexibility benefits of martial arts, but looking at the grim faces of those on the king's council, Gaby knew that was only an excuse.

The class was a good idea, since by the time they knew if the war would reach them personally, it would be too late to start training. People deserved a chance to at least defend themselves, if possible. After dropping off her tray, she signed up for a time slot soon after breakfast.

She had just enough time to brush her teeth and clean her room before she had to be back in the cafeteria. The tables had been folded and leaned against the wall so the floor was available for practice, leaving the basement for council meetings.

At the front of the room, Alex and Tom were already stretching. Gaby lined up with the others and tried to copy the teachers. Her fellow students were adult and teen, fae and human, but by their expressions, she could tell who knew they were already in a war and who had only heard vague rumors of mild trouble with the peace negotiations. She didn't know if she should envy the local students who had gone home for the summer, or if she should feel sorry they had less information.

After stretching, Alex and Tom demonstrated some basic body positions and moves, followed by a few self-defense maneuvers. Despite their different training styles, they worked as a team, sometimes pausing to discuss how to adapt a discipline for the newbies. Alex's judo was more rule-based, while Tom used a no-holds-barred style meant for actual combat. He was terrifying to watch, even when he slowed his movements for demonstration.

Gaby awkwardly tried to get her arms and legs to behave, with limited results. She always seemed to go left when everyone else was going right, and she couldn't figure out how to blend the positions into motion. Eventually, when the others were more or less following Tom successfully, Alex came and nudged Gaby's limbs into the proper places.

"You're doing fine," Alex whispered. "It's only the first day, and people have different abilities."

Gaby wrinkled her nose skeptically. As far as she could tell, she had *no* ability in this class. Which was par for the course for P.E. classes, actually. She had been the despair of her teachers and her athletic brothers.

Alex grinned. "Really. If U.N. was here, you'd see what I mean. Two left feet, that boy. Raise your arm a little higher, but drop your shoulder." She kept up the murmured instructions and physical nudges until Gaby was almost moving with the others.

A few minutes later, Tom dismissed the class.

"You'll get better," Alex promised, patting Gaby on the shoulder.

Yeah, sure. But Gaby would keep attending, because poor defense skills were better than nothing. Anything she could learn might help protect her family in the future.

As the next class streamed in, she shook out her aching arms and legs, then made her way upstairs. Tom wasn't even winded, though Gil took Alex's place beside him to help teach. That surprised her a little, since she hadn't known Gil had any training. Though since the fae had been planning to conquer Earth, it made sense to train their people.

In Shar's office, he and Ned were reviewing the reports from the small fae spying on the enemy camps. So far, nobody had been caught, and the ambassadors had collated the reports before passing them on. Nothing stood out to Gaby as important, though the fae would have a better idea of what was useful data.

"Did you want me to scribe now?" she asked Shar, mindful of his request the day before.

He put down the stack of paper and rubbed his face. "At the moment, I'd rather you go talk to Miles about fae interactions with food. See if you can make a list of mild poisons meant to debilitate rather than kill. Scribe for him as well as translate and research, if you please. Bring me a list by the end of the day, even if you aren't finished."

"Sure. By dinner or bedtime?" She clutched her new notebook tightly.

"Dinner if you're finished, bedtime if you aren't," he absent-mindedly said, already reading through the reports again.

Ned waved as she left, but Shar didn't look up. Being king seemed like a lot more work than reward, and he didn't get a castle or a private plane or anything. Poor Shar.

Gaby took the stairs down so a little more exercise would strengthen her legs for the new training. If she couldn't be coordinated, maybe she could at least increase her stamina and strength.

She found Miles in the human nurse's office instead of his own, frowning at the computer and stabbing at the keyboard. His office didn't have a computer, since he wasn't comfortable using one. Clearly, that hadn't changed.

Gaby tapped gently on the door frame. "May I help?"

His head shot up, and he stared blankly for a second. "Oh, Gaby. Do you know how to use this, um, innerweb?"

She giggled. "The internet? Yeah. What are you trying to find?"

He vacated the desk and moved to a nearby chair. "Chocolate, for one. And hot sauce. And—"

"Hold on!" Gaby said. "Let's take them one at a time. And are we researching something about them, or where to buy them?"

Miles puffed out his cheeks and ran his fingers through his hair. "Yes?"

"Okay." Gaby flipped her notebook open to a new page. "Let's start with a list of every item you already know, and then we'll go from there."

She wrote down chocolate and cayenne, then added caffeine, cinnamon, and more as she and Miles determined the correct ingredients or translations for foods that had given the fae difficulties so far. Though no one ingredient was dangerous to all of them, most fae races had at least one problematic allergy to an Earth food. Maybe that wasn't surprising, considering the human tendency to push the safety boundaries.

Personally, she didn't see the appeal of danger, whether it be jumping out of an airplane or scorching her taste buds beyond the point of flavor. If she had her way, her life would be boring. Until recently, she'd had a good chance of that, but now? She sighed and typed in the next search term.

By bedtime, she gave Shar a printed list and an electronic file of the most likely fae allergens, with pictures of what they looked like or where they could be found in nature. The commoners in the right locations could forage for the things that grew wild.

"We'll finish the shopping list for major countries tomorrow," she promised, covering a yawn.

"Well done," Shar said.

Gaby stumbled to bed and fell asleep almost instantly. Her dreams featured lavish meals that caused all the diners to keel over dead.

In the morning, she picked the blandest food offered for breakfast before stumbling through the defense class and reporting to Miles.

FINISHING the list actually took her and the healer another day and a half to complete, and by then, more bad news had emerged.

Not just one, but multiple wildfires had lit in Greece. It seemed the fae had changed their strategy, either to add as much trouble as possible or because their weather mages were exhausted for the moment. Gil tried explaining the difference between disasters, but all Gaby understood was that storms required continuing energy, but fires would feed themselves. And with several fires, there was a lot to feed.

Everyone gathered around Nik for support, though his home was on an island at the other end of the country. If the fae had resorted to fire, there was no guarantee they would stop in one place, and his family might still be in danger.

Gaby bit her lip, imagining a similar fire sweeping through Boston. How could they win against power like this? She itched to return home, even if she could do nothing to actually help her family beyond keep track of her younger brothers during an evacuation.

Over the next two days, the fires spread until more than eighty separate blazes were burning on Saturday. Almost thirty people died, and more were injured. The fire in the Greek national park was the biggest single wildfire recorded in the European Union since the year 2000, covering more area than New York City. The official cause was unidentified, though some people blamed arsonists and some thought climate change was responsible. At the school, those theories were soundly hooted down during dinner.

"Fire mages," Gil muttered, "or phoenixes, or salamanders, or cherufe, or..." He trailed off with a sigh. "With so many fires, the lords might have collected every fire fae they could find."

"But the President will agree the climate is to blame," Gaby said bitterly. "How much longer before we can move against the armies?"

Would nothing convince him of the real danger? How long would he sit on his hands and do nothing? Since he wouldn't help — or couldn't — Miknon's plan was the only strategy they had. The longer the fae went unopposed, the more damage they would do, and the more entitled the lords would feel. And yet, attacking before Miknon's commoners were ready would only doom them to failure.

"We have one chance, and only one chance," Shar said as if he were reading her mind, which was possible, though rude. And he wasn't touching her. More likely, everyone was thinking the same things she was, comparing their resources to the enemy's. "If we lose, everyone loses. We must take the time to get it right."

She shuddered. "Can we win?"

"It's a good plan," Miknon said. "We have excellent reasons to do our best. I feel confident, as long as we have full support." She raised her eyebrows at Shar.

"We're working on it," Shar promised. "Half the supplies are already gathered. As we speak, they are being divided and repackaged while the fae are trained on their use."

He turned to Zee, who had come for dinner with a dazed look and twitching fingers. "How are the circlets coming?"

Zee rubbed her face and blinked twice. "Um, we're having difficulty making new ones, so there's a limited supply to work with. Not everyone even brought them down from the ships." She sighed. "They didn't think we needed them anymore, now that we're not traveling."

"How impractical," Ned said. "We should have brought all resources."

"Be fair," Chantelle said. "A lot of the barges crashed into the water, and we couldn't save much from them at all, besides the people."

"We also expected not to need to work together so closely anymore," Zee's father said. Ike, that was the alias he was using.

"Well, things have changed." Shar rolled his shoulders and stretched his neck. Dark shadows lined his eyes, and half his meal was untouched. "Chantelle and Meg, if you will coordinate with Zee to divide the circlets, I'll arrange for them to be delivered to as many locations as possible."

"Yes, Sire." The siren and Gil's mother immediately rose with their trays.

Zee shoved the last of her dessert into her mouth and followed them. Though he hadn't been mentioned, her father also wheeled away from the table.

Shar watched them go with a frown. "I meant after they finished eating." He dropped his fork onto his tray and turned sideways on his chair, one hand braced on the table.

Before he could stand, Gaby blurted, "Take your own advice."

She slapped her hand over her mouth, feeling her cheeks burn. Shar raised his eyebrows, and several of the fae gasped. Gaby bowed her head and hunched her shoulders. When would she learn to mind her words?

Gil chuckled and shoved the king's tray closer to him. "She's right. Eat before you collapse. I know you aren't getting enough sleep, so you'd better get enough food and water." At Shar's caustic look, he bowed. "Sire." The obedient pose was ruined by another shove of the tray.

"You are a bad subject," Shar said.

"Yes," Gil agreed, "but a good friend. Eat!" He demonstrated with a large forkful of his own lasagna.

Head still ducked, Gaby finished her vegetables, watching Shar from the corner of her eye. He leaned back in his chair and emptied his glass, then reached for his fork.

Plate empty, Gaby rose with her tray, then stole Shar's glass while he was glaring at Gil. After taking care of her dishes, she refilled the glass and returned it to the table.

"I see this is a conspiracy," Shar said.

Gil winked at her. Gaby shrugged and blushed again, then hurried to the kitchen to wash dishes.

ON MONDAY, Alex started the next semester of college and was unavailable to help with the defense classes. Though Tom pulled in one of his warriors to assist, Gaby struggled to keep up without Alex's personal help.

At the end of the practice, Tom raised his hands for quiet. "We are dividing the classes into different levels. Everyone should sign up again. The list will say what level you are assigned."

He waved at Wes, who waved back with a clipboard. The students gathered into a rough line, chattering and stretching to cool down. When Gaby reached the front, she found "beginner" next to her name. No surprise there. Without comment, she signed up for an easy class taught by a human instead of a fae warrior. At least their capabilities would match hers better.

Since Miles no longer needed her, she went upstairs and knocked by Shar's open door.

"Come in." The elf glanced up from his computer. "What can I do for you?"

"That was my question," Gaby said quietly. "Do you need any help?" She glanced around the door frame to make sure she hadn't missed anyone in the corner. "It looks like everyone else is busy?"

"They all have work to do, yes," Shar said. "I'm compiling reports, but if you want to type while I read, that would be faster."

"Sure." Gaby took the chair he vacated and checked the screen to see exactly what he'd been doing. Each country had a section of notes, organized by what they needed, what they already had, and what the spies had seen.

Shar moved to another chair and lifted his feet to rest on a third. Flipping through his lapful of papers, he selected one. "Let's read Freya and Jin's report first, and you can tell me if I missed anything."

She mentally weighed the stack of papers he held. They'd be here all day. No, there would surely be more reports coming. They'd be here all week.

Well, she didn't have anything else to do, anyway, and maybe they would find a way to protect her family.

They had to. Somehow.

As Shar dictated, she typed rapidly, her fingers not keeping pace with her racing worries.

Chapter 14

In Which the Time Has Come

August 30, 2023

Gil checked the clock for the tenth time. Class was still not over. How could it not be time?

Ever since school started two days ago, the hours had crept by as slowly as days. Today, he'd already suffered through Spanish, PE, and a simplified biology class, and now English had trapped him in a prison of time. He bared his teeth at his homework and wrote that example of a metaphor.

With only a third of the students left from last year, the teachers had been reduced and the schedule simplified, and the fae teens took half or more of their classes with each other, with or without humans. Zak was taking an advanced numbers class that used letters, and those taking a second language class varied in their selection, but for much of the day they saw the same faces. At least it was easy to help each other with the homework.

He checked the clock. Had it even moved? Maybe it was broken. He turned over his phone to check the time there, and Ian kicked his chair from behind.

Fine. Besides, his phone said the same time, so the clock must be right. Gil clutched his hair and tried to pay attention to his homework. Didn't they have more important things to worry about than the difference between metaphors and similes?

The lords had increased their attacks in both intensity and frequency. A week ago, the Greek fires had increased to the hundreds. An island by Spain had been the next to be hit, and seven percent of it was still burning. Fires also hit Italy, and extreme heat was threatening half the country.

As if that wasn't enough, the storm mages must have gotten enough rest. Austria was flooding at hundred-year levels, and a storm named Idalia — why did the humans name their weather? — was threatening the southern border of the United States. Apparently, Kishar thought that was far enough away from him.

Gil squirmed and tapped his pencil on his homework. He would much rather collect the council and find a way to thrash the lords. But most of the younger council members were here in class with him, and even Taras, Shalla, Miles, and Mother were seated in the back. Only Nik and Izdu knew too little English to participate, so they were supervising as the graduated students handled the translation and reporting duties upstairs.

At least this was the last class of the day, and as soon as the clock moved — he glared at the seemingly frozen tool — he could get back to more important matters. He squirmed toward the edge of his seat, ready to bolt when class ended.

Across the aisle, Shar turned his head enough to send a warning glance at Gil. Argh! Fine! Gil bent over his paper, dragging his pencil across the page as sharply as a knife. And there was a simile. See, he was paying attention. He leaned on his free elbow, raising his hand to block his view of the timepiece on the wall. If he didn't finish in class, he'd be stuck with homework, and that wouldn't help anything.

By exercising his willpower until he was ready to explode, he finished the assignment just before the bell finally blared. He darted from his chair, dropped the paper on the teacher's desk, and ran from the room.

Then he had to wait in the hallway for everyone else to exit more slowly. Ahhh! He leaned back against the wall and closed his eyes, breathing in and out, in and—

"Okay, Gil," Shar said. "We're ready."

"Okay!" Gil jerked upright and bounded for the stairs, too impatient to wait for the elevator.

At the last minute, he recalled his manners and slowed for Shar, who was walking at a slightly more dignified pace. Only slightly; the prince stretched his legs in long steps that covered ground rapidly without actually running.

"I have an offer for you," Shar whispered. "Or a request, if you prefer."

"What's that?" Gil asked.

"I'd like to give you a permanent place on my council when this is all over."

Gil almost tripped down a stair in shock. "I appreciate the honor, Sire, but I'd rather not. I'm looking forward to exploring Earth and having some fun. Once the treaty is signed and peace is assured, my job is done. Mother and Miknon and I have plans."

"Your contribution doesn't have to end," Shar said. "Think about it. I value your advice as well as your friendship. You were right about this world and right about the direction our society needs to go. You are friends with everyone and can keep me informed of their opinions. Not spying, just sharing their concerns."

As the rest of the group followed, the footsteps clattered on the stairs until the echo was too loud for conversation. Gil shook his head firmly, and Shar sighed. Gil shook his head again. Though he was sorry to thwart his prince and sorrier to disappoint his friend, he had no desire to wallow in diplomacy and bureaucracy for the rest of his life. The last year had been quite enough to drive him mad.

Since school was back in session, they had to wait for the last slow student to clear the basement PE room, though they filled the time by fetching water and snacks and setting up chairs. By the time everything was ready, Izdu and Nik and the upstairs translators had also arrived. Only Nikos and Alexandria were missing, since they had their own classes at college.

Gil sat on the edge of his chair and tucked his hands under his legs to keep them still. Miknon took her usual place on his shoulder, with a balancing hand on his ear. If he didn't behave, she was all too inclined to pinch. As if he didn't know how important this all was. Mouth clamped shut, he waited for Shar to begin.

"Idalia has become a hurricane," Shar said. "That's a very bad storm, worse than before. It's causing floods and downing trees. We can't afford to keep waiting for the circlets, no matter how handy they might be." He tipped his head apologetically at Zak.

"I regret we could not move fast enough," Zak murmured.

"What we have will have to do." Shar turned to Gaby, who flipped her notebook open. "We have gathered all the supplies Miles recommended, have we not?"

"Yes, Shar. And trained everyone in their use, and packaged them for transport."

"We plan to poison all the food," Miknon said, "not just that of the mages and warriors. That will avoid suspicion falling on anyone, as well as make them too sick to be forced to fight."

"And we've trained everyone on sabotage and self-defense?" Shar asked Taras.

"Yes, Sire." The naga bowed his head.

"We need everything to happen as much at the same time as possible," Shar said. "We hope you humans will handle the coordination with your tech."

"Sure thing," Ian said.

"Certainly," Gaby agreed. "We'll get other students to help."

"We sent the rocs last week," Shalla said, "with my instructions in their heads. Each will find a designated contact. The dragons and their drivers left two days ago. Everyone should be ready by now."

"While the others handle the army camps," Miknon said, "I'm going after Idalia. Rood will take me and Bal."

"No," Gil blurted. Even with Amarud to carry them and Balasi to protect her and battle whatever fae was causing the storm, she would be in too much danger.

Miknon promptly twisted his ear. "And why not, dear brother?"

Mother covered her mouth with trembling fingers, but she shook her head at Gil. And that was the final word.

Squelching the arguments that cramped his heart, he pried off his sister's fingers. "Ow. No reason. Go ahead and chase the storm."

He didn't want her to get hurt, but she had the right to make her own choices, and this battle was important to her. If Mother wouldn't stop her, neither would he.

But if she didn't come back, he'd make her sorry.

"Who's going after Kishar and Zaidu?" Gil asked.

"Nobody yet," Shar said. "They have only a few people with them and will be easy to capture once their armies are defeated. Surely they will surrender at that point, ending the war without a face-to-face battle."

Mother looked dubious, but nobody argued with the prince. The council quickly tried to plan for every possible problem, though once it was in motion, any number of surprises could emerge. What they couldn't predict, they must adapt to.

After the meeting, Gil, Miknon, and Mother gathered for a private farewell.

"Be careful," Mother said. "I've already lost one—" She choked to a halt.

Miknon kissed her on the cheek. "I will. I promise." She flew to Gil and wrapped her arms around his neck in a choking grip. "Be good, brother."

"Only if you come back," he threatened, swiping at the lone tear betraying him.

She pinched his ear and flew toward the mage and pilot waiting discreetly around the corner. Gil sank to the floor and buried his face against his knees. Mother huddled beside him, leaning against his shoulder.

Father had died on the old world, and Ram was already lost to them here. If Miknon didn't return, only the two of them would remain.

Gil kissed Mother and dragged her to her feet. "Come on, let's get to work. If we don't keep everyone on track, Miknon will never forgive us."

Mother scrubbed at her face and gulped. "After you."

Hand in hand, they hurried upstairs and found a room that needed more people on the phones. On the other side of the world, only a few hours remained until daybreak, and the small fae must poison the food and sabotage the supplies of many armies before breakfast.

THE TEXT SAID,

> First pixie found cookpot. Sending in poison.

Gil did not respond. Though all phones had been put in silent mode, nobody wanted a notification making a screen light up at an inopportune time. Unless the saboteurs needed instructions for an emergency, he could do nothing but wait. He'd been waiting for more than an hour, and he was going crazy.

Behind him on a blanket on the floor, Zak mumbled in her sleep and rolled over. Next to her, Gaby was silent, one hand tucked under her cheek. To let them sleep, the room was lit only by the last bit of sun glowing around the edges of the closed blinds. In the dimness, the phone screens glowed brightly with any message. Mother's phone beeped, and she read silently, moving her lips as she struggled with the task.

"The dragons just dropped the last group," she whispered. "Everyone is deployed."

Gil nodded. "Leave me your phone and go tell Shar," he whispered. "See if there is any fruit left, please. The girls might be hungry when they wake."

That should take her a few extra minutes and distract her thoughts. When she left, he dropped his head to the desk. Every room on this side of the hallway was full of humans and fae taking turns monitoring or sleeping. The other two residential floors had similar hallways doing the same. They had ears all over the world, but the one place Gil wanted to hear from was silent. Not only was Miknon too small to carry a smart phone, but she couldn't put technology that close to Amarud or Balasi and expect both tech and magic to work. Obviously, that also kept the mage and the pilot from using a phone.

Gil wouldn't know if his sister survived until she came back — or didn't.

His phone beeped, and he jerked upright before checking his texts.

First poison delivered.

One down, in one location. The council had decided the food must be poisoned with the selected mix of ingredients before attempting any sabotage, to reduce the number of people moving around. The last thing they needed was for their people to be caught before they had completed any of the other tasks. The tactic was sound, but it was making for a long night. After delivering the poison, each crew would have to decide if they dared start damaging weapons and supplies or if they must hide until morning and see if enough soldiers became sick. Neither choice was a guarantee of success.

Would the small fae have enough time to get everything done? If not, could they manage enough to still disable the armies? And even if they succeeded in one location, would they prevail everywhere? The task seemed impossible, but if they lost, all Earth would lose. The fae's new home would be ruined, the alliance broken, and peace a forgotten dream.

Gil snorted. Fourteen months ago, he had talked Shar into letting him sneak off the ship to make a treaty with Earth. It was supposed to be easy — just make an alliance with the humans before the lords could ruin everything. But one thing after another had delayed the treaty, and now they were still facing war.

At least he had saved Miknon's life with the escape.

His phone beeped with a weather alert. Hurricane Idalia was now spawning tornadoes. Was this a result of a magic battle between Balasi and the weather mage?

Miknon was probably in the midst of the danger. His heart clenched. She could be dead already. This was as bad as waiting to learn if she survived the trip back to the spaceship to bring down the rest of the fae children. At least then she wasn't fighting anyone, just hiding. He shoved his chair backward, scraping it on the floor, and Gaby stirred and sat up.

After a look at Zak, she whispered, "Is it time?"

"Not yet," Gil whispered. "Go back to sleep."

Gaby shrugged. "I'm awake now."

The door clicked, and Mother slipped in, hands full of apples. She set them on the desk and checked her phone.

"Nothing more," she murmured. As if he hadn't checked already. "Shar says most locations are at about the same point in our strategy. Now we wait."

Gil snatched an apple and bit it ferociously. He hated waiting. And no text would tell him if his sister still lived.

Zak bolted upright, breathing heavily.

"Hey, Zee," Gaby whispered, "you're okay." She gently touched Zak's elbow.

"Yeah, okay," Zak muttered. She rubbed her eyes and stumbled to her feet. "What's the update?"

"Everyone has landed and is working on the cookpots," Gil summed up. "Same everywhere."

Zak nodded sharply and took two apples, tossing one to Gaby. "Why don't you two get some sleep?"

"Oh, no," Gil protested.

"Oh, yes," Mother said. "We can't afford to have you groggy later."

Grumpily, he finished his apple and took Zak's blanket. Mother traded places with Gaby and closed her eyes. Gil copied her, but his mind kept racing, even when sleep dragged him down.

He eventually woke as abruptly as Zak had, and shot to his feet in alarm. "Where's—" But his sister wasn't here.

"Shh." Zak held a finger to her lips and nodded toward Mother, who was still sleeping with worry wrinkles carved into her forehead.

Gaby offered her notebook, and Gil read the neatly tallied details quickly. Where breakfast had already occurred, the poison had left behind groaning armies more concerned with the closest hygiene trench than attacking anyone. Ash had bound the only sentry who refused to eat on duty.

Everywhere, progress was being made. They had a chance, though still a slim one, to win this war.

But nobody had heard from Miknon yet.

Chapter 15

Troubles

August 31, 2023

Ian waved goodbye to Alexandria, who now caught a ride to college with Nikos every morning after seminary. He checked his texts as he trudged the few blocks to school, yawning wildly. As if six in the morning wasn't bad enough to start classes, he'd spent half the night coordinating guerilla attacks and collecting reports. Four hours of sleep was not enough, especially when he woke with nightmares.

And he still didn't know if they'd won. By the time he collapsed into bed, a few armies had already eaten breakfast on the other side of the world, and a lot of soldiers were too sick to move. And the healers couldn't fix anybody because they were already exhausted from the lords forcing them to strengthen the warriors for Earth's gravity.

At school, he stuffed his scriptures into his locker and grabbed a quick breakfast, which he ate on the way to science class. He dropped into his seat and covered another yawn. Who cared about ecology when they were trying to stop a war?

Halfway through class, his phone beeped with a text. Mrs. Hahn didn't care if he checked his phone, as long as he didn't become disruptive. She'd worked with the fae enough that she always assumed he was translating an unusual word for someone. She was usually right.

But not this time. Shar had sent an update about the small fae. With the combatants too sick to stop them, the saboteurs were running through every camp, destroying supplies and weapons. Granted, that didn't stop magic, but few could concentrate enough to cast a spell when they were puking out their guts. By the time they did recover, magic would be the only resource they still had. It wasn't a perfect solution, but at least it bought some time. And Freya had knocked out a whole contingent of guards in China with her lightning.

Reluctantly, Ian put away his phone and focused on Mrs. Hahn. He didn't even look at her cute baby, who accompanied her to class both because Ms. Maxwell had decided a real-life example of infancy would help the fae, and because the perk had convinced Mrs. Hahn to teach for another year. They didn't have so many great teachers that they wanted to lose one because she had a new baby. And unlike in a regular high school, the students here tended to focus instead of getting distracted, baby or no. Anyone who wouldn't follow the rules had already been transferred.

Despite dozing twice, Ian turned in his homework on the way out the door.

Next was algebra, which was not his favorite subject. Adding unknowns to math didn't improve it. And he didn't have any close friends in class with him, since Gaby was ahead of him and Zee was only in Algebra I. Honestly, that was still impressive, since all of the other fae were still in basic math.

Ian slumped in his chair and stared at the textbook. These weren't even real problems, as far as he was concerned. Stop a war — that was a real problem. Learn how to fight the lords' magic after the armies were out of the way. Discover if Miknon survived. Complete the Fae dictionary.

Stop dreaming about Dad.

Why did Dad have to send him that stupid letter? Ian had been happy for a year, but now his brain decided he needed to remember all the mean things Dad ever said. Useless, spoiled, undisciplined, lazy. Wasting time on languages. A sissy who got laid out by simple headaches. Not even his haircut passed Dad's approval, and it was just hair! Ian turned the page of the textbook harder than it deserved. Nobody cared about Dad! He dug his fingers into his "too-long" hair and tried to focus on his math.

Unfortunately, he didn't finish that homework during class. At lunch, he sat in the basement between Gaby and Gil. While Ian struggled through algebra and she silently pointed out errors, they listened to the latest update on the guerilla war.

The small fae were moving through the army camps again, freeing those who swore not to fight against the prince. Those who could drag themselves away were leaving, though others would have to wait until they recovered from the food poisoning. Anyone who would not promise their allegiance was bound or maimed to prevent them from fighting.

Ian winced, picturing slashed hamstrings like Miknon had demonstrated. The healers could mend that, apparently, but not until the war was over. For that matter, nobody had found most of the healers yet.

The warning bell rang, and Ian hurried to his locker and then to his language class. Here, too, Gaby was ahead of him, but considering he didn't have a native speaker as a parent, he thought Spanish III was pretty good for a sophomore. This was his easiest class of the day, and he zipped through his homework before the teacher finished the lecture. After he turned it in, he was free to scan his texts again for more updates.

The healers were finally showing up, mostly under bushes, as if they had fallen from exhaustion and been abandoned to crawl under the closest shelter. Not only were they exhausted, as everyone had expected, but they were suffering from some kind of illness. They had chills, fever, joint pain, increased heart rate, and reddened skin that shed in large sheets.

Miknon's saboteurs had decided to stay at their various locations another day or two to monitor both the poisoned fae and the healers. Miles sent question after question to pin down what was wrong with his colleagues, but the answers were unhelpful.

On his way to English, Ian stopped by the healer's office. "Any luck with the healers yet?"

"I don't understand," Miles said. "This illness is new. I don't know what caused it, much less how to fix it. I need to actually see the problem and run some tests."

"Maybe it's because you're on Earth," Ian suggested. "We have smaller tides and an actual night. It could be a biorhythm problem? Or some of our different plants and animals? Something in the diet?"

Miles furrowed his brow. "So many differences. It could take years to track the cause."

The warning bell rang. "Let me know if I can help," Ian said before darting to class.

English was also easy, and Ian listened to the teacher with only half his attention. Reddened skin sounded like sunburn, which fit lying in the sun for hours or days. But "red skin" also fit a lot of other illnesses, too.

Nonetheless, the idea of sunburn stuck in his head. When Gil and Miknon had first landed on Earth, Gil ended up with a blistering sunburn, despite his black skin. The fae weren't human, even those who could pass in a crowd, so it was foolish to expect them to respond like humans.

A picture of a vampire turning to smoke joined the memory. Most of the legends about vampires were wrong. They didn't feed on blood or turn other people into vampires, they could go out in the sunlight, and they weren't immortal monsters. But as healers, they did *taste* blood to analyze it — which was amazing — so maybe some of the other stories had a grain of truth.

Maybe the legends about sunlight dissolving them were only exaggerated, not completely wrong. Maybe they got sunburned very badly or something. And maybe Miles didn't know about it because their old world had a red sun instead of a yellow one. Maybe it was an allergic reaction to different light waves.

But how did that connect to the joint pain? And skin peeling in sheets instead of flakes? Was that because they were fae instead of human? Ian scribbled the last of his homework and retrieved his phone for research. If Alexandria weren't at college, she'd love helping with this.

Quickly, he checked the weather first. Hurricane Idalia was dying.

His shoulders relaxed another notch. The plan was working, one step at a time.

So, if he could help Miles diagnose the other healers, they'd have another asset on their side and be that much closer to success. He switched to a medical database and typed in the symptoms. When the bell rang half an hour later, he was still analyzing the results to find what diagnosis might fit the best.

He left the room, gaze fastened on his phone. Turning the corner into the main hall, he bumped into someone's back.

"Sorry," Ian said automatically, but the person didn't reply and didn't move out of the way. In fact, he moved backward, pressing Ian against the wall.

"Hey," Ian protested. He looked up and froze. Everyone in the hall was silently backing up to make room for a litter carried by a horned baubau and a highborn Ian recognized as one of the dragon drivers. All the dragons were supposed to be helping Miknon's army. What was important enough to bring him back?

The fae woman on the litter was only partially covered with a sheet. Her exposed face was blistered, red with rash and black with severe burns, and the bare arm lying on top of the sheet was peeling in hand-sized patches. Ian's stomach churned, but he couldn't look away. In the shocked silence, the sound of gagging echoed.

"Go away," Ian shouted at the students. "Chores, homework, whatever. Starting by the math rooms. Go, go, go!" For the first time, he was thankful to be counted as faculty for more than teaching the Fae language classes. At least he had enough authority to clear the halls.

The most distant teens stirred and turned away. Those nearest the cafeteria doors disappeared inside. Ian forced his way through the students who couldn't yet leave and pushed open the door to the healer's office.

"Miles—" he started, but the healer was already dropping his phone onto his desk and rising from his chair. Ian swung the door all the way open so the litter could fit through.

"Put her here." Miles flipped back the sheets on a cot.

Gently, the three men transferred the injured fae. In the process, Ian saw a lot more of her injuries than he wanted. The blisters and peeling covered every exposed inch of her, and her ankles were grossly swollen. Bile rose in his throat. This was the worst case of sunburn he'd ever seen. Maybe the legend of vampires burning in the sun wasn't much of an exaggeration. If the rest of her body was as bad as what he could see, how could she live?

"I'll get the nurse," Ian blurted, then fled through the now-empty hall.

A quick phone call assured him the nurse was on her way. He crammed his books into his locker, then joined Gil and his other friends in Shar's office. Gaby was answering emails to Shar's dictation while the others worked on homework, but everyone stopped when he walked in and sagged onto a chair.

"I just left Miles," Ian said. "I guess a dragon flew back one of the healers so he could get a better look."

Gaby pushed back her chair. "I'll go help."

"I really, really don't recommend that." Ian gulped a glass of water from the desk.

Shar stood. "I will go."

Ian opened his mouth to protest, and Shar raised an eyebrow.

Ian closed his mouth. "Yes, Sire." The title seemed appropriate.

After Shar marched out, Gil asked, "Is it really that bad?"

Ian grimaced. "Worst thing I've ever seen." He pulled out his phone. "I'm researching possible diseases besides sunburn. Gaby, thanks for helping me with algebra at lunch so I don't have homework now."

"Sure, no problem." The dark-haired girl returned to the emails, but her typing was now hesitant.

"Can I help?" Zee asked.

The short gremlin scooted next to Ian with her phone. Ian recited the list of symptoms for her, which made Gaby's typing slow even more. Gil threw his half-eaten peach into the trash can, and Nate curled into a ball with all his noses hidden under his coils.

"Hey, here's something," Ian said. He read aloud the article on erythrodermic psoriasis, which matched all the symptoms. "It can be triggered by stress, infection, or sunburn. That fits. I don't know exactly how the healers do their magic, but I wouldn't be surprised if all those forced healings overworked their immune systems as well as their magic."

He scrolled as Zee leaned over his shoulder. "Ew. It can affect 90% or more of someone's skin, with a high chance of developing pneumonia or sepsis. And it can—"

He turned off his screen, but he was too late.

"—lead to death in 9% of cases," Zee whispered.

"Well, it won't this time," Ian said. "I'm sending this article to Miles right now. If this is what it is, then we just need to find a cure."

"Give me the link," Zee said. "I'll take it to him in person and translate the hard words for him."

"Good idea." Ian texted the link to her. "Good luck, and let me know if I can help."

"If any of us can help," Gil said.

Gaby and Nate nodded soberly. Zee left with her phone clenched tightly in her hand.

"I'm sure they'll figure it out," Ian said. Miles had magic, right? There had to be a cure. He changed the subject, hoping for good news. "When will Miknon be back?"

Gil jerked his shoulders in a frustrated shrug and frowned harder. "No word."

"Sorry," Ian murmured. He sat between Gil and Nate and helped them both finish their homework while Gaby handled the office tasks and tallied updates from the small fae. It seemed petty to worry about homework at a time like this, but what else were they supposed to do?

The dinner bell rang, and everyone slumped downstairs. Despite Hurricane Idalia slowly fading and the successful sabotage of the army camps, victory seemed so far away. The healers were badly ill, the reluctant enemy had been damaged in order to stop them, Kishar and Zaidu had yet to be faced, and nobody had heard from Miknon yet. Ian's heart ached, and he could only imagine how the fae felt.

War stunk. He jumped every time the television came on or his phone beeped, sure there would be more bad news. His stomach churned, and his migraines hovered in the background almost every day. Reluctantly, he pointed at the first meal option without looking at it, and found a seat by Mom and Alexandria, who was back from college for the day.

"Not a good day?" Alexandria murmured, switching her chocolate milk for his regular. He hadn't noticed he'd grabbed the wrong one.

"I hate all this," Ian said. "The fighting, the injured, the disasters. Wondering when people will die. If casualties will be my friends or friends of my friends."

His head pounded, and he pushed his tray far enough away to rest his head in one hand. Mom rubbed his shoulder but said nothing.

"Yeah, I know." His sister poked his chicken with her fork. "You still have to eat." After a bite of her own food, she said, "I often wondered what was floating around in Dad's memories. He would never talk about it, but it must have been bad to mess him up that much. I hope he finished his therapy, but I guess I won't know until he contacts me about coming to my graduation."

She sighed and continued eating, nudging the chocolate milk closer to him between bites. Guilt flooded Ian. Maybe he should have told her about Dad's letter. No, no matter what else Dad was or wasn't doing, he wasn't being nice yet. She didn't need that back in her life any more than he did, and she would have a harder time ignoring Dad.

At a pat from Mom, he picked up his fork and slowly ate, but his thoughts raced faster. Dad had actually been in the middle of war, not just on the edges like Ian. What nightmares had he seen in real life? Alexandria was right to wonder what memories haunted him. Not that they excused his meanness, but maybe they explained it. If everyone he saw felt like an enemy or a failing ally, then where was his peace and safety?

Peace *should* have been with his family. But Dad clearly didn't see things that way. He only saw people who wouldn't fight *with* him and must therefore be fighting *against* him. Ouch. His own family had told him he was crazy. He must have felt abandoned and surrounded by enemies. Ian drained the chocolate milk, but it didn't make him feel better.

To be fair, Dad's theories *were* crazy, according to all the information anyone had. But, in the irony of the century, his invading aliens turned out to be not a complete delusion. The aliens were certainly real. The invasion was rather half-hearted. Most of the fae would be happy to make peace if the lords would let them.

Why couldn't everyone stop fighting? Dad, the fae, Russia, and everybody else. What was so great about winning because you killed enough people to frighten the rest into pretending they followed you?

His cake tasted like sawdust, and he pushed it away. Without comment, Alexandria collected his tray with hers and dumped them both.

"I have lessons to plan," Mom said. "Come get me when Nikos arrives."

"Sure, Mom." Ian dropped his head onto his arms and breathed slowly in and out. Where was *his* peace?

A phone rang, and Gaby's quiet voice answered. "Hello, Jin. What's up?" She gasped. "What? When? How?"

Ian sat up straight as Gaby put the phone on the table and pressed the speaker button.

Jin continued in almost a shout. "I don't know. I went to get her for dinner, but she wasn't in her room. I can't find her anywhere!"

Instantly, Shar and his council gathered around the table.

"Freya?" Shar mouthed.

Gaby nodded.

"They must have stolen her again," Jin screeched. "I don't know how they found us here. What are we going to do?"

"Jin," Shar said. "Please look for clues. We will get back to you as soon as we have a plan. Can you do that for me?"

Jin sucked in a ragged breath. "Okay. Okay, I'll go look. We have to get her back." The phone clicked off.

"Who? Why?" Ian stuttered.

"Kishar," Tom said like a curse. "Without an army, he needs another way to fight. War mages are rare and usually able to defend themselves. Only Freya was young enough to be vulnerable. Now he will have his own war mage to attack us directly, besides depriving us of her talents."

"Freya wouldn't do that," Gaby protested.

"She will after he breaks her mind and turns her against her friends," Tom said grimly.

Gaby burst into tears and ran from the cafeteria.

Numbly, Ian stared at the king's chief warrior. Like Dad, he meant. Tortured by war until he turned against his family.

CHAPTER 16

IN WHICH THEY MUST USE TECH

SEPTEMBER 1, 2023

FRIDAY WAS A SCHOOL HOLIDAY, in addition to the actual holiday on Monday, though Zak thought getting out of work to celebrate work was an odd concept. Wouldn't it make more sense to choose a worthy work to fill the day? Humans were rarely logical. She didn't regret the vacation, though, because it gave her a chance to catch up on news of the war. Elsewhere in the world, uncommon heat waves swept across whole countries. The fires in Greece continued.

In Allentown, the temperature continued to be pleasantly warm, which only meant Kishar wasn't yet ready to fight in his own backyard. Was he waiting for Freya to join his side? Did that mean he was still torturing her into submission? Zak's heart ached for her prior roommate. How long could her friend withstand against the magic of Lord Kishar?

Or perhaps he would merely use more physical persuasion. That prospect was only slightly better, since she might resist a little longer at great cost to herself. How much pain could she withstand before she broke? Vince had lasted only a few minutes, but Freya was considered more valuable and thus should be treated with a little more care.

If they were all very lucky, maybe Freya was yet again delaying the enemy by playing stupid or demanding a new wardrobe as the price of cooperation. But whatever accounted for the delay, it wouldn't last forever. They needed to rescue her before it was too late.

They had no way to do that.

There was a very slim chance Shar could arrange to have Freya assassinated to prevent her being used against them. So far, he had not agreed to Taras's tentative suggestion to try. No one dared discuss it with him further.

The worst part of being king was being forced to make terrible decisions in search of the least terrible answer. Was Freya's life worth the risk to so many others? Zak didn't know how Shar could face the question, since thinking about it made her stomach climb up her throat.

With no classes to occupy the students, the king's council gathered to discuss possible solutions for the many problems they faced. Zak joined them but sat in the corner with Gaby and continued her research on treatments for the healers. Every lead was immediately texted to Merodach for trial, though she expected to need to translate the hardest words for him later. So far, nothing had worked, alas. Merodach had kept his colleague alive, but her condition had not improved.

"Most of the army camps are now neutralized," Taras said. "Those merely sick might recover in a few days, but the injured will be out of the way for weeks. The small fae are now focusing their efforts on finding the healers and releasing any common fae that have sworn to not fight the king."

"Where are they going when they leave?" Shalla asked. "Do they have safe locations to hide?"

Nik nodded. "Some are staying in their local countryside under the direction of the ambassadors. A few with specialty skills are being shipped to more advantageous locations."

"Okay," Shar said. "Let's keep doing the same things for as long as they keep working. Tell me if anything changes."

While the updates continued, Zak kept reading. The next article made no sense, though the search terms had been promising.

Zak whispered to Gaby, "What is UV?"

"Ultraviolet?" Gaby suggested, peering over Zak's shoulder to confirm. "Basically, a part of sunlight that isn't visible. To humans, anyway. I don't know about the fae."

"If sunlight caused the problem," Zak murmured, "how could it be the cure?"

"Oh, all UV isn't the same," Gaby explained. "See, it's saying UVB helps but plain sunlight doesn't, probably because sunlight has other wavelengths in it, too. Plus, it's recommending shorter exposure times." She tapped the screen. "This might actually work. It says it slows the growth of skin cells, reducing symptoms. We should try it."

"How do you separate the sunlight?" Zak asked, hope rising.

"UV light can be produced by machines," Gaby said. "We can probably buy one, though we might have to experiment to find the exact wavelengths that will help."

"Help what?" Shar asked.

Zak looked up and discovered everyone staring at them. Their voices must have risen, interrupting the meeting. "Pardon, Sire. We might have found a possible cure for the healers. If we may be excused to investigate more?" She closed the laptop, stood, and bowed.

"Is there anything we must have Zee or Gaby for right now?" Shar asked the council. They shook their heads, and he waved toward the door. "Keep me informed of any progress."

"Yes, Sire." Zak bowed again and nearly bolted for the door, with Gaby right behind.

Instead of waiting for the elevator, they used the stairs at top speed. In Merodach's office, they divided the research. Gaby shopped for machines and compared features, availability, and prices on the healer's computer, while Zak and Merodach used her laptop to slog through the technical recommendations for therapy in order to compose strategies and sort them into an order to try. When they got stuck on vocabulary, Gaby jumped in to translate as much as possible.

By lunch, they had ordered a machine and sent one of Mak-swill's soldiers to pick it up. Even if they found a successful wavelength, Merodach expected multiple sessions would be necessary for a cure. Though Zak dutifully reported the difficulty to Shar while they ate, she remained hopeful. He nodded thoughtfully and requested updates of the slightest improvement.

After lunch, she collected Father and took him to the basement classroom used for technology. While Merodach worked on treating the healers, she needed to turn her attention back to the abandoned circlets. It was most likely too late for them to be useful to the common fae, but if she could adapt one for Shar's magic, it could make the difference when they confronted Kishar and Zaidu. Sadly, Grandmother had only tuned the circlets for the talents she needed to run the fleet, not for magic in general, and command voice hadn't made the list.

By now, Father knew where each tool and part was kept, though he still struggled to remember the Earth words for them, especially those that had no Fae counterpart. Once, Zak had thought she could offer her technological expertise as an asset for the treaty, but by now, she knew that was a useless idea. Humans knew much more about technology and machines than she did, perhaps more than she ever would. Even Father was a novice compared to them.

Nonetheless, her desire to know more, *do* more, remained strong. Though she might never contribute to human knowledge, she could still become the best among the fae contrivers and help them make a place in this new world. She still dreamed of combining magic and tech for more effective contrivances. But not until the war was over.

"What is your plan exactly?" Father spun a circlet idly in his hands, but his gaze was piercing.

Zak shrugged helplessly. "Try something else. I don't know; I'm only guessing. If only we had the king's crown that was already tuned to him, we might be able to boost the power of his magic instead of just combining it with someone else's. I don't know if that's possible, but trying is better than nothing. Do you have any ideas?"

Father sighed. "I hate to admit it, but you have surpassed me." He raised a hand. "Let me clarify. I am thrilled you have surpassed me. I hate to admit I have nothing to add to your attempts, as I am better at working with contrivances than at inventing them. If Mother were here, or any—" He sucked in a breath. "Or anyone else with more experience and talent, perhaps they could help. Since we have no one else, I will follow your lead."

"But I don't know what to do, either," Zak protested.

"I know. But you have learned things from the humans, have you not?"

Zak nodded.

"Then tell me about them," Father said. "Perhaps the attempt to explain to me will suggest something we can try."

"Fae technology isn't really made for this," Zak said.

"It was less so when Mother began her experiments." Father waved at the tools and supplies. "Please, begin. You said you wished for the king's crown because it is tuned to Shar's bloodline. Is there a way we could tune a common circlet instead?"

"I don't know," Zak said. "That might be a good question for Mero, once the treatments begin working on the other healers."

"Will they work?" Father asked.

"If they don't, we will try something else," Zak promised. "What if we tried different forms of power, like the UV machines make different wavelengths of light?"

"Do you think it would work?" Father asked.

Zak shrugged. "I have no idea."

"Then let us try," Father said.

By DINNERTIME, Zak and Father had tried a dozen different things with the circlet. None of them worked enough to test them on Shar, though they had still learned much and had a dozen new attempts planned for later. She pushed Father to the cafeteria, helped him with his tray, then took a seat beside Gil.

"Have you heard from Miknon?" she murmured discreetly.

Gil shook his head, the single jerk making his worry apparent. She nodded and dug into her food, unsure what to say. It was possible Miknon and her group were still battling, despite the dying storm, or they might have moved on to another location to help someone else. It was also possible they had perished in the attempt.

How many of the fae would die before they won? Or lost.

If they lost, the fight would pass to the humans. Magic would battle technology, and the winner was very uncertain. The only sure fact was that the death toll would rise among fae and humans until the rotting stink buried the few survivors.

If Miknon had not survived, Zak would weep, as she had wept for Vince and might still weep for Freya and all of Earth. After eating half of her meal, she couldn't stomach another bite. She desperately needed to do something useful — anything that would support her friends and allies. If she couldn't aid Miknon or Freya, then she would help elsewhere.

Father was still talking while he ate, so she slipped to the infirmary with a fresh tray of food. As she suspected, Merodach had not stopped working to eat. Very slowly, he was typing into the computer, frequently pausing to mutter to himself. The keyboard, of course, had no Fae characters, not that Merodach knew how to read Fae anyway. As a commoner, that privilege would have been kept from him. And though he had taken the English classes with her, she wasn't surprised his reading skills lagged behind, since he had other duties to keep him from practicing as much as she had.

"Eat," Zak said. "I'll type and translate as you dictate."

She set the tray on a small table a short distance away, conveniently located between the desk and the cot occupied by the patient.

Merodach rubbed his forehead before rising. "That would be faster."

As she sat, Zak pointed at the tray. "Eat."

The healer took his assigned place and neatly cut his food. Zak occupied herself by reading his notes and correcting a few words. After chewing and swallowing two bites, he continued in Fae, detailing the trials so far, with times and machine settings and results. He spoke slowly, giving her time to translate between his bites.

Zak typed equally slowly, making sure her English was accurate. Apparently, the therapy had been drying to the skin and had caused irritation, but with adjustments to the wavelength and duration of the treatment, Merodach was finally seeing improvement.

Zak glanced over her shoulder at the sleeping healer. From here, the damage seemed as great as before, but she trusted Merodach to have a better idea of the whole situation, including what was going on inside the other bloodworker.

By the time she finished typing the entire report, Merodach's plate was scraped clean, and the healer looked more cheerful.

"Okay," Zak said, "what's the next step?"

"Can we get more of these machines?" Merodach rubbed his slim hands on his knees. "Around the world, I mean. If we can treat all the healers we've found so far, that would be better than waiting for them to be brought back here."

"You're sure this is working?" Zak asked.

"Positive," Merodach said. "It will take more treatments, and time for the skin to heal visibly, but I expect a full recovery in a few weeks. Perhaps sooner, if other settings prove more advantageous."

"Then I should report to Shar and see about getting more machines." She scooped up the empty tray. "Should I text you the reply?"

"Not unless there is a problem," Merodach said. "Otherwise, I shall assume you have taken care of everything." He smiled and opened the door for her.

The cafeteria was empty, so Zak took the tray into the kitchen and left it with the dishwashers. She reported to Shar, who nodded briskly.

"And the small fae have continued their rescues," he said. "By the end of the day, I expect most of those we can save to be in safe locations. That is four military assets we have stolen from the lords — soldiers, supplies, healers, and some of their magic."

Not all the mages and elementals had been in the army camps, but those who had been there had been neutralized, one way or another.

"Including the hurricane," she added.

"Yes," he agreed, though his smile faded into worry wrinkles.

She did not ask if they had yet heard from Miknon, because the answer was clear.

Zak's next stop was Mak-swill's office. The principal cheered and immediately called the general to arrange for more UV machines to be delivered to every ambassador currently hosting an injured healer. She carefully noted Zak's specs to be sure the machines and settings would be correct.

Once it looked like there would be no more questions for her, Zak left the principal's office. She should report to Shar in person, but she leaned against the wall and merely texted him instead. Looking at the worries etched on his face had only made her remember her own heartaches.

Within weeks, if not sooner, the healers would be on their way to recovery. But would that be soon enough? The armies were currently at a standstill. Winning, or at least not losing, seemed more within reach of the king's allies than it had since the treaty negotiations fell apart. The biggest obstacles remaining were the mages who had escaped, the lords themselves — and Freya.

They would continue to fight the mages the best they could, and losing the support of the army would at least hamper the highborn. Zak still couldn't make the common circlets boost one mage's power rather than combine the magic of several, nor did it work for Shar's magic, so facing the lords remained a dangerous proposition.

But if Kishar turned Freya against her prince and friends, her lightning magic would protect the lords, especially since her former allies would be reluctant to strike her down. Zak was more thankful than ever to not be a warrior, forced to decide between striking at a familiar face or letting a friend betray them.

And yet, sooner or later, someone must make that choice. Kishar would make sure he turned Freya against them. Zak's former roommate and friend would become her enemy.

Even if Zak discovered how to strengthen Shar's magic with a circlet, a bolt of lightning would fry him in an instant. And no one else had even a chance of withstanding the lords.

They were doomed. Taras was right about the wisdom of assassinating Freya.

Zak slid down the wall and cried into her knees. Was there no way to save Freya? To save them all?

CHAPTER 17

TRANSFER

SEPTEMBER 2, 2023

GABY'S PHONE RANG, showing Mamá's picture. She excused herself from the council and stepped into the hallway to answer it.

"Bonjour, Mamá."

"I have good news," Mamá said. "We've been talking to Grand-mère, and she finally agreed you can prove you are no traitor by leaving the school and coming home. It's still early enough to transfer to the local high school."

"Oh." Gaby's heart sank. Leave the school. Leave her friends. Abandon her science translations. And go home to share a tiny bedroom with Grand-mère again.

"Gaby?" Mamá asked.

"I want to stay," Gaby said. "You agreed this was important work."

Mamá sighed. "It was, but the ambassadors have graduated, and there are more people to help now. They don't need you anymore. And we don't know if the school will stay open until you graduate, so you would be better in a school that will stick around. Transferring as a junior or senior is hard."

If Gaby went home, she would be in a better position to help her family if war came their way. And if she didn't, Grand-mère's suspicion might force her to transfer to another boarding school until graduation or until Grand-mère died. And though old, she was perfectly healthy. Homesickness swept through Gaby, and she pulled the phone away to look at Mamá's photo on the screen. As much as she loved her friends, she would rather have her family.

"Okay," Gaby said. "I'll come home. I can be packed by the time you get here." She checked her watch. The drive would take them five or six hours, which would put their return fairly late. "Did you want to stay the night and go home tomorrow?"

"Oh, not today," Mamá said. "I wanted to give you time to pack and say goodbye to your friends. The twins have practices today, so we'll come Monday. We can be there by lunch."

"Okay, Mamá. I'll be ready. Je t'aime."

"Je t'aime. Everything will be fine. See you Monday." The phone turned off.

Gaby leaned against the wall. She was going home. How would she tell Zee? Or any of her friends. She shoved her phone into her pocket and took a deep breath. She still had two days. The news could wait. For a little longer, she could help with the ongoing efforts to end the war.

But as she turned to head back into the room, the council exited in a rush. Zee pushed her father and Tom pushed Ned to the elevator at a speed unsafe for wheelchairs. Gil grabbed her wrist and towed her toward the stairs amid the rest of the crowd.

"What—?" Gaby blurted.

Gil lengthened his stride. "Miknon."

Gaby twisted to look at U.N., who gave her a thumbs-up. Good news, then? Gaby pulled her arm free and pounded up the stairs between the boys. At the top, Gil zigzagged around everyone and pulled his mother faster, heading for the front door.

The door opened, and two tall figures slipped inside. The pilot and the mage who had gone with Miknon. But where was the pixie?

Gil and Meg screeched to a halt, panting for breath. Gaby clutched U.N. and prayed. The newly arrived elves looked haggard and exhausted, with sweat-soaked hair and ripped clothing. She had never seen a highborn look so terrible.

And what about Miknon? Gaby bit her lip and glanced at Gil and his mother, but they were already moving forward again. And then the elf in the back moved around the other one, revealing the small body in his arms.

Gaby's heart stopped. U.N. patted her arm, and Miknon stirred and sat up. And then the little pixie disappeared from sight as her brother and mother swarmed her. Laughing and crying in equal measure, they took her from the pilot and headed for the stairs without another look at anyone.

The elevator doors dinged, and the last of the council emerged. As they spotted the returned highborn, their faces bore the same relief that weakened Gaby's knees.

"Welcome home," Shar said to the fae who had leaned back against the front door as if too tired to step forward. "Are you available to report now, or do you need to rest first?"

"If we could get food and water," the mage said, "we can last a bit longer."

"Come on." Gaby hauled U.N. toward the cafeteria.

"But I want to hear," he protested.

"The others need to be there more than we do," Gaby said. "But if we hurry, we'll still catch most of it."

"Fine." U.N. stepped faster. "I'll get water if you find snacks."

Gaby nodded. Though the fae were no longer starving, the last of them had landed only a couple of months ago and were still underweight. The cooks kept a cupboard stocked with easy snacks for those fae and for the shapeshifters who needed to eat every time they shifted. While U.N. filled pitchers with water, Gaby loaded a tray with the most substantial snacks available, including packaged and fresh options.

Ready at almost the same moment, they hefted their burdens to the basement, where the council had gathered as usual. When they walked in, Tom jumped to his feet and helped Gaby settle her tray onto a folding table. Chantelle filled two plates, handing the first to Gaby and carrying the second herself. U.N. poured two glasses of water. Within minutes, the highborn each had a plate on his lap and water in his hand.

When they both drained their glasses immediately, U.N. set the full pitcher between them.

As Gaby expected, the report wasn't over yet. Shar wanted to know every detail of their quest to destroy the hurricane. Gaby could only follow a little of the technical magic details, but she gathered the fight had been more difficult than expected, accounting for their late return.

Once their story had been told and analyzed, they wanted an update on the other attacks. This was old news for Gaby, and she soon grew bored. Even after Meg arrived and joined the other adults, they got no news of Miknon.

Seated along the wall behind the adults, all the students fidgeted, glancing out the door as if debating escape. But what if the council actually got around to something new? What if they decided to assassinate Freya, her being the second-to-last obstacle remaining to ending the war? Gaby wanted to know if they did, and apparently the others felt the same urgency to remain.

Eventually, Gil appeared at the doorway. He ducked his head around cautiously and waved. From his position, it was doubtful either Shar or the adults could see him, but the gesture caught the attention of all the students. He waved his hand in a circle, then beckoned.

Zee nudged U.N. and tipped her head at Gil. U.N. elbowed his sister, then tiptoed out the door with Nate's wagon. The girls followed quietly.

Gaby cast a look over her shoulder as she left. Shar was watching them go, but he said nothing. The adults weren't looking their direction.

In the hallway, Gil beckoned again. Silently, he led the group upstairs to Shar's office, which was empty while the council was in the basement. Miknon sat on the desk, gorging herself from a tray of food. Gil shut and locked the door.

"Sit, everyone," he commanded.

Rather surprised at his serious tone, to say nothing of holding a meeting without the prince, Gaby sat, as did the others.

"Gil told me about Freya." Miknon licked fruit juice from her fingers. "And about Tom's suggestion to eliminate her."

"I hate it, too," Zee said, "but how long can she last? We can't afford to let her fight us."

"Can't we save her?" U.N. asked. "This isn't fair!"

Gaby nodded vigorously. It was very unfair. Freya didn't *want* to hurt them.

Gil pounded his fists together. "Kishar is certainly keeping her close to him, and Shar won't send a rescue party into enemy territory when we don't have enough information. We can't lose anyone else to the lords."

"Understandable." Despite her apparent agreement, Alex's fists were clenched and her narrowed eyes were an angry green.

"But—" U.N. wailed.

Alex put a hand on his shoulder. "I know. It's not fair."

"Can we get more information?" Gaby asked softly. "I mean, with magic or something?"

"Those who have that kind of magic will obey the prince," Miknon said. "We're her only chance. I want to go see if she's still alive, still sane, still an ally. If there is any way to get her back, we can tell Shar."

"Who, us?" Gaby blurted. "We're just kids."

"Yes," Gil said. "We're the only ones who know what's going on but can be spared from other duties. And we're the only ones on our side who dare defy Shar."

"Aren't you worried about us getting captured?" Gaby asked.

"I wasn't planning to be seen." Gil looked far too innocent. "Just a little spying, that's all."

"We don't have school on Monday," Alex said. "That gives us two days to plan."

Gaby sighed. She'd be gone on Monday. She would have been no help, anyway, being nobody special.

Gil shook his head. "I want to go today. The longer we leave Freya at Kishar's nonexistent mercy, the less chance we have of ever getting her back sane."

Gaby straightened her back. Today. She could go today. One last chance to help before she abandoned everyone. "Count me in."

"Nikos could drive us," U.N. offered.

"Don't be ridiculous," Alex said. "Nikos is much too responsible to be involved. I'll borrow the truck."

Gaby surveyed the room. "Can we fit all seven of us in it?"

Gil nodded. "Miknon always sits on my lap, and Nate can sit on the floor. A seatbelt wouldn't fit him, anyway."

"Should we leave Nate?" U.N. asked. "No offense intended, but you don't run fast, Nate."

"I'm the lookout." The little hydra grinned with several heads and winked with the others. "I can watch in all directions at once." He wove his necks in an elaborate pattern to demonstrate.

Gil nodded as if that was obvious, and Miknon rolled her eyes. Gaby recognized the older-sibling gesture. How much mischief had those three been in before to know their parts without discussion?

"Are we going now or after dark?" Alex asked. "What excuse are we giving Nikos? What's the plan when we get there."

"We'll leave just before dark," Gil said. "You create the excuse. As for the plan..."

They spent an hour developing a strategy they hoped would work, then returned to their usual activities as normal. Almost as normal. During lunch, U.N. dropped his silverware multiple times and babbled like crazy, languages criss-crossing in a scrambled mess. Gaby hoped she didn't look that nervous.

Gil, Zee, Miknon, and Alex were apparently more used to subterfuge. Not only had they been full of ideas for spying and hiding their plans until it was time, they now acted completely innocent. Nate — well, she didn't know how to read hydra body language very well.

Okay, so Nate was lookout, and U.N.'s language skills were too important to skip. The others seemed to be experts at this sort of sneaking around, plus Alex was needed to drive the truck.

Why did they include Gaby? She wasn't fae, wasn't experienced at spying, wasn't expert at anything pertinent to the mission. Being good at math didn't help in a rescue.

And yet, she had been asked, and she hated to disappoint them. In two days, she would be gone forever. This was her last chance to help, and she didn't want to leave Freya with the enemy.

She crammed her shaking hands into her pockets. If she couldn't control herself, nobody would believe nothing was wrong. She would spoil everything. But where could she hide that wouldn't tip off the adults?

THE WAR OF THE FAE 161

The garden. With Abe gone as well as most of the students, the school had gone from non-stop production to the minimum needed to supplement the kitchen and keep hands busy. Though students took care of it for chores, she could probably find something to do.

A quick question to the cooks established a need for tomatoes and peppers for dinner, so she grabbed a bucket and made herself scarce. Even the hot sun was better than ruining their plans.

Hours later, the cooks were fully stocked for days, the tomato patch was perfectly weeded, and the compost pile had a whole new stack of dead plants covering it. Gaby scrubbed her hands clean, though green still stained her skin.

During dinner, U.N. ate without such obvious nerves, possibly because Alex nudged him every time he opened his mouth. Gaby ate because she needed the energy, not because the delicious tomato and basil risotto had any appeal.

Casually, their secret spy team dumped their trays and drifted to the front hallway and then outside. The bright blue truck was parked halfway through the lot, between the faculty cars and the buses used to transport mass numbers of students.

Alex jingled keys. "I told Nikos I was taking you on a field trip, so if anybody asks, we talked about the water cycle and the river, okay?"

"Do we need to be able to answer questions?" Zee asked.

Alex laughed. "I emailed you all a cheat sheet. Are we ready?"

Gil lifted Nate into the back seat. "Ready."

With Alex driving and Gil navigating, Gaby sat between U.N. and Zee. Nate curled at U.N.'s feet, though no one in the back seat had long legs. The twenty-minute drive to the park in the next town was silent, except for the rumble of their wheels on the road and the inevitable traffic sounds.

Instead of driving around the park, Alex took the road through it, as planned. They would park on the edge and sneak the rest of the way on foot. Though risky, they had decided it was still better than letting Freya, whose current loyalties were in question, see the memorable blue truck.

They had almost reached the end of the grass when Alex slammed on the brakes.

"What—" U.N.'s question died in a croak.

Gaby followed his gaze out the window, but Gil was already scrambling from the car and running toward a tall statue.

No, not a statue. A troll turned to stone. Vince. Gaby blinked against sudden tears.

U.N. and Alex tumbled out one side, and Zee climbed down the other. Once her way was clear, Gaby followed, leaving the door open for Nate to see.

"Oh, Vince," Gil sighed, placing a hand on the stone.

If Vince had been a real statue, Gaby would have been very impressed by the sculptor's skill and the detail involved. She wouldn't have been impressed with the sculptor's taste, since Vince was frozen in an endless scream of agony. One hand was raised as if to fend off an enemy, and a finger was missing. Gaby swallowed hard against the bile rising in her throat. The statue hadn't been broken; Zaidu had maimed Vince while he was alive.

He still looked much too lifelike, except he was dead, heated only by the summer sun. Even his tunic and pouch had turned into stone, though his hemline looked delicate enough to break at a touch. Inside his pouch, a rectangle object pressed against the stone fabric.

"There's his phone," Gaby whispered. "That explains why it died."

"I thought they killed him." Zee's voice cracked.

"Isn't he dead?" U.N. asked.

Miknon leaned half out of the pink backpack hung on Gil's chest. "Yes, but this isn't something Kishar or Zaidu can do."

"This is troll magic," Gil said. "He must have turned himself to stone to prevent being forced to talk."

Gaby sucked in a breath. And now it was Freya's turn to face Kishar's persuasion. If Vince couldn't withstand it, how could Freya?

"Can't he turn himself back?" Alex asked. "Now that it's safe?"

"No," Zee said. "When they change a fist for a punch or a foot for a stomp, yes. But when heart and head are stone, they no longer have the will or magic to return."

"Oh." Gaby formed the word silently. Poor Vince.

Gil let his hand drop and turned back to the truck. The others followed. Nate scooted back from the doorway and resumed his place at

U.N.'s feet. The click of seatbelts was the only sound until Alex started the truck.

Gaby stared out the window at Vince until the statue was out of sight. Poor Vince, who could only choose between betraying his friends and death. Her heart ached, selfishly not just for him, but also for herself.

She was also betraying her friends, abandoning them in two days. Her work with the science vocabulary would be done, and any measly help she could offer the war effort would end. But going home now was her only chance to return to her family. She needed to be with them, especially if the war continued.

And she wasn't brave like Vince.

Chapter 18

In Which They Spy

September 2, 2023

Gil pointed to a parking spot behind a couple of trees, and Alexandria pulled over. They wouldn't be completely hidden, but it was the best they could do.

Turning around in his seat, Gil examined all his friends in the dimming light. In contrast to their dark clothing, the humans were paler than usual, apparently still in shock about Vince. The fae were sad but unsurprised, having been raised on tales of the vengeful highborn.

"Once we reach the building," Gil said, "we'll wait until dark before we spread out. Remember, we are spying only. Whatever we discover, we'll take back to the adults to decide what to do next. Don't be seen, and definitely don't get caught. We just want to find where Freya is and how she's doing. If we see the lords, we'll report what we can, but don't go near them. Does everyone remember their assignment?"

"Upper floors," Miknon said.

"Back lookout." Nash didn't look nervous about his dangerous task.

"Front lookout," Zak said.

If anyone saw her, she could at least pretend to belong long enough to give her a chance to get across the road to the park. The humans would be identified immediately.

Gil nodded and assigned each human a side of the building, leaving the last for himself. "Okay, be careful. Just see what you can and get out. Are your phones on silent?" He checked his own, then double-checked. "Text if you need help, and remember to watch for Miknon and Nate."

Miknon was too small to carry a heavy phone, and Nash didn't have hands. Zak and the humans checked their phones and climbed out of the truck. Gil lifted Nash down, and the hydra slithered away without waiting.

Anxiously, the others waited a few minutes, then Gil motioned Zak forward. The gremlin walked through the trees and nearly disappeared, no magic involved. Her dark blue jeans looked like shadows, while her green shirt and skin blended into the leaves, and she was small enough to hide behind a bush with little effort.

Gil's phone lit up.

Clear.

He nodded at the humans and slid his phone back into his pocket. The four of them tiptoed through the park, moving slowly to avoid tripping in the fading light. The temperature was finally starting to fall, though it would take a while yet to be comfortable. Within moments, they had to split up to reach their assigned spots around the old hotel.

Gil made his way to the side closest to the garden, the area most likely to have enemy fae roaming around. His nose gave him a better chance to detect problems before it was too late. Now he either needed a handy tree to give him cover while he spied, or an opening to approach the windows.

But before he could find either, a familiar scent wafted his way. Ram! Gil dropped flat behind the closest bush and waited. When nothing happened, he cautiously raised his head and peeked around the bush.

His brother was wandering around the garden, occasionally pulling weeds or smelling flowers, but mostly walking at a speed slightly faster than a snail. Only Gil's good night vision in the faint light streaming from windows and Ram's slow motion revealed him as more than a very short tree. Despite wearing human clothing all year at the school and enjoying it more than Gil did, he was now dressed in a traditional kilt, bare-chested, with his hair as close to a traditional style as the shorter length allowed. He looked completely normal and unconcerned, as if he hadn't betrayed his prince, his family, and his people. As if he hadn't led Kishar to Vince so the troll could be tortured and killed.

A low growl rumbled in Gil's chest, and he held his breath to keep himself silent. If Ram heard him, he would call for help, and then everyone would be caught.

Ram lifted his face and sniffed. Gil dropped his head again, pressing his hands to the grass in preparation for a lunge. Ram called no alarm, and his scent did not grow closer.

Even more carefully, Gil peeked again. Now Ram had a flower pressed to his nose, and he had turned his back to stare up at the tall building. False alarm, then.

Gil took several deep breaths to calm his nerves. If Ram hadn't already proven himself utterly worthless, Gil might have approached him and asked for help. As it was, the only thing that kept him from killing the traitor was the inadvisability of leaving a dead body lying around when he was trying to be unobtrusive. And the prospect of telling Mother what he'd done.

Still smelling the flower, Ram wandered toward the back door of the old hotel. Gil texted Zak and the humans, then sneaked after his brother, bending low to remain unseen. If he could follow even a little, he might narrow down the important sections of the building. The more information he could gather — and survive to report — the more chance someone would have to rescue Freya later. Peeking around the corner, he watched until Ram disappeared inside. Gil waved toward the bushes that probably hid Nash, then patted his phone. Yes, already sent the alarm. A bush rustled, but Nash stayed hidden.

Gil crept to the door and laid his ear against it. No sound from the other side. Very, very slowly, he cracked open the door. When nobody shouted, he peeked inside. Ram's elbow showed around the closest corner, vanishing as Gil watched.

He waved at Nash again, then slipped inside, closing the door silently and kicking off his sandals. Shoes in hand, he tiptoed after his brother. At the corner, a careful glance revealed Ram at the bottom of a stairwell, examining a picture on the wall. With another sniff of the flower, Ram headed upstairs, turned a corner, and vanished.

As he followed, Gil texted a short update to the others. If he disappeared, they should at least know what had happened to him. This was stupid, but he kept following his brother anyway.

At the top of the stairs, Gil saw Ram's foot as it went through a door. Though Gil was being very quiet, something must be occupying Ram's mind to keep him from noticing his twin's scent behind him. He deserved to be wracked with guilt. Or maybe the distraction was just the flower he kept smelling.

Gil started to follow, but as he stepped onto level ground, Ram's voice echoed in the hall.

"Greetings," Ram said. "How is our prisoner today?"

Gil flattened himself against the wall and tried to breathe silently. Prisoner! Freya? Unless the lords were collecting prisoners, which was possible.

Someone grunted. Probably a guard. Fortunately, the door into the main hall kept Gil from being seen.

"Has she zapped you yet?" Ram asked.

That was almost certainly Freya. Gil quickly texted the others.

> Freya is on the second floor, maybe. Try the back by the garden.

With any luck, someone would find a way to tell Miknon to concentrate her efforts there. As soon as they had enough information, they could all leave and let Shar make a rescue plan.

"She's still recovering from the last session," the guard said. "I hope she surrenders soon, because I'm tired of standing here all day."

"Would you like a break?" Ram asked. "I could get my weapons and come back to relieve you for a few minutes. I'm sure you could use a drink by now."

"I don't know," the guard said thoughtfully. "You're not much bigger than she is. She could overpower you and escape."

"I am a wolf," Ram said. "She isn't likely to overpower me, and she certainly can't kill me fast enough to keep me from screaming. If you give me the key, I'll lock this stairwell, and the main stair is too well guarded for her to escape. You could get a drink and sit at the bottom of the other stairs. If something happens, you'll get here so fast nobody will know you left."

Gil immediately texted the others.

> Main stair is guarded.

If he got caught because of his own stupidity, at least Shar would have the most information possible.

"I suppose that would be acceptable," the guard said. "I'll wait for you to get your weapons."

"I'll be right back." Ram's footsteps raced softly through the hallway.

Gil quickly texted again.

> Ram wants to interrogate Freya. I'm going to eavesdrop.

In only a couple of minutes, Ram was back again. "Okay, take your time. She's always quiet after a session with Lord Kishar."

"Who wouldn't be?" The guard grunted a laugh. "Remember to lock the door."

"Right."

Gil pressed himself against the wall as a shadow moved under the door and the handle jiggled. Ram moved away again. Heavy footsteps marched down the hall toward the middle of the building.

Gil tiptoed closer to the door. If only he could get through right now, he might have a chance to rescue Freya. But he didn't have lock magic or a key. He should go now, before he got caught.

Another door opened, somewhere nearby.

"Haven't you had enough?" Ram asked.

"Go away." Freya's voice was weak but cranky.

Gil pressed his ear to the door.

"Why don't you obey the lords?" Ram's voice sounded almost more curious than angry.

A noise on the stairs made Gil whirl around, hand on his dagger. Alexandria raised her finger to her lips in warning, even as she stepped silently toward him. Behind her, Ian, Gaby, and Zak tiptoed extravagantly. Miknon fluttered above them. Gil scowled and pointed outside. All five shook their heads. Ian folded his arms and scowled back.

"Because they are cruel and unfair," Freya said.

Alexandria's eyebrows shot up, and she again motioned for silence. A few more quiet steps brought them all to Gil's side.

"They are powerful and irresistible," Ram countered. "It's better to obey. It's certainly less painful."

Gil motioned Zak forward and pointed to the handle, miming unlocking it. Zak grimaced but silently bent to examine the knob. She gently wiggled it, then frowned and turned harder.

To Gil's surprise, the door opened immediately. Zak held it nearly closed, and everyone froze.

After a minute, Ram asked, "Do you think you can escape Kishar's will?"

Freya sighed. "Vince did."

Everyone looked at Gil. He rapidly evaluated the situation and the amount of trouble they would be in if they attempted a rescue, and weighed that against the chance of losing her the way they lost Vince.

"I don't recommend his method," Ram said.

"It's better than working with you," Freya snapped back with some of her usual spunk.

Gil closed his eyes. He couldn't leave her, not while she was still herself. He met the gazes of the others and nodded sharply. They nodded back.

"I'm bored of talking to you," Freya said. "Are you finished yet?"

"I will never be finished." Ram's voice was heavy.

Gil pointed to himself and Alexandria and raised two fingers, moving them toward the door. She nodded and rolled her shoulders to loosen them. With four fingers on the other hand, he indicated the others coming behind. Zak nodded and moved aside, still holding the door knob.

Taking a deep breath and drawing his dagger, Gil stepped in front of the door. "Now," he mouthed silently.

Zak let go of the door, and Gil and Alexandria burst through it. He immediately scanned the hallway, looking for Freya's room, which couldn't be far since her voice carried to the stairs. Indeed, it was the next room over, and Ram stood in the open doorway.

In unison, Gil and Alexandria slammed into the traitor, carrying him into the room and against the far wall. Gil pinned his arms while Alexandria covered his mouth, hoping desperately the thud of impact was too quiet to attract notice.

Right behind them, the others poured in. Zak closed the door and leaned against it, and Gaby and Ian spread out. No weapons were available in the room, not even a wastebasket or chair. Freya lay on a bare mattress that was the only furnishing.

"Don't move," Gil threatened. "I don't care if I kill you."

Ram shook his head, widening his eyes at Alexandria. His hands lay still under Gil's, and he didn't struggle. Gil yanked Ram's dagger from his belt and tossed it onto the floor.

"Gaby, is Freya okay?" Gil asked without taking his gaze from his brother.

"Oh." Gaby choked on the word and stopped talking.

"I think okay is a very relative term." Ian sounded ill.

Leaning harder on Ram, Gil risked a quick look sideways. Freya still hadn't moved. Bruises, burns, and blood covered her face, and her ripped clothes were dirty and just as bloody.

"Why do you torment me with more illusions?" Freya closed her eyes tightly.

If Shar were present, he could touch her mind and prove they were real. After all Kishar's magic, what could convince her without the prince?

"Gaby? Zee?" Gil asked. "You were her roommates. Any ideas?"

"Against Kishar's magic?" Zee said.

Gaby sucked in a breath and dropped to her knees by the mattress. She reached for Freya, stopping before they actually touched. "When you wake in the middle of the night," she whispered, "you make a lightning ball to chase away the dark before you go back to sleep."

Freya chuckled weakly. "Kishar wouldn't know that, so you must be real. I thought you were asleep." Tears washed mucky tracks on her cheeks.

Gaby shrugged. "My grandmother shared a room with me and often woke at night."

"Can we escape together," Zak asked, "or do we need to leave Freya for a later rescue?" She didn't mention the assassination option, for which Gil was thankful.

Freya's tears turned into quiet sobs, but she didn't move. "Do what you must."

"We can't leave her," Gil said.

Alexandria bowed her head in relief, though she kept her hands firmly across Ram's mouth. "What about this one? Do we knock him out or... kill him?" She grimaced.

"We can't leave him, or he'll tell what happened." Gil's stomach churned. "Well, traitor? Death now, or an execution later?"

Alexandria eased one hand from Ram's mouth and loosened the other enough for him to speak.

"How can I fight Alex?" Ram murmured. "I remember how fierce she is, how she beat me the last time we fought."

As she covered Ram's mouth again, Alexandria shot Gil a confused look. He hid his own confusion. The last time the two fought, Ram almost won. Only trickery by Zak and Jin had thrown him long enough for a combined effort to bring him down. What was he planning now?

"Don't trust him," Miknon said. "He already betrayed us twice. Death is the only sure remedy."

Her voice was cold, but her wings trembled as much as Gil's stomach was churning. This was — had been — their brother, before he was the traitor.

"If he's dead," Ian said, "that's the end. You'll never get another chance for anything."

Gil thought back to the letter he'd thrown away for Ian. A bad relationship was better than no relationship at all. Wasn't it?

Though there was no chance to redeem his brother, he would rather not execute him personally, and Shar would appreciate any information they could strip from him before he died.

"We'll take him, too," Gil decided. "Zee and Gaby, can you help Freya? U.N. and Miknon, scout the halls and handle the doors. Alex, you're with me." He paused for another look at Ram. "Freya, do you care if we ruin your dress a little more?"

"No," Freya said. "I hate it."

"Gaby," Gil commanded, "use Ram's dagger to cut Freya's skirt to the knees. Slice the rest into long strips, please."

Gaby and Ian quickly shredded the lower edge of Freya's dress and passed the resulting lengths to Gil, who bound and gagged Ram. After checking him for other weapons, Alexandria took one of his arms and Gil the other.

Gaby and Zak hauled Freya to her feet and draped her arms over their shoulders. Ian let Miknon into the hallway and watched her through the cracked door.

"Okay, let's go." Ian threw the door wide and ran ahead for the stairwell.

The girls went next, hurrying as fast as Freya could stumble. Alexandria, Gil, and the prisoner brought up the rear, with Gil's dagger conveniently against Ram's side. As she left, Alexandria reached behind, locked the door, and closed it. Good. Making everything look normal might delay pursuit.

The hall was quiet, and Freya's pained breathing echoed too loudly. Ian waved frantically at the door he held open, checking back and forth between Miknon ahead of him and the others following. Though he was anxious to escape, Gil held Ram to a pace slower than Freya's. If someone did discover them, the traitor would make a good shield for a moment.

But nobody came, and they made it down the stairs and outside without being noticed. Gil emerged last into the dark, and nobody was in sight. Had his friends and adopted brother been captured?

"They went ahead," a voice hissed, low to the ground. A rustle followed, snake scales whispering in the grass.

Good, then they were all together. Their escape would be faster if Gil could carry Nash back, but he couldn't leave Ram with only Alexandria. Besides, Freya couldn't run, either, and it was easier to keep the dagger against Ram at a walking pace.

The trip back to the truck seemed to take a year, but they made it without getting caught. With two extra people, everyone couldn't fit in the seats of the truck. Alexandria had to drive, and they didn't dare let Ram sit in the open back. To ease Freya's trip, they laid her in the truck bed with Gaby and Zee. Ian took the front passenger seat, and Miknon, Gil, and Nash watched Ram in the back seat.

So as not to hurt those in the truck bed, Alexandria drove slowly. Nobody spoke, unwilling to give any information to the traitor.

At the school, Ian hopped out and ran inside the school. In a minute, he was back with a crowd of people. Merodach scooped up Freya and carried her off. Taras and his fellow guards dragged Ram away. The remaining family and leaders blocked the door and glared at the spies.

"Wait," Gil said. "You aren't executing him before you question him, are you?"

Shar folded his arms. "Were you seen by anyone else?"

"Absolutely not," Gil said.

"Then go to bed," Shar ordered, clipping each word sharply. "We'll talk in the morning. Rather, *I* will talk and *you* will listen." The prince was obviously furious, jaw set and eyes almost burning silver.

Gaby, Zak, and Nash sidled around him and ran for the door.

"I'm not tired yet," Mama Helen said. "We will talk tonight."

She pointed to the truck, eyes blazing. Alexandria handed the keys to Nikos and climbed into the back seat with Ian. Gil and Miknon silently joined them. Mama spoke briefly to Shar, then took the front seat. Nikos started the car without speaking. Mama kept her lecture short, finishing before they reached their apartment. She was disappointed, they were stupid, and punishment would be discussed tomorrow. The teens kept their mouths shut and merely nodded.

Once in bed, Gil stared at the ceiling, listening to Nikos and Ian breathing as they fell asleep. Though capturing Ram carried its own problems, it had also ended one. And now Kishar didn't have a lightning mage on his side. Alone, the lords would at least be easier to defeat, though not easy. The prince and the common fae had a chance to prevent war now.

As soon as the war was ended and the treaty was signed, Gil could return all responsibility to Shar and finally be free to explore Earth, be a zookeeper, and play with his friends. If only he had his twin at his side, he'd have everything he ever wanted.

He dragged his pillow over his face to keep his sobs from disturbing the only brothers he had left.

CHAPTER 19

CHOICES

SEPTEMBER 3, 2023

CAREFUL NOT TO DROP HIS tie into his cereal, Ian slid into his seat next to Alexandria. Unlike weekdays, on Sundays they ate at home and would make only a brief stop at the school to drop off Gil, Miknon, and Nikos on the way to church.

But that didn't stop them from discussing issues as a family. Mom was already lecturing again, apparently not convinced she'd scolded them enough for being stupid. Not that she called them stupid, unlike Dad. Her terms were careless, foolishly brave, and "what were you thinking?!"

Nikos was scowling ferociously, either from worry about his adopted siblings or because he hadn't been invited on their expedition. Probably both. If Ian had thought Nikos would go along with their "foolishly brave" plan, he would have been the first to vote to include him. Think how much easier it would have been to drag Rafe out of there! Or carry Freya instead of making her walk. Besides, Nikos always made Ian feel safer.

Once Mom paused for breath, Gil opened his texts and read updates aloud. Apparently, many of the common fae who had been drafted into the army and then mildly poisoned by Miknon's saboteurs were now recovering and sneaking away. Nobody knew exactly where they had gone, and nobody on the good side was looking very hard for them. Once the lords were defeated, there would be plenty of time to bring them back. In the meantime, being missing meant they were both safe and unavailable to fight against the prince.

Ian kept his mouth shut and didn't look at Mom. See, they were helping. Miknon had shut down the army, pretty much, and Freya was safe again. And everyone had made it home safely. When everyone finished eating, Mom took the keys from Nikos and stalked outside. Ian rolled his eyes at Alexandria and obediently followed. The teens took their seats in the truck and buckled without comment.

At the school, Shar was sitting on the front steps, and he hopped up as soon as the truck stopped. Uh-oh, more trouble. Ian wrinkled his nose at Gil in sympathy.

The prince of the fae opened the back door of the truck. "If I could borrow Alex and U.N. for a few minutes, please?"

Alexandria stiffened, and Ian ducked his head. Them, too? Great. Mom would only ground them for the rest of their lives, but fae rules were different. They could be expelled or banned or turned to stone. Nobody would actually agree to the last one, right?

Nikos and the fae slid out, too, since they'd be staying at the school for the day. As Nikos passed Ian, he patted him on the shoulder. Mom rolled down the window and raised a warning eyebrow at Shar, prince and mage regardless. Of course, she had survived Dad, more or less, so she had courage in plenty.

Shar waved Gil and Miknon into the school, with a glare promising they weren't off the hook. Then he eyed Ian and Alexandria. "Tell me your version of last night."

"We're on our way to church," Ian protested weakly.

Shar folded his arms. "Talk fast."

"We were just going to discover where Freya was so somebody else could rescue her," Alexandria said. "But then we found her with only Rafe as a guard, and the opportunity was too good to pass up."

"You saw nobody else at all?" Shar asked.

Ian shook his head hard enough to rattle his brains. "Nobody. Promise. Nobody was around, and we were really careful."

"Careful." Shar said it like a curse word. "Can you tell me anything useful?"

"I've been pondering all night," Alexandria said. "This was all too easy. I suspect a trap, like the Trojan Horse."

"What do you mean?" Shar asked.

"Ask Nik about the Trojan Horse," Alexandria said. "Rafe didn't even fight back. He claimed he was afraid of me, but I doubt that."

Ian nodded. "When Gil texted us that he was following his brother, we all expected him to get caught, which is why we followed."

"Stupid," Shar bit out.

"Yeah, I know." Ian rolled his eyes. "But then we didn't see anybody at all, like we said, and that seems odd. And Ram left the doors unlocked, so I agree with Alexandria. It's all very suspicious."

"I will ask Gil about that," Shar said. "Along with a few other things."

He clamped his lips together, and Ian suspected Gil was in rather a lot of trouble.

"Is that all?" Alexandria asked. "We do need to go."

Shar nodded briskly. "Get out of here."

"What will you do with Rafe?" Ian asked.

Shar turned and walked away.

"Let's go," Mom said. "We'll be late."

"But I want to know," Ian said. "And will Freya be okay?"

"You weren't invited," Mom said. "Stay out of it and mind your own business."

Heaving a sigh, Ian watched the door close behind Shar. But Freya was his friend, and so was Gil. It was his business, wasn't it?

Alexandria slung an arm over his shoulder. "Come on."

Reluctantly, he climbed back into the truck, ceding the front seat to Alexandria without a fight.

They made it to church just in time, but Ian couldn't concentrate all during sacrament meeting, pondering what the fae would do about Rafe and Lord Kishar and if Freya would recover from her torture. Not until Alexandria dragged Ian to Sunday School did he pay attention, mostly because his sister elbowed him every time his mind wandered.

He rubbed his side and glared at her, but she only jerked her chin toward the teacher, who was still talking about the body of Christ mentioned in Corinthians.

"Paul's analogy of a body is one way to consider family unity," the teacher said. "Differences should be cherished, because we need all kinds of strengths and talents working together to make it through life. Any thoughts about how these verses suggest we should treat our family members?"

Ian smothered a snort. Not like Dad did, that was for sure. Dad thought everyone should be like him and like the things he liked. He despised Ian for being different, which was exactly why his letter belonged in the trash.

And yet, Ian couldn't seem to forget about Dad or the letter. Why not? Why keep going through this misery of remembering? He squirmed until Alexandria cocked her elbow for another nudge, and then he forced himself to sit still.

Though careful to pretend attentiveness to the class discussing family relationships, his mind still raced. Why did he care what Dad thought? Dad didn't love him. Dad didn't even like him, so his opinion counted for nothing. Leaving Dad had been the biggest relief of Ian's life. So why couldn't he forget about him? Dad was no better than Rafe, the traitor. Okay, maybe a little better, since he hadn't tried to kill anyone.

How did Gil deal with his brother being so awful? Not by forgetting him, Ian was sure, despite the fae punishment of erasing Rafe's name from their society and pretending he didn't exist. Gil was the most open-hearted person Ian knew, with friends and adopted family everywhere he went. Not that Ian minded, since Gil was now *his* brother, too, as far as either of them were concerned.

And Gil had all sorts of family woes to deal with. Rafe remained a living worry, while Gil's grandfather and father were dead. Gil mourned his grandfather, who had been with him for most of his life, but Ian knew he also wished for his father, who had never even made it on the ship when Gil was a day old. For that matter, Miknon and Zee had also lost parents.

Which option was better — suffering bad memories, missing good memories, or having no memories?

Despite the agony in his own heart, he wasn't sure what would hurt the most. He did have some good memories of Dad. Before Afghanistan, Dad had played frisbee with Ian, helped him with math homework, and taught him Russian. True, he thought one extra language was enough and always pushed Ian toward science, but he hadn't been all bad.

Before the war broke him, like this one might have broken Freya. Would Freya recover? Or would she still turn into an enemy like Dad had, and hate those she once loved?

Scooting a little farther from Alexandria's elbow, Ian wrapped his arms around his torso and curled in as much as he dared. A long time ago, Ian had loved Dad, too. Pain radiated from his chest to his throat, and he tried to swallow the lump that was suddenly choking him.

When they'd left Dad after the divorce, Ian was sure it was the right choice. Never talking to Dad again felt like the perfect solution. No more fighting, no more derision, no more meanness. Never having to worry about hiding or defending. Free to stretch his talents and be himself. Free to be happy.

He hadn't realized no more Bad Dad would feel like no more Good Dad, either.

How did Gil deal with the ache of three lost family members when Ian couldn't even handle one? And not even a nice one! Ian should be happy Dad was gone.

But this felt way too much like grief. Too much like missing someone he loved. How could he love someone who had treated him so badly? He shouldn't care. He didn't care.

Alexandria's elbow alerted him to the closing prayer, and he mechanically folded his arms and closed his eyes. Instead of hearing the classroom prayer, he remembered Mom praying for Dad, even as they prepared to leave him. After the way he treated her and ruined the family, she still wanted his heart and mind to heal.

Could Dad heal? Could Freya?

Could Ian?

Still aching, Ian followed his sister to find Mom and return to the truck. He let them chatter in the front seat while he leaned against the window and tried to keep his chin from quavering. He wasn't crying. He wouldn't cry. Dad wasn't worth a single tear. He swiped angrily at his face, erasing the evidence.

Mr. Abernathy, the so-called language expert, had been as mean as Dad, but once he left the school, Ian forgot about him pretty easily. Why couldn't he forget Dad the same way?

Because he didn't love Mr. Abernathy. But he didn't *want* to love Dad. All it did was make him hurt more. After all, there wasn't any way to save their relationship now.

Was there?

Was it worth trying?

Mom parked the car at the school. "Who wants to get Nikos? I imagine Gil and Miknon will be busy longer today, though if they want to come now, that's fine. Otherwise, we'll come back for them when they're ready."

Yeah, busy deciding what to do with their scummy brother. Why did they both have rotten relatives? Ian scrubbed at his face again. If Gil caught sight of him, he'd know something was wrong. But he didn't need to worry, because Alexandria was already hopping out of the truck.

Ian turned his face away from the school and concentrated on breathing slowly. Before Nikos got in the back seat with him, Ian had better not look like he'd been crying. Having Dad gone was supposed to be a good thing. By the time Alexandria returned with Nikos, Ian had his body under control. His mind was another matter entirely.

While the others chattered on the way home, Ian pondered. He kept thinking all the way into their apartment and all through lunch. Finally, when Mom and Nikos cleared the table, he gave up on being ready and jumped in.

"Can we have a family council?" Ian asked.

"I'll go read in my room," Nikos volunteered.

"No, I need the whole family," Ian said. "I mean, I know Gil and Miknon aren't here, but they aren't staying with us forever, either, and they don't know enough about this topic to help. You're indopted, Nikos, so you're stuck with us forever."

"I'm not adopted," Nikos said, "though I'm okay with forever."

"IN-dopted," Ian emphasized. "That's like adopted without the paperwork."

"I don't think I've ever heard the term," Nikos said.

Alexandria rolled her eyes. "That's because Ian made it up."

Nikos laughed. "Okay, sure. I'm indopted."

Mom sank into the chair next to him, forehead wrinkled. "Now that we've settled that, what's wrong, honey?"

Raising their eyebrows at each other, Alexandria and Nikos took the chairs across from Ian and on his other side and fixed their older-sibling stares on him.

Ian rubbed his hands on his pants to dry his sweaty palms. "I — I got a letter from Dad."

"The skunk." Alexandria slammed her fists on the table. "He wasn't supposed to do that. Why didn't you tell us?"

Nikos clenched his jaw and inhaled deeply, flexing his shoulders. Some of Ian's tension dropped away. His family was on his side, what-ever that meant.

"I trashed it," Ian said. "I never wanted to talk to Dad again, so it didn't matter."

Mom put a gentle hand on his arm. "That's okay, honey. You don't have to."

Ian nodded jerkily. "I know. But I've been thinking."

"Big surprise," Alexandria teased. "But Ian, you don't have to talk to or about Dad if you don't want to."

"I know," Ian repeated. "But I can't stop thinking. Not just about Dad, but about Freya and Rafe."

"What's the connection?" Nikos asked.

"I can guess the connection to Rafe," Alexandria said. "They're both rotten apples. I know how close you and Gil are, and I bet you see how much he's hurting because of his brother's actions, right?"

"And I see the similarities to Freya," Mom said softly. "She and Troy are both damaged by war."

"Oh," Nikos said. "Okay, then what are you thinking about your father now?"

"Families are supposed to be together forever." Ian raised a hand to stop the comment Alexandria was ready to make. "Yeah, that's already ruined, and no, I don't expect the family to get back together, because Dad messed up pretty thoroughly."

Alexandria closed her mouth.

"I'm happy with you guys," Ian said. "I don't want to go back to Dad, I promise. But I can't stop thinking about him, and that's making me sick." He rubbed his forehead but waved off Mom's reach toward his meds in her pocket.

"I don't want to let him ruin my peace of mind," Ian said, "but what is better? Giving him a chance to compensate for his actions — but maybe making things worse — or never talking to him again, never knowing if he *would* try to fix things?" He slumped in his chair, and Nikos clasped his shoulder.

"That's a good question," Mom said. "Opening yourself for opportunity always involves opening yourself for risk. You might succeed, or you might fail. You must decide if the opportunity is worth the risk."

"Yeah, that's what I don't know," Ian said. "I thought maybe you all could help me."

"I've already decided to move on," Mom said. "I still love Troy, but I can't trust him. I don't know if I'll ever find someone else, but if not, I can be happy with just my children."

She put one hand on Ian and stretched the other to Alexandria while she smiled across the table at Nikos.

"I'm still waiting to contact Dad until I'm eighteen," Alexandria said. "That gives me almost three months to plan what I want to say. I'm not in any hurry to see him again, though if he keeps going to therapy, I'll consider inviting him to graduation next year."

"I'd be happy never talking to him again," Nikos said, "though I wouldn't turn down punching him in the nose."

Mom gave Nikos a disgusted look before turning to Ian. "You have a long time before you turn eighteen. You don't need to decide before then. Take your time and be sure you know what you want."

Ian wrinkled his nose. Yes, but what *did* he want? Why wouldn't they tell him what would be better? Would Dad improve with another chance or keep being mean? Was broken better or worse than missing?

As for waiting until he was eighteen, he didn't want to suffer this turmoil until then. He'd rather find an answer sooner.

"What if we can't stop the war, and Dad gets pulled into it and dies?" Ian asked.

"Then that's his own fault," Nikos said. "Don't let his choices ruin your life."

But Dad's choices had already messed up Ian's life. He just wanted to know if anything was fixable or not. He bit his lip and blinked back tears. If Dad died, would Ian ever regret not having a chance to change his mind and talk to him again? Or would it be a mercy to have the question settled for good?

Alexandria leaned across the table, eyes the bright sage green that indicated strong emotion. "*You* decide," she said. "*You* get to say how much Dad you ever want in your life again. *You* set your rules and boundaries. *We* will make sure Dad sticks to them. If he hurts you again, we'll bounce him on his backside faster than the Fae spaceships can travel."

Despite his worries, Ian chuckled. "That's impossible," he said. "Humans don't move that quickly."

Alexandria folded her arms. "Don't care. Nikos will help me."

"Sure will," Nikos said.

"Take your time," Mom repeated. "I love you."

She rose and pulled him into a hug, and Nikos and Alexandria ran around the table to add their arms to the family embrace.

Of all the things Ian might regret in his life, his siblings, indopted or otherwise, would never be among them. Now he needed to decide how to be less sorry about Dad.

CHAPTER 20

IN WHICH RAM HAS A SECRET

SEPTEMBER 3, 2023

ZAK FINISHED her breakfast by the time Gil and Miknon arrived Sunday morning. A few minutes later, Shar called a council meeting of only the fae members. Ah, then the topic must be not war but betrayal.

Not at all to her surprise, Zak arrived in the basement and found the traitor already present, surrounded by guards. His clothes were wrinkled from sleeping in them. Assuming he had slept at all, considering the dark circles under his eyes. Head bowed, he waited without struggling.

Like the other fae, Zak remained standing until the prince sat in a folding chair at the front of the room. Once everyone settled and their greater heights no longer blocked her view, she scanned the crowd.

Gil and Miknon were on the front row, but Maia was absent. If Zak were to guess, the traitor's mother couldn't bear to watch the trial and execution of her once-son. How could Gil and Miknon endure the fate of their brother?

"You have all heard the latest report," Shar said grimly, "so I won't repeat it. Now is the time to question the traitor."

He turned his gaze on the white shifter, who paled even more. With power echoing in his voice, Shar said, "Tell us everything you know about the lords and their plans."

Shalla jumped to her feet. "If Kishar commanded him not to talk, this could break his mind. You should work up to the big questions gradually."

"His mind is the least of my worries," Shar declared. "Talk, traitor. Do you have anything useful to say, or should we execute you right now?"

Zak held her breath, unsure if she should hope for a few more minutes of life or a quick end. Someone whimpered. Probably Gil, from the sound of it.

Head still bowed, the shifter said, "The humans won't like you killing me."

"I have a stonegazer waiting for a chance at you," Shar said. "You will live as stone for weeks before you starve. I will tell the humans you are still alive." He raised his eyebrows. "Further, the humans have no authority over us, since they haven't signed the treaty yet. Thanks to you and your masters, so enjoy the consequences. Nothing will stop me from dealing with you. Now, will you talk or die?"

Ahead of Zak, Gil's back was curled in misery. She was too far to reach him for a comforting touch, but Miknon wrapped her arms around his neck.

"I will talk," the traitor said. "May I reach into my pocket?"

"No," Shar said.

The shifter turned to Taras, who held his left arm, and leaned his hip toward the tall naga. "Please empty my pocket."

Taras switched his dagger to his left hand and slid his fingers into the kilt pocket, pulling back with a folded bunch of paper. Human paper, from the thin blue lines on it.

"I was bound from reading the battle notes," the traitor said. "I couldn't take the whole book, but I retrieved those few pages before the lords could find somebody else to read them. All that is left is homework and science vocabulary. They won't learn anything from the remaining words."

Stealthily, Zak slid her phone from her pocket and texted Gaby that her notes had been found. Without that guilt dragging on her, maybe she would feel some relief.

"We already changed the plans," Taras said. "Your offering is useless. Your betrayal was worthless."

"Good," the traitor said.

Shar blinked and straightened a little. Zak wrinkled her brows in puzzlement. Good?

The shifter bowed as much as possible with the guards holding his arms. "I apologize for betraying you and trying to reveal your plans. I regret my choices."

Shar narrowed his eyes. "Are you going to plead for your life?"

"No," the traitor said. "I've betrayed you twice now. I expect no mercy. I just wanted you to know I'm sorry." He turned his head a little in Gil and Miknon's direction.

"Is your escape some kind of trap?" Shar asked. "Is this a delay to give the lords time to attack?"

"No trap," the shifter said. "I did not plan to leave yesterday, with or without Freya. I'm sure they've noticed her absence by now, though they might think I stole her rather than suspect you."

Shar leaned back in his chair and pursed his lips. "After your steadfast loyalty to the lords, why this change of mind now?"

"I supported Lord Kishar because he upheld tradition," the traitor said. "Though you are the king's son, Kishar was also designated an heir. He wanted to continue the old ways, and you do not. The choice seemed clear. Therefore, I gave the plans to Lord Kishar and returned with him to rally his warriors." He sighed. "I regret the death of Vince, though I did not understand how he could believe in your rebellion so strongly."

He rolled his shoulders but didn't struggle against the guards. "But after living under Kishar's rule for a short time, I discovered the way we lived on the ship was *not* the traditional way. King Arishaka had already loosened customs and increased equality, and we simply had nothing for comparison. The traditions I longed to keep were already new."

Gil snorted. Zak agreed with his skepticism. Had his brother never listened to the stories their elders told of the old world? The highborn had ruled by whim with absolute power.

The traitor bowed his head. "Under Kishar and Zaidu, the

commoners were little more than slaves. Only the most useful gained a little immunity, and then only as long as they continued to be useful. Those with minimal magic were less than slaves, nothing more than objects. I saw pixies like my — like those I knew on the ship, broken and discarded like the human light bulbs."

Zak smothered a sob with her hands, both for the deaths and the traitor's inability to reference the adopted sister that could no longer acknowledge him. Ahead of her, Miknon buried her face in Gil's hair. He reached to pat her with a trembling hand.

"This was what some of the lords want to restore." The traitor's voice cracked. "I could no longer tell myself the old ways are better. I could no longer support their treatment of our people. But it was too late for me to return home."

He sucked in a deep breath. "So I pretended I adored Kishar. I told him I had not been trusted since my first betrayal and had been unable to learn any secrets. I said our prince had commanded me not to speak, which was true, but claimed the magic blocked more subjects than it did."

Tired of looking at the backs of heads, Zak watched Shar instead. Though his mouth was still grim, his eyes were sad, and his fists were clenched on his knees. And still the painful report continued.

"I lied about my current capabilities as a warrior," Gil's brother said. "I said I hadn't been able to practice at the school and must be retrained. I was assigned to be a servant while I trained, and I pretended it was an honor to serve. They trusted me and let me wander freely. Between my assigned duties, I watched them training." He straightened his shoulders. "You should know the lords are practicing their magic together as well as alone, though I can't guess at their purpose."

"They have never worked together," Shar said. "It was one of the few advantages we had."

"What could they be doing?" Taras asked. "Zaidu's water magic is powerful, but Kishar's best talent is his command voice. How could they combine those?"

Shar waved him off. "We will discuss possibilities later. Continue your story, traitor."

Ram — Zak found she could no longer maintain the custom of

thinking of him without a name — sighed again. "I couldn't go home without being executed on sight. I didn't have the internet to research other destinations, but I was determined not to stay. I had to escape somehow, even if I must live as a wolf forever and never talk to anyone again."

"They weren't watching you in the garden," Gil croaked. "Why didn't you leave then?"

Ram turned his head partway again, though not enough for Zak to see his face. "I still hoped for a chance to catch Kishar alone and rip out his throat. Then his death would pay for my sins."

"His guards would have caught you and killed you," Gil said.

Ram shrugged, a weary gesture rather than an angry one. Zak's stomach clenched into a ball of misery. Vince had died because he didn't see another way to avoid betraying his friends. Ram didn't care if he died because he *had* betrayed them. How many more friends would she lose before this war ended?

Shar shook his head. "I can't believe a word you say."

"I know," Ram said. "Nobody will ever believe me again. My family is lost to me, my friends hate me, and I betrayed my prince twice. I am ready to die. But first, Sire, I have one gift for you."

"A *gift*?" Shar's eyebrows shot up his forehead.

"I told you they trusted me," Ram said. "They didn't restrict my movements, even while I cleaned the lords' rooms. I looked for anything that might help you, though I didn't know how I would pass any information to you."

Shar's fists tightened, but he said nothing.

"Kishar keeps all his plans in his head," Ram said. "There was nothing to find in his room. But in Zaidu's, I found something belonging to the king."

A murmur of surprise ran through the room, and Zak couldn't hide her own gasp. Zaidu had stolen something? Or did Ram only mean information?

Ram bowed his head. "If I may have the use of my hands for a moment, I will return it."

With a twitch of his finger, Shar indicated permission. Taras and the other guards let go of Ram, though they did not step away.

Ram slowly reached for his leg. He placed both hands on his thigh and pressed his thumbs in and downward, smoothing his kilt. No, moving something *under* his kilt, around his leg! When he reached his knee, he let go and shook his leg. With a clatter and a glint, the hidden object fell to his bare foot.

Taras jerked forward, but Ram merely lifted his foot and stepped aside, hands outstretched and empty.

On the floor, a circle of metal gleamed in the harsh light. Shar hissed in a breath, but it took Zak a moment longer to recognize the king's crown. The old king's crown, since Shar had never had it in his possession.

"Zaidu probably wanted a hold over Kishar," Ram said. "Now it is yours again, Sire. I am ready to die."

Slowly, he dropped to his knees and bowed his head to the floor, hands stretched in front of him. Only the rapid rise and fall of his back revealed his distress.

With his attention still on Ram, Taras handed the crown to Shar. The uncrowned king turned the circlet in his hands, watching the light shine on its curves. The council was as motionless as the traitor, and Zak had to remind herself to breathe.

The last time anyone but Lord Zaidu had seen the crown, including Shar, had been when Arishaka had worn it. Memories must be flooding Shar right now, both good and bad. Like Zak, Shar had no memories of his mother, but at least she still had her father.

"This is good news, Sire," Shalla tentatively said. "With the crown, you can prove your lineage. The lords can no longer call you an illusion or an imposter."

Shar clenched his hand around the circlet. "And if Zee can use this to enhance my magic, I might have a chance to beat them."

He beckoned Zak, who rushed to his side. In truth, she wasn't so confident she could make the tech work on his crown, but she must try.

Bowing, she said, "Yes, Sire."

"Shall I call the stonegazer now?" Taras glanced toward the back of the room.

Zak bowed again, turning her face away from Ram, who had not moved since he knelt. Could she use the crown as an excuse to leave now? Though he had never been a close friend, she could not bear to watch Gil's brother die.

"Wait!" Gil sprang to his feet so fast that Miknon fell off his shoulder and had to beat her wings frantically to avoid hitting the floor.

Zak straightened and sent a warning glance his direction. Shar was in no mood for impertinence, even from his best friend. Gil ignored her and kept his gaze on the prince.

Shar glowered. "I am not interested in another plea for mercy."

Gil bowed low and stayed there. "I know, Sire. I have a question for — the condemned." His voice cracked on the last word.

"You will answer his questions as you answer mine," Shar commanded Ram.

Ram nodded against the floor.

"You said this wasn't a trap," Gil said. "But did you know I was following you? Did you lead me to Freya and deliberately avoid raising the alarm?"

Ram said nothing, though his body shook with the effort of staying silent.

"Speak." Shar's voice echoed with power.

"Yes," Ram croaked, face still to the floor.

Zak blinked and tightened her grip on the crown. That explained why they had escaped so easily. But why had Ram done it?

"Didn't you think we would just kill you there instead of capturing you?" Gil wailed.

"Yes." Ram's admission sounded like it had been torn from his throat.

Gil sucked in a breath audible to everyone in the room. "Didn't you *care?*"

Ram shuddered so hard his head banged on the floor, but he said nothing.

"Naram." Shar used his true name for the first time since the traitor had been outcast.

"No!" Ram whispered. "I hoped you would kill me and rescue Freya. If you didn't find the notes and crown on my corpse, they would be buried with me, out of Kishar's hands."

With a smothered cry, Gil collapsed into his chair. Zak turned her face away and bit her lip to fight the tears stinging her eyes. At least

Maia wasn't here to see her son like this. Either son. And Miknon had settled on the floor, curled under her wings until nothing showed but her feathers.

"Sire?" Taras asked.

"I must think," Shar said. "Take him away and keep him out of my sight. And feed him something. He's not allowed to die until I say so." He sat straighter and glared at the council. "All of you, leave me alone!"

He stalked from the room without a backward glance. Taras murmured to his guards, and Ram was dragged to his feet and out the door. As the council trailed out, nobody looked at Gil and Miknon. The two siblings eventually struggled to their feet and stumbled out. Finally, only Zak and Father and one guard were left.

"Are you ready?" Father asked softly. "We still have most of the day to work."

"Right." Zak rubbed her eyes and took a deep breath.

She slid the crown over her arm to have her hands free to push Father's wheelchair. Unlike the rest of the council, who must go upstairs, her destination was in the basement. Without a word, the remaining guard followed, taking a watchful stance by the door of the tech classroom.

At the back, her Fae radio had been joined by two tables of her projects, including the circlets. By now, everyone in the school knew this was her space, and nobody touched it. Here was where she had reverse-engineered how Grandmother had created the circlets to combine the efforts of mages to generate enough power to drive the spaceships. With that knowledge, she had tried to make them work for Shar, but she had failed. At least her attempts had allowed her to duplicate a few more circlets to be used in the war.

Now they had the king's own crown, tuned to his bloodline. This was her best — and last — chance to enhance Shar's powers enough to allow him to battle the full-grown and well-practiced lords. If she took Grandmother's work and Father's experience and her own knowledge of Earth technology, could she combine them all in the crown?

Just as importantly, could she succeed before the lords gathered their armies for attack? She had mere days to try, or perhaps only hours.

She and Father tried the same things they had done with the

commoner circlets, but they didn't work. The human tech would not integrate with the crown created by magic instead of fae technology. Father knew no more of magic than she did, and less about human tech.

If she couldn't figure it out, then the war might still end in defeat. But she was out of ideas.

Exhausted and starving, she left Father downstairs and went after a late lunch for them. Brains needed fuel, the science teacher said, so they might as well eat as they pondered their next attempt.

Though she could hear the chatter and laughter of students in the rooms she passed, the halls were mostly empty, and she traveled without a word to anyone. The feeling was very familiar. Her whole life had been spent almost in isolation, hiding her gender from everyone lest the lords kill her like her contriver grandmother. Father still disapproved of the humans and avoided them as much as possible.

In the kitchen, she stacked a tray with food, water, and dishes, then carefully balanced it for the trip back downstairs.

With nothing to do on the spaceship but study, she had become a master of her chosen profession. But it wasn't helping her now. She wasn't good enough. She didn't have time to become good enough. Her failure might doom her people.

She walked back through the empty halls and pushed the elevator button with her elbow. If only Father knew more about human technology.

The elevator dinged and opened its doors, but Zak stared without seeing it. No matter what Father said, she couldn't do this herself, or even with him. Why was she surprised? Everything so far had taken teamwork, not just one or two people working on a task. Learning Earth languages, negotiating the treaty, even rescuing Freya. She needed someone who knew more about human tech.

Her eyes widened as the answer hit. She needed a human. And she knew who to ask.

The elevator doors closed. She blinked and pushed the button again.

Back in the classroom, she settled the tray on the teacher's desk and grabbed a sandwich, then set her phone in front of her and opened her email.

Kirill, she typed, *I need your help.*

CHAPTER 21

BATTLE

THE ALARM CLOCK BEEPED, and Gaby smacked it. Today was her last day at the school, and she still hadn't told her friends. Before they went spying, she had been too upset to talk about it, and afterward, everything was too chaotic. Her problem was inconsequential compared with everything else. She was the only one who would be hurt by Grand-mère's edict.

Across the room, Zee's bed was still empty. After sharing a room with Grand-mère, Gaby always woke when her roommates did. Since she'd slept undisturbed, that meant Zee had never come to bed. She must still be working on the king's crown, poor girl.

If Gaby were an engineer instead of a mathematician, she would have helped, but she didn't have any useful skills. And now she was out of time to even be an extra pair of hands, because her parents would leave any minute to take her home. Lunch would be her last time with her friends.

It wasn't fair. She'd worked hard and done everything she was asked. She learned the Fae language and already had a list of scientific words no one else knew. And she helped rescue Freya. She had earned her place here.

Why did Grand-mère have to be so terrible? Gaby pressed her face into her pillow until she ran out of air. Reluctantly, she headed for the shower, mentally checking her packing from last night. Physically, she was ready to go, but she dreaded breaking the news to her friends. Sighing, she turned off the water.

As she dressed in the bathroom, she listened for Zee, but the bedroom was silent. She scooped up her toiletries and pajamas and plodded to her bed. After dumping her armload, she flopped her loaded suitcase onto her bedspread. Two minutes to pack, half an hour for breakfast, then a few hours before her family arrived. As if to emphasize the passage of time, the numbers on her clock flipped. And Zee was still gone.

Gaby froze, pajamas still in her hands. It wasn't fair. Everyone else was working to end this war before it spread across the world, and she was running home like a coward. All because of Grand-mère, who had already made her life miserable. How long would she let herself be pushed around as if she didn't matter? No more!

She dropped her pajamas and grabbed her phone from her nightstand.

"Bonjour, Mamá. Have you left yet? Well, turn around the car and go home. I'm staying here." She put the phone on speaker, then started unpacking her suitcase. "Yes, I'm sure, Mamá. Hola, Papá. I don't care what Grand-mère thinks. You tell her I'm protecting the family by staying. Actually, never mind; I'll tell her myself."

"I don't think that's a good idea," Papá said. "Let us talk to her."

"I can do it," Gaby said. "Go home and tell the boys I'm sorry I won't see them for a while."

She hung up and took a deep breath before dialing again. "Bonjour, Grand-mère. This is Gabriela."

"Your parents are on the way," Grand-mère said in French.

"Not anymore," Gaby said in English. "They're coming home, and I'm not. I'm not a traitor; I'm protecting Earth. If you don't like it, that's your problem. But if you want to see me again, you'd better be nice. To everybody, not just me."

Grand-mère gasped and spluttered. "But Gabrielle—"

"And my name is Gabriela," Gaby interrupted. "Say it right. I love you, Grand-mère."

She hung up and flopped face-down on her bed. She'd meant to be firm, not rude, but her anxiety and long frustration had betrayed her. What were the chances of Grand-mère talking to her again?

She groaned and pushed herself up. Ten minutes later, room restored, she walked into the cafeteria and grabbed a tray. From across the room, Alex pointed to an empty seat next to her, since the school holiday also applied to colleges. With everyone available, Gaby expected a council meeting to be called, whether or not Zee succeeded with the crown.

But breakfast passed quietly, and Alex and Gaby spent the time chatting about math and astronomy. Since Gaby hadn't mentioned she was going home, she didn't have to reveal her change in plans. After dumping their trays, the girls went upstairs to Shar's office, which was empty.

"That's strange," Alex said. "He didn't summon the council. Maybe he's planning his birthday party for tomorrow."

"He didn't summon *us*, you mean," Gaby said. "Maybe he doesn't trust us after we snuck off. Or maybe the adults think everything is too dangerous for us now."

"Well," Alex huffed, "that's too bad, isn't it?"

She marched for the stairs, and Gaby followed nervously. As they reached the bottom of the stairs, they heard the adult members of the council in the PE room. Alex texted all three of her brothers, Zee, and Nate before squaring her shoulders and charging in. Gaby crept after her.

"Execution is the safest," Tom was saying, though he stopped when he saw the girls.

"Can we help you?" Shar asked.

Alex waved her hand casually and took a seat, pulling Gaby with her. "Our invitations got lost in the mail, but fortunately, we made it anyway."

"You weren't invited," Tom said.

"And yet, here we are." Alex leveled a stare at Shar, lips pressed into a straight line.

Gaby slid down in her chair and debated a quick retreat. Though she wanted to help, she didn't want to intrude. How could Alex face all those glares without cringing?

"This doesn't concern you," Shar said gently.

"I think it does," Alex argued. "You're discussing a student. We're students. And we're *concerned* about the effect your decision will have on our friends."

Grasping the sides of her chair, Gaby braced herself to stay.

Rapid footsteps echoed in the stairwell, and Alex smiled. "In fact, I think we're about to be joined by more *concerned* people."

Shar rubbed his forehead. "You didn't."

"They deserve to be here," Gaby whispered.

The boys rushed in, grabbing the door frame to swing into the room without slowing. Most of them sat next to or behind the girls. Gil continued to the front of the room and bowed to Shar.

"Sire, we humbly request admittance." Despite the polite words, his posture was rigid.

He didn't wait for an answer before joining the other students. They crossed their arms and braced their legs, clearly unwilling to leave. Nate wrapped his tail around the legs of Nik's chair and glared with all nine heads.

"Fine!" Shar raised his hands in surrender. "You can stay, but you won't like it."

Gil snorted. "What's new?"

Shar motioned to Tom. "Continue." Before the naga could do so, more footsteps pounded down the hall. "What now?" Shar asked.

Zee stumbled into the room, smudged with oil and dust, green hair falling out of its braids, and dark circles under her eyes. She clutched something to her chest, though Gaby couldn't see anything besides a metallic gleam. Behind her, her father slowly propelled his wheelchair.

Shar and Nik both rose and offered their chairs, but Zee fell to her knees in front of the prince.

"We did it," she croaked, presenting the object.

Shar eagerly examined it. Somehow, Zee had bound the king's crown to another ring of metal, though Gaby couldn't tell what or how.

"Is this one of the common circlets?" Shar asked.

Zee nodded, and Nik helped her to her feet and into his chair.

"It was Kirill's idea," Zee said, "to use it as an intermediary. It works by... Um." She waved her hands in the air in random motions. "I don't think I can explain it. But it translates the human power to the crown's magic."

"I need to test this." Shar clutched the altered crown like a life preserver. "But how?"

Gaby rose and headed for the door, determined to be useful while they thought. She ran to the kitchen and gathered food and water, choosing some of Zee's favorites to make sure she ate. By the time she reached the basement again, Wes had joined the council, though the teen highborn looked rather confused.

"You want me to do what, Sire?" Wes asked.

"Hold your shield against me for a minute," Shar said. "Protect your mind from me. I won't hurt you, but I want you to resist my commands."

"Sure," Wes said, "but you'd have to use my name in front of everyone."

"Don't you trust them yet?" Shar asked.

Wes grunted and surveyed the audience. Gaby put her tray on Zee's lap and pressed a glass of water into her hand. If Wes hadn't yet learned how to be friends with humans, nothing she could do right now would convince him. She put a peach into Zee's other hand. A damp napkin would have improved Zee's cleanliness, but too late now.

With another grunt and an ostentatious eye roll, Wes raised a magic shield, wrapping the nearly invisible shimmer around himself.

Crown in hand, Shar said, "Wedaneus, drop your shield." As usual, his voice echoed with power.

Wes yawned but did not move.

Shar clenched his fist around the doubled crown until the low spikes drew blood, then put the joined circlets on his head. "Wedaneus, drop your shield and bow."

Though his voice was no louder than before, it shook Gaby's bones.

Even with the wrong name, she had to grip her chair to avoid the compulsion to stand and bow.

The shield vanished, and Wes doubled over like a puppet whose strings had been cut. The rest of the fae gasped.

"Well," Shar said, "it works."

Zee's shoulders trembled. Gaby patted her arm in congratulations, then handed her more food.

"May I get up now?" Wes asked.

"Yes." Shar raised the crown above his head and shook it like a trophy. "It's time to stop this war. I want this ended by tomorrow, when I come of age and take my place as king."

Humans and fae all cheered. Gaby's heart raced, and her stomach turned inside out, but she still yelled as loudly as the others.

Shar slung the crown around his elbow, then pulled out his phone. "Maxwell," he said, "the time has come to face the lords. As king of the fae, I require the bus drivers to transport my troops to the edge of the park. We welcome the humans as allies if they wish to join us, but we do not require them to fight."

"This is a very bad idea." Ms. Maxwell's voice over the speaker was controlled but obviously distressed. "You've been telling us for a long time that you can't face their magic. Why now?"

"Zee has provided us with a new weapon," Shar said. "This is our chance to stop the war before it gets any worse. Further, this is not your choice; it is ours. We don't want to wait until the enemy thinks they have an overwhelming force."

Ms. Maxwell's sigh echoed through the phone. "I will talk to Major General Anthony about our troops." The phone clicked off.

Shar turned to Tom. "I want to leave in an hour, with or without the humans. Gather our warriors."

Tom bowed and instantly left the room.

"Anyone who is going should prepare now," Shar said.

The room emptied in a rush. Gaby was one of the last to leave, hands full of Zee's tray while her friend continued to eat. The two took the elevator to their room, and while Zee showered, Gaby perused her own closet for anything suitable.

She finally settled on a long-sleeved shirt and her thickest jeans.

While not armor, it was the most protection she had available. Once clean, Zee chose a similar outfit, and both girls hurried downstairs.

Ms. Maxwell, Shar, Miknon, and Tom were already in conversation, ignoring the crowd that gathered in the hallway. Numerous fae uncharacteristically had weapons. Granted, most of them were daggers instead of swords, but had they been hiding those in their rooms for the past year? All Gaby had was a phone, and that was useless in a battle.

Miknon spotted her and beckoned. Confused, Gaby approached.

"Do you have something to make voices louder without magic?" Miknon asked.

"Like a microphone or speaker?" Gaby asked. "Sure, I can find something."

She ran, anxious to return, though if they needed the microphone, they wouldn't leave without her. In the library, she found both a mic and a battery-powered speaker to make it even louder and packed them in a handy bag.

To her relief, nobody had left when she returned. In fact, the hallway was more full of troops sitting against the walls. The fae mingled with humans in military fatigues or ordinary clothes. Even Freya was there, looking rather worse for wear, though Miles the healer was at her side.

From her perch on the principal's shoulder, Miknon nodded at Gaby and nudged Ms. Maxwell.

Ms. Maxwell raised her hands for attention. "Okay, everybody. The general says he'll only allow volunteers, so if you don't want to go, you're dismissed."

Nobody moved.

"If you aren't trained as a soldier, I highly recommend you stay here." Ms. Maxwell looked at the students. "This particularly applies to those of you who are still underage."

Nik crossed his arms and grinned. "I'm an adult. I've missed everything else, and I'm not missing this."

Alex glared with eyes of warning green, and U.N. stretched to be as tall as possible. The fae teens just stared.

Meg, Gil's gentle mother, stepped forward. "We know this is dangerous, War Lady, but so is letting the war continue. This is what we've been fighting for. I can't stay home, and I can't forbid my children from helping." She narrowed her eyes at Gil. "But if you don't be careful, Kishar will be the least of your worries!"

From around the closest corner, just out of sight, Ms. Ellison appeared. Her children immediately flattened themselves against the wall with guilty looks.

"I wish I had any hope of making my children stay home," Ms. Ellison said, "but I suspect they would sneak out. So I will go along to keep my eye on them."

Alex blushed scarlet, and U.N. paled. Nik put his arms around his adopted siblings and nodded briskly.

If Gaby needed permission from her parents, she was sunk. Not only were they not here, they would never agree. Regardless, she had no intention of staying behind. She wanted to help, and now was the time. Honestly, she wasn't sure what she could do, but if she stayed behind, she couldn't do anything.

Gaby clutched the bag of electronics and prepared to argue she was needed for tech support, but Ms. Maxwell waved everyone outside and assigned buses without further discussion.

Gaby and the other students clumped together at the back of their bus.

"Are we crazy?" Gaby whispered.

"Yes," Alex said, "but it's a good crazy."

"I like crazy," Freya snarled.

Twenty minutes later, they arrived at the far side of the park and unloaded, and the military passed around walkie-talkies to every tenth person.

"English or Fae?" U.N. squeezed his walkie-talkie so tightly his knuckles turned white.

"Mix it up," Ms. Maxwell said. "That should confuse anybody but us."

She ruffled U.N.'s hair before marching away with the troops that would clear bystanders from the park and then sneak around the back of the fae apartments.

"We'll give them a while to get into position," Tom said. "Everyone here should be quiet and stay put."

U.N. repeated the instructions into his walkie-talkie using a brilliantly confusing mix of English and Fae. The warriors hid behind bushes or trees or otherwise tried to be inconspicuous. Gaby and the other students copied them.

Across the road, the old hotel was quiet. No cars were parked there, since none of the fae could drive and the lords had already sent away all the humans.

"How can we get the lords to come outside and face us?" Shar murmured. "I expected a sentry to alert them to our presence."

In the distant sky above the hotel, a plane swooped gently downward. A tug at Gaby's elbow drew her gaze to the grass.

"Bring the loud speaking," Miknon whispered.

Slowly, the pixie flew from tree to tree toward the building. Shar shrugged and nodded, so Gaby followed, sweating ferociously and trying to stay hidden. At the edge of the park, Miknon waved Gaby down behind a large shrub.

"Set it up here," Miknon said.

"Why?" Gaby pulled out the sound equipment.

Miknon grinned evilly. "We need to draw them out, right?"

As if that explained anything. Gaby set up the microphone and speaker, then set the mic on the ground by Miknon.

Miknon took a deep breath and leaned in. "I am Miknon the pixie," she shouted in Fae. The speaker enhanced her voice so it could probably be heard halfway across the park. The fae would certainly hear her. "I call upon all commoners to rebel. The time of the lords has ended; the time of equality is upon us. Thus says our king, who is indeed alive."

She pointed dramatically back at Shar, though Gaby doubted anyone could see the pixie, much less her tiny arm. Just in case she was in the way, Gaby flattened to the ground.

Miknon continued. "Our troops have damaged the lords' armies and rescued the healers. This is the last outpost. You are alone, and you are surrounded. Surrender now, and make a better world."

The distant plane turned slightly toward them, and Gaby absently tried to figure the math for their flight path. What airport were they trying to reach? But planes didn't matter, because the doors to the fae building were opening. Gaby scooted backward and ran into a warm body. Hands touched her legs until she stopped moving. She cast a frantic gaze behind her and discovered Nik at her heels and a crowd on their knees behind him. Shar and U.N. were in the middle, with Freya, Gil, Alex, Tom, Nate, Wes, and a dozen fae warriors surrounding them.

Shar rose to his feet, and everyone automatically copied him. Nik pulled Gaby behind him, though he left Miknon at the microphone.

A fae peeked around the open door, then ran into the yard. Behind him ran more and more common fae. Their hands were empty, though a few carried knives at their belts. Instead of drawing their weapons, they lowered their heads, pumped their arms, and headed straight across the street to where Shar waited. Without any other options to defend herself, Gaby clenched her fists.

The first commoner to reach them bowed to the prince and spun away, flinging himself up a tree like a monkey. Gaby blinked and relaxed her hands a little. The next commoners also bowed and moved on, though most of them chose bushes instead of trees or kept running.

They were all defecting. Could Shar really win this battle without a fight? Gaby sucked in a breath.

She relaxed too soon, because the next to emerge from the building were highborn mages and armed warriors. Shar's bodyguards closed tighter around him.

"That's Zaidu," Gil said in Gaby's ear.

The lord he pointed to wore a knee-length, embroidered tunic edged with a rainbow of jewels. His golden hair was elaborately braided.

"And Kishar," Gil said.

The infamous Kishar had no embroidery or jewels, and in a movie, Gaby would have guessed his costume to be Greek or Roman. His dress, whatever it ought to have been called, fell to his feet in a shimmer of brilliant blue silk. His silver hair was merely tied back in a low ponytail with a gold ribbon.

Kishar stopped in the doorway and raised his arms. "Miknon, I command you to be silent." The lord's voice echoed like Shar's when he was using magic.

Miknon leaned in and said something in Fae that Gaby didn't recognize.

"What does that mean?" Gaby asked Gil.

He pursed his lips. "It's not polite."

Behind them, Alex said, "Why didn't that command work? Is Kishar weakened somehow?" Her voice was hopeful.

Gil chuckled. "Miknon isn't her name. Mother adopted her as a baby, and we had to call her something."

"Then it's been her name for seventeen years," Gaby protested.

Gil shrugged. "Still doesn't count."

Now the stray airplane was closer and lower, clearly lost. With the sun behind them, all Gaby could see was the reflection of the window and a vague, oddly shaped silhouette. But unless it crashed, it didn't matter how odd it was.

Gaby darted around Nik and grabbed Miknon and the sound equipment, then retreated to relative safety by the prince.

Shar crammed his crown onto his head and took the microphone from her. "Zaiduramman, Kisharnizir, I command you to stop fighting."

The two lords paused, but only briefly.

"See, he does not have enough power to be the king," Kishar shouted. "You have been deceived by an imposter."

Zaidu raised his hands, and a nearby fire hydrant exploded. He directed the stream of water at Shar. Wes blocked it with a magic shield, though the water continued to pour. Kishar laughed and pointed to the water, which began to boil mid-flow. The steam crept along the airborne river, closer and closer to Shar. Tom ran toward the lords, and Gil jumped between the prince and Wes's shield.

The steam reached the shield, which exploded in sparkles that broke the stream of water. Wes collapsed onto the grass. Gaby crawled toward him, hoping he was still alive.

Kishar and Zaidu raised their hands again, and this time, there was no one to stop them.

CHAPTER 22

IN WHICH NOBODY RECOGNIZES A SHIP

SEPTEMBER 4, 2023

GIL SPREAD HIS ARMS WIDE, shielding Shar, though he knew he couldn't stop a river of steam. They would all die. He frantically stepped backward, but they had no time to get out of range of the lords' magic.

"Start running," he begged uselessly.

"Kings don't run," Shar said.

Somehow, he didn't even sound afraid. Gil was terrified, but he stayed where he was, unable to abandon his friend.

Taras attacked Zaidu, who grinned wickedly and threw a new blast of water at him. The naga was blown off his feet, and Zaidu refocused his magic at Shar. Within seconds, Gil and Shar were drowning on their feet from the deluge. For now, the water was cool, though strong enough to make Gil stagger even coming from across the road.

Then Kishar pointed at the water, which again turned to steam. The cloud moved along the water, closer and closer to Gil and Shar. The lords hardly ever worked together, and combining their magics was even more rare. This must be what Ram had mentioned them practicing. If they were going to be traitors, why couldn't they stick with their non-cooperation policy and fight separately?

Gil pushed backward again and slammed into Shar, who had not retreated, as promised.

"Get out of the way," Shar said. "This is not your fight."

Gil didn't look behind him. "Not a chance."

The prince was more important than a lowly zookeeper, and maybe Gil would block the heat long enough for Taras to recover and eliminate one of the lords. Assuming the naga had a chance against the magic. Besides, if Gil died, he wouldn't have to worry about what to do with Ram.

The steam was now close enough to heat the air on Gil's face, and Shar still wouldn't move back. Gil closed his eyes and hoped Mother was busy elsewhere on the battlefield. She already had enough nightmares in her life without watching them die.

Something thumped softly, and water hissed. The heat on Gil's face vanished.

"Who is that?" Shar exclaimed.

Gil opened his eyes. Just in front of the lords, a blocky airplane had landed on the street between the park and the hotel yard, and water now steamed from its hull. Barely small enough to land on the road due to its stubby wings, it looked like someone had tried to turn a barge into a dragon, or vice versa, then covered it all in ceramic tiles like dragon scales. Zaidu and Kishar detoured around the plane and curved the stream of water to redirect their magical attack.

"Hey, U.N.," Gil called. "What country makes planes like that? Are they friends or enemies?"

Ian stopped hovering behind Nikos and Alexandria and ran to Gil, swinging his walkie-talkie like a weapon. "Humans don't build airplanes that look like dragons and maneuver like helicopters. It must be a fae spaceship, though I don't know why it didn't land months ago."

Shar kept watching the battle across the road. "It's not ours. We don't put wings on barges, and all our ships have landed or been emptied. Forget the plane until the lords are defeated."

Taras rolled to his feet and lunged at Kishar, who dodged and blasted a stream of heat at him. Without Kishar's magic, Zaidu's river of water stopped boiling, though it was still hot enough to hurt as it hit Gil again. Did it make a difference if he was cooked or merely drowned?

Freya growled and cast lightning at Zaidu. The lord yelped and translocated himself three feet away, landing unevenly and falling on his rump. His hair stood on end, but he unfortunately seemed unharmed. Suddenly free of the river, Gil shook himself hard to shed the water and clear his eyes. He gasped for breath, hearing Shar do the same behind him.

"He knows how to make the most of a small magic," Mother said bitterly. She transferred her glare from Zaidu to Gil. "I saw what you did," she said. "We'll talk later."

When had she gotten so close? Gil ducked his head from her wrath, but he didn't move away from Shar as Mother turned to guard them. As if she could do more than Taras could. He was the best warrior among the fae, and Mother wasn't a soldier at all. As soon as the lords got rid of Taras and Freya, they would attack the prince again, and nobody could stop them.

"Maybe we need more volume." Zak grabbed the microphone from Gaby and the crown from Shar and sat on the ground to frantically tinker with them.

"What are you doing?" Gil asked. "We need to get Shar out of range."

"I don't have time to explain," Zak said, "and you wouldn't understand anyway. Just keep the lords away from me for a few minutes."

"Use the plane as a shield," Nikos suggested.

Shar moved a bit sideways, dragging Zak with him. Nikos relocated Wes before returning to guard position. Mother, Gaby, Nate, the Fitches, and the king's bodyguards spread out in front, keeping watch on the battle. Across the road, Freya attacked both lords with lightning, which hampered Taras's efforts but kept Kishar and Zaidu distracted. More fae warriors joined Taras to harass the lords and their tiny army, though they couldn't win against them.

The commoners tackled the enemy warriors and mages in small groups, overwhelming them by sheer numbers rather than technique, weaponry, or magic. Even the commoners who had worked for the lords were lobbing stones from behind bushes. A few of the enemy fell, but so did more of the commoners. Gil couldn't tell who was dead and who was merely injured.

At the back of the fae apartments, human military streamed into the building. U.N. raised his walkie talkie and alternately listened and spoke. Curtains opened in the building to signal rooms cleared one by one as the soldiers flushed out anyone still hiding. Wisely, they left the magic users on the grounds for the fae to deal with.

To save as many commoners as possible, the fae warriors dispersed to combat the enemy warriors and mages. Only Taras and Freya kept fighting the lords. It was a losing battle until Zak finished her alterations, but it did keep Kishar and Zaidu from helping their army.

Still guarding Shar and Zak, Gil kept one eye on the plane that had unexpectedly landed. After it touched down, it hadn't moved at all except to cover its windows with unfolding tiles. The fighters were avoiding it, possibly because it made them as nervous as it did Gil. Despite Shar's command, they really needed to know if they needed to split their forces to guard against it.

"If the plane isn't ours and isn't yours," Gil asked, "whose ship is it? And whose side is it on?"

"Maybe it landed here by accident," Gaby said, "and now they don't want to emerge into the middle of a battle."

"Do we have *more* aliens?" Ian sounded both worried and weary.

"Could it be tech?" Zak didn't look up from the crown as her fingers raced to finish whatever tech miracle she was attempting. "Like a rowbutt?"

"Robot," Ian corrected absently. "That would explain why nobody has emerged yet, but AI doesn't usually handle landings safely."

"I told you to forget about it," Shar said. "As long as it doesn't attack us, we can figure it out later. Whoever they are, we'll build a three-way peace on Earth."

Ian groaned. "We haven't even finished the first treaty yet!"

Gil hid his own sigh. The fae had worked with the humans for almost a year to learn their languages before they got to the actual negotiating. If this new ship held a whole new race, then everything just got very complicated all over again. Assuming the newcomers were willing to agree on anything.

Across the road, Taras and the warriors were slowing, and Freya looked ready to drop with exhaustion. On the grass, most of the enemy were motionless, either injured or bound. Many of their own soldiers lay beside them. The two enemy lords, however, were still fighting.

Zak popped to her feet, crown extended. "I'm done." The microphone wire dangled from the combined circlets like a mouse tail.

Asking no questions, Shar slapped the crown crookedly on his head and shouted into the microphone. "Zaiduramman, Kisharnizir, I command you to stop fighting."

Kishar and Zaidu stumbled but didn't stop.

Shar grimaced. "Still not enough power."

"But it was closer," Gil protested.

"More power," Zak said. "More power, more power." She danced from foot to foot. "I don't know how to add more power."

More power! Of course!

Past the plane, Freya staggered to her knees. Gil ran forward and pulled her arm over his shoulder. Hauling her to her feet, he dragged her back across the road to the prince.

"But Zaidu," Freya gasped.

"Taras," Gil bellowed, waving at Zaidu.

Ian shouted into the walkie-talkie, and fae warriors and human military streamed toward the abandoned lord.

"They'll distract him for a minute," Gil said. "I need you to zap Shar's crown."

"My lightning shorts out magic," Freya said. "Remember?"

"Zee combined the circlets to allow technology to enhance magic," Gil said, "so hopefully now the crown won't break. Right, Zee?"

"That's not—" Zak took a deep breath. "More or less, I suppose."

Wearily, Freya held out one hand. "Okay, give me the crown."

"No, I mean, zap it while he's wearing it," Gil clarified.

"Are you out of your mind?" Shar barked.

Maybe. Gil winced. Hopefully not.

Freya pulled her arm free and stared at Gil as she wobbled on her feet. "You want me to hit the prince with lightning?"

"Just a little." Gil held his finger and thumb a short distance apart. "For more power."

"Lightning?" Shar repeated. "I don't think so. If I didn't know better, I'd ask if your brother put you up to this."

Gil shrugged. "Okay, I'm out of ideas." He drew his knife and settled into a balanced stance. With the warriors so tired and Freya out of energy, the lords would attack again soon. The king's side would probably lose, but he was determined to die fighting.

Shar raised his eyebrows at Gil, then turned to Zak. "You, I trust. Would this insane idea work?"

Zak bit her lip and hunched her shoulders. "Maybe? Lightning *is* power."

Shar sucked in a deep breath. "Then let's try it."

Gil sheathed his knife so his hands would be free to help Shar. If there was any help he could give. He scanned the crowd and beckoned urgently for Merodach. Having the healer nearby was probably a good idea when electrocuting the prince. Was there any part of "electrocute the prince" that *was* a good idea?

"I still think you're crazy." Freya raised her hands. "Now?"

"Just a minute." Shar removed his signet ring and thrust it at Gil. In command voice, he thundered into the microphone, "I hereby disavow Kishar as heir and cast him from my family. I designate Gil as my heir until such time as I have my own children."

Mother turned around and stared. Freya and Zak bowed, but Ian stifled a giggle.

Gil groaned and pushed Shar's hand away. "Please, no."

It was bad enough Shar wanted him on his council. If Gil were heir, he would never be free again. And he was nothing but a common shapeshifter and zookeeper. Nobody would follow his rule.

"This was your idea," Shar said. "If I die in this battle, I won't leave Kishar as my heir, so who would you suggest?"

"Wes?" Gil motioned to the unconscious body nearby. "He's highborn."

Shar rolled his eyes. "Yes, Wes is so trusting and unbiased."

His grasp of human sarcasm was clear, but he was right. Wes had made progress, but he still had problems considering commoners and humans as valuable. Gil hoped that would change in time, but for now Wes would be nearly as bad of a king as Kishar, just less powerful.

"There must be someone else," Gil protested. "Freya? Anyone else?"

Freya raised her eyebrows and shook her head.

"This *whole treaty* was your idea," Shar said. "You convinced me to give the humans a chance for peace. *You* are responsible for our present, so be responsible for our future."

"That's not fair," Gil said.

"I wasn't trying to be fair." Shar presented his ring again, one eyebrow raised.

Fighting despair, Gil stared at the signet. Though he had carried it for almost a year to indicate the authority Shar assigned him, he hadn't missed it or the responsibility. Once they beat the lords, they just had to finalize the treaty before they could find homes for all the fae, and then he would be free.

But if Shar died and Gil became king, he faced a miserable load of duties every day. Could he stand the weight of responsibilities and public judgment? Everyone looking to him for guidance, taking his time and attention, wanting more of him than he had to give. He didn't mind being Shar's best friend, since that was more about making sure the prince — the king — got in a little fun from time to time instead of turning into a boring mushroom. Being heir was a nightmare. Why couldn't he go back to being a carefree child instead of being forced into premature adulthood?

But though more of the fae, especially the students, liked the humans now, did he dare trust them to aim for peace above all else? Or would they eventually listen to the lords and fall into darkness like his own brother had?

Slowly, Gil took the ring, though his hand shook.

Shar clasped him on the shoulder, an unusually intimate gesture. "If I fail, don't let Kishar win."

"And how am I supposed to stop him?" Gil complained.

He shoved the ring onto his finger, but it jammed halfway. He tried two more fingers before it finally fit. Last year, he had strung the ring on his silver chain, next to the silver wolf emblem of his family, but the heir must not hide the signet behind his shirt collar. He squared his shoulders, though curling into a ball was more tempting. Hiding was no longer an option now that Shar had ruined his life.

Gil bowed to his prince, then glanced at Zak. The navigator had bitten her lip until it bled. Not a good sign, but she didn't say anything. She would say if she had changed her mind about it being a workable idea. Wouldn't she?

Gil turned to Freya. "Nobody wants me as king, so this had better work. Just a little lightning, mind. You don't want to turn the prince into a lamp post."

"No kidding," Freya snapped. She flexed her fingers and reached for the crown on Shar's head.

CHAPTER 23

KING

As FREYA STRETCHED UPWARD, Ian bit his lip. Electrocuting anybody was a bad idea, much less a prince. Should he get Mom or Alexandria or Nikos to stop it? But it wasn't any of their business, and somebody needed to defeat the evil lords. But what if it didn't work? Worse, what if Freya killed Shar?

"Wait," Zee said.

Oh, good, someone was stopping this madness. Freya lowered her hands, but Zee only shoved the microphone into Shar's hand.

"I increased the volume," the gremlin inventor said. "We might as well use every advantage we have."

Freya nodded and reached up again.

A thought struck Ian. "Wait a minute." He quickly reviewed the little he knew of magic, but the answer he wanted wasn't there. He just didn't know enough.

Freya sighed and lowered her hands again. "What now?"

"If we're using every advantage," Ian said, "then Shar should use all his magic, not just his voice. More magic is more magic, right? We need more power, Zee said."

"How would light or illusion help?" Shar asked. "And I'm too far for my weak mind-touching. Besides, we never mix magics."

"Kishar and Zaidu learned how to combine theirs to be more effective," Ian argued. "And didn't Zee say the other circlets were designed to combine powers?"

"Not like that," Zee said. "Multiple users of the same power, not different powers."

Ian shrugged. "What will it hurt to try everything at once?"

"I don't think it will help, either," Shar said.

"Okay, never mind." Ian didn't even know how magic worked.

Shar squared his shoulders. "I'm ready, Freya."

"I'm not ready," Freya muttered, reaching for the crown again. She took a deep breath, and lightning sprang from her fingers and ran around the joined circlets. Sparks danced like fireflies across Shar's hair. He howled, a terrible rising shriek like the hounds of hell were being tortured. Freya jumped back and covered her mouth. All across the park, the scattered battles halted, and people turned to stare.

With shaking hands, Shar raised the mic to his mouth. He lit up like the lamp post Gil had warned about, flickering in and out of visibility as he screamed into the microphone. "Zaiduramman, Kisharnizir, STOP! I command you to stop fighting now!"

The words echoed and re-echoed, not only in Ian's ears but crawling inside his head and rattling his bones. Apparently the light and flickering weren't a side effect of electrocution, but only Shar's magic. Despite his claims it would make no difference, he had evidently decided to try everything at once anyway.

The magic shook Ian even harder, like an earthquake inside his head. He clutched his head and fell to his knees as his skull split open. Okay, his hands said his head was still in one piece, but his head didn't believe it. His vision blurred, and his stomach heaved. Maybe combining light and telepathy with Shar's voice was a very bad idea.

Shar collapsed and lay absolutely still. From the park to the fae apartments, other people fell, some silent and some thrashing. Kishar and Zaidu froze, and Tom and his warriors ran — or crawled — to capture them.

"Oh, good," Ian mumbled, trying not to vomit, "we won. Didn't we?"

Or was Shar dead and their victory hollow? Death sounded very peaceful and painless right now.

Gil stumbled the two steps necessary to reach Shar, falling on his knees beside him. He placed trembling fingers on Shar's throat, then laid his ear on the king's chest. Ian tried to go help, but every muscle trembled, and the slightest movement made his vision swim and go black. All he could do was watch through half-closed eyes.

"He's alive," Gil croaked. Without raising his head, he pulled the crown from Shar's head and tossed it to Zee. Then he removed the signet ring from his finger and forced it back onto Shar's hand. His body went limp, but his back still rose and fell.

Oh, good. The fae wouldn't have to find a new king before they even crowned the old one. Yay. Ian couldn't rouse any enthusiasm under the flood of pain and nausea. Unable to remain partially upright any longer, he collapsed sideways onto the grass and covered his eyes with one arm. Thank goodness Shar was alive, but Ian wasn't sure he wanted to be. Death would hurt a lot less, wouldn't it? Whose dumb idea had it been to have Shar include telepathy and light in the call? Why hadn't somebody slapped Ian for being stupid?

He wasn't sure how long he lay on the grass, though it felt like an eternity. After a decade or so, somebody touched his shoulder. His stomach rebelled at the slight jiggle, and he whimpered.

"Don't touch me," he begged.

"Okay," Mom whispered. "Are you injured anywhere?"

Ian groaned. "Just inside my head."

"I should have brought your meds," Mom said, "but I put bear spray in my pocket instead."

Ian chuckled and instantly regretted it. "Did you get to use it?" he whispered.

"No." Mom sounded sad. "I mostly helped the deserters find hiding places or makeshift weapons."

"Good job, Mom." That sounded a lot more fun than fighting, actually. And way more fun than meddling with magic. Apparently, the fae were wise to not mix magics blindly.

The grass rustled, and a shadow fell across his face, dimming the light just enough to be less than torture. Mom's hand gently scooted next to his, barely brushing the skin. It still hurt like touching sunburn, but Ian didn't move. If moving didn't make his head fall off, he would have grabbed her hand like a little kid crossing the street. He wanted to ask about his siblings, but someone had added another hammer to the dozen already pounding inside his skull. Mom would have told him if they weren't okay, so they would show up sooner or later.

"Hail, Lord Shar!" someone shouted. "Shar is king!"

Ian groaned and covered his ears, but he could still hear the others echo the call. More and more voices, strong or weak or trembling, repeated the words.

"They're all bowing," Mom whispered, "except Kishar and Zaidu, who haven't moved a muscle since Shar commanded them to stop."

Then they had won, or so it seemed. Ian ought to be happy, but now that everything was over, all he could think about was the fae he had seen fall to the enemy. How many of them were dead instead of merely injured? How many would still die from their wounds? In all the chaos, he hadn't been able to keep track of everyone he knew. Sure, Mom would say if Alexandria or Nikos was dead, and he'd seen Gil breathing, but what about everyone else? Had they all survived, or would he be mourning friends and acquaintances as soon as they compiled the lists of the dead?

And what if Mom was only waiting until he recovered to break the bad news? What if his siblings *had* died, or been permanently injured?

He would have nightmares for the rest of his life. Even if the only dead were mere acquaintances, he would still remember the horror forever. Like Dad? Was this what he was suffering? Only worse, because he'd been at war for years, not just one afternoon. How could he bear it?

Well, clearly, he couldn't. That was why he had PTSD.

Ian shuddered, then clutched his stomach to keep from puking at the movement. Would he be like Dad for the rest of his life? Would he ruin everyone else's life because he couldn't deal with his own trauma? Because, honestly, Ian wasn't dealing well at all. Horrid pictures of the battle pranced across the inside of his eyelids, but he couldn't open his eyes to get rid of them. He'd never sleep like this, either.

Poor Dad.

But no way would Ian be like Dad. He'd go to therapy for a decade if that's what it took, but he couldn't live like this. Wouldn't.

If this migraine didn't stop, he was pretty sure living wouldn't be one of his problems at all, so he wouldn't have to worry about Dad.

Assuming he lived, what should he do about Dad's letter? Ignore it? Write back and tell Dad to jump off a cliff? Or talk to him? The dilemma had been difficult before, but now he felt more sympathy for Dad than ever before, and he hated every minute of it. It was easier to believe Dad was terrible because he was a bad person. Sure, Mom and Alexandria had said it was the PTSD, but all Ian saw was the cruelty. Dad didn't *have* to be mean.

But maybe he didn't see how much he was hurting his family. He *had* been right about aliens coming. Maybe he honestly thought he had to be strict to save everyone.

Even when they told him how they felt? Why couldn't he listen to them? Would he listen now or would he always be a jerk?

With the migraine that wouldn't quit, Ian couldn't find his way out of the maze of confusion. Was his relationship with Dad worth trying to fix or not?

A cool hand touched his head, and the pain and nausea slowly drained, leaving Ian limp. It was too much trouble to open his eyes, but he took a deep breath.

"Thank you, Miles," Mom whispered.

"Thank you," Ian echoed.

After a minute, he rolled onto his back and cracked open one eye. Mom sat by his side, as he already knew. Nikos stood at his feet, clearly in guard position, and if Ian leaned his head back a little, he could see the familiar patch on Alexandria's jeans. Oh, good, Mom hadn't been waiting to break the bad news.

Ian rolled his head sideways and scanned the park, still only with one eye. Miles was working his way around the battlefield with amateur helpers. Many people, including Wes, stumbled to their feet in his wake, but some lay still. Ian's chest ached, and he clamped his lips together to keep from crying.

On the other side of Mom, Zee was slowly detaching wires from Shar's crown and handing them to Gaby to stuff into a bag. Shar was sitting, more or less, leaning against Gil while Tom guarded them. Not that there was anything left to guard against, since nobody was fighting.

Ian squinted past the landed airplane. Yep, the lords were still there. Now they were so coiled with rope that their clothing could barely be seen. They looked like spools of thread with doll heads stuck on top.

A crazy giggle threatened to burst out, and Ian held his breath until he could control the impulse.

"Are you ready to get up?" Mom asked softly.

Slowly, Ian pushed himself to a sitting position. His head didn't explode, so he rolled to hands and knees. From either side, Nikos and Alexandria grabbed him gently and hauled him to his feet. They kept their hands on him until he stopped wobbling, then slowly let go.

"Are you okay?" Alexandria asked.

Ian rocked his hands in a more-or-less gesture. At least his head was still attached. Nikos examined him with a pained squint. Apparently satisfied, he rubbed his head and returned to watching the crowd. Ian was willing to bet he hadn't been the only one to be knocked flat by a sudden migraine.

"Did we win?" Ian asked.

"Approximately," Alexandria said. "The lords are defeated. Now we just have to deal with all the leftovers." She grimaced as she surveyed the park.

"If you're okay, I'll go help the healers," Mom said. "Don't leave without telling me."

"Yes, Mom," Alexandria said.

Nikos nodded, then winced. Ian didn't bother moving his head, but he waved as she left.

"So," Alexandria said, "what are we doing about that airplane?"

Ian groaned. "Nothing? Maybe Zee is right about it being a robot, because it hasn't moved since it landed."

As if on cue, the tiles over the windows unfolded again. Unfortunately, the glass was so thick and wavy that nothing but colored shadows could be seen. But something was definitely inside. Or someone. And probably not a robot.

Gil helped Shar climb to his feet, and Zee struggled upright with Gaby. Tom whispered urgently in the king's ear, then drew his sword.

The door remained closed. They still had a minute — for something, though Ian had no idea what the plan was.

"Okay," Alexandria said, "go slow and try not to look dangerous. That means you, Tom. Try a friendly welcome, then we'll try to learn who they are and what they want."

Of course she had a plan. She always had a plan. Ian would have rolled his eyes if they hadn't been stretched wide with fear. Thank goodness Dad wasn't here, because he would probably have exploded the ship by now.

With any luck, it didn't need to be blown up. But Tom didn't sheathe his sword, and Ian's heart sped.

"U.N.," his sister said, "you're the language expert. See if you can learn how to say hello."

"Thanks a lot," Ian muttered. "Gil, you ready?"

The werewolf was probably the next best at learning new languages quickly. Carefully, Gil slipped his shoulder out from under Shar's arm. The prince stayed upright, though he swayed a little. Nikos moved back to stand near Shar, though he didn't touch him. Gaby subtly drifted to Shar's other side.

"I'm here." Gil clapped Ian on the shoulder, then moved to stand by Tom.

Together. They could do it together. They had learned how to speak to each other, after all. Ian took a deep breath, then another. At least his brain was working again. Sort of.

"I've decided," Alexandria said calmly, "that adulthood stinks."

"You aren't even an adult yet," Nikos teased.

"You know what I mean," she tossed over her shoulder. "Always something else to do, someone else who needs help. More deadlines, more responsibility."

She was way too accurate, and Ian's shoulders sagged under the weight of expectations. But neither could he walk away and leave everyone else to carry the load. He'd seen what happened when Dad gave up, and he wanted to be better than that.

Stupid adulting. Being a kid was easier.

He squared his shoulders and edged a little closer to his sister. He wasn't alone. And if he could face aliens — twice — then he could certainly face Dad again. In fact, he wanted to introduce his friends to Dad, to prove aliens weren't necessarily dangerous. And if Dad didn't like the fae, then Ian would know there was no chance for reconciliation with his father. Then he wouldn't have to worry for four more years, because he would know the answer. Yes, that was a good plan. Alexandria would probably approve, both of the plan itself and *having* a plan.

And in the meantime, he'd be plenty busy learning *another* alien language. Oh, please, let these aliens also not be dangerous. They hadn't blasted anybody yet. That had to be a good sign, didn't it?

The door of the small spaceship cracked open. They were out of time. Though new aliens meant no actual translation would be possible for now — maybe not for months — they'd better learn very fast how to communicate their peaceful intent. And hope the aliens had the same goal.

Alex and Nikos joined Tom and Gil on the front row. Ian took a deep breath and followed. Behind him, Zee, Shar, and Gaby drew closer.

Chapter 24

In Which the Ship Opens

September 4, 2023

Zak set her hand discreetly on the sharpest tool in her pocket kit and kept right behind U.N. With one foe defeated, must they face another? She cast a glance over her shoulder to confirm Shar was staying safely behind her and Gaby.

From inside the barge, a pale hand reached through the narrow opening and pulled sideways. Slowly, the door creaked open more. Taras cast his own warning look at Shar and shifted his grip on his sword but didn't raise it. Now two hands reached around the edge of the door, which began to slide a little faster. In a few seconds, the gap was wide enough for a glimpse inside.

Zak gasped. Despite its strange design, it was indeed a Fae ship. At least, it was full of fae. From where she stood, the flickering pixie light was too uneven to identify all of them, but there were nearly fifty fae of many races, including a few gremlins. The hands on the door belonged to a white shifter with the long ears of a wolf, sitting on the floor and grimacing as he pulled.

Sheathing his sword, Taras crossed his arms and watched.

"What are we waiting for?" Gil asked. "They're no enemy; they saved us." He bounded forward and pushed the door open the rest of the way. "Greetings. Welcome to Ki. May I help you up?"

Breathless, the older werewolf nodded, reaching up as Gil bent to lift him. Once back on his bunk by the door, the newcomer stared at Gil through the messy white braids hanging across his face. He touched Gil's face with trembling fingers. "Where is the mapmaker?"

Shar sucked in an audible breath, and Zak looked over her shoulder to see what was wrong.

"U.N.," he said, "go get Zee's father and find *all* of Gil's family."

"Why?" U.N. asked. "And Rafe and Ike are back at the school."

Yes, why? Zak's father was the navigator, not the mapmaker who had discovered and preserved the long-ago seer's map to Earth.

"Go!" Shar roared, not quite using command voice. He winced and pressed a shaking hand to his head.

"Okay, okay." Ian darted away a little unevenly, dragging his siblings with him.

Gil shrugged. "I don't know the mapmaker."

"Oh." The newcomer dropped his hand and bowed his head.

Taras walked to the open door, and Zak crept after him, Shar close on her heels.

"I don't know if she was ever on the ship," Gil continued.

The older werewolf howled in anguish. "You lost her?"

Shar darted around Taras, ducking his Companion's lunge at him, and slid into the ship, landing on his knees in front of the pale shifter. "We did not lose her, I swear. Give us time to bring her." His voice vibrated with power, though he spoke nearly in a whisper.

The werewolf raised his gaze to the doubled crown on Shar's head. "You are not Arishaka, and what did you do to his crown?"

"He was my father." Shar bowed his head. "I regret he died on the journey."

"Gil." Zak tugged on his elbow. "Wouldn't it be easier to talk if we took them outside?"

"Gil?" The pale wolf looked past Shar. "Like— And your face... But you do not know the mapmaker?"

"I'd like to," Gil said. "That's always been one of my favorite stories."

222 Marty C. Lee

Shar nudged Gil's knee. "You should stop talking now."

With a large sigh and rolling eyes, Gil sarcastically closed his mouth. He and Shar linked their arms together and carried the pale shifter as if on a chair. Taras lifted the next fae, and Zak headed for the first person small enough for her to transport.

On her second trip, Zak sent Gaby away and waved off the other humans, to avoid alarming the newcomers. There would be plenty of time to introduce them later. Obediently, they returned to their work on the battlefield. A few more fae came to help, but most were dealing with the injured and the prisoners. Between the limited help and the cramped quarters that meant they must go single file in and out of the ship, it took nearly an hour before everyone had been settled gently on the grass under the trees.

On her last trip out, Zak carried two pixies from the back corner. The empty ship was crammed wall to wall and floor to ceiling with bunks, supplies, and a smaller navigation radio she yearned to examine. Unlike *New Kunisu*, there was no room for even a single tree, though berry bushes grew in large barrels with mesh keeping them secure during times of weightlessness. The small garden, the size of her school bedroom, had grain in three different stages of growth and a variety of vegetables. Taps extended from the walls of the ship for the typical fae trick of using the necessary water storage to also shield them from radiation. Not that fae science knew what radiation was, but they knew how to be safe in space.

Like the bigger ships, they still needed pilots to move the ship, navigators to find the way, heat, shields, light, healing, clean water, plant magic, and more. With fewer than fifty people to run this entire ecosystem — ha, Gaby's science lessons had worked — they must have been busy all the time, taxing their magic to the limits. That much was obvious. Perhaps that explained the tiles covering the ship. The more they could do with technology, the less they must do with magic.

The burning questions remained. Who were they? Where had they found another ship after the fleet had taken every one the fae could build? How had they found Earth without the mapmaker or the map on *New Kunisu*?

Zak laid the pixies on the grass and stood where her shadow would filter the sun for them. It had taken her weeks to get used to the blinding light on Earth, and all the new fae were ducking their heads or shading their eyes instead of looking at their new surroundings. Many of them wept silently, either in relief at reaching Earth or in distress at the bodies still littering the grass as they waited for a healer or a burial.

To be polite, Zak watched them only from the corner of her eyes. They seemed neither starving like the passengers of *New Kunisu* nor well-fed like the rest of the fleet. Too thin, but still healthy. They had done well, considering the limited space they had for supplies and gardens.

"How—" she started, then closed her mouth. If Shar wasn't ready to ask questions, she should be patient. She shoved her hands into her pockets and concentrated on squelching her curiosity.

Gil bounced on his toes, obviously as curious as she was, but Shar sat on the grass beside the first white shifter and a female who looked like an older relative, waiting patiently. For what?

From the direction of the road, figures hurried. U.N.'s blond hair shone like highborn silver. Behind them came Maia pushing Father's chair, Miknon, and Ram flanked by Alex and Nik as well as a couple of fae guards.

"Ah, here they are." Shar rose and paced forward. "I told you we didn't lose the mapmaker."

"Where?" Gil craned to see. "Who?"

With an amused lift of an eyebrow, Shar pointed. The new shifter pushed back his braids to get a better look at the approaching people. Zak frowned. Despite scrunching his face against the sun, he somehow looked familiar.

"Ike?" Gil asked. "No, he's just the navigator. The mapmaker was a girl, according to the story."

Maia smiled at Shar, then spotted the newcomers. She stopped pushing the wheelchair and froze, mouth hanging open. With a wail, she darted around the wheelchair and ran to the shifter, falling to her knees and throwing herself into his waiting arms.

U.N. took over pushing the wheelchair, but once she knew Father wasn't abandoned, Zak gave all her attention to the scene in front of her. Sobs racked Maia as she clutched the shifter like her life depended on it. Tears streamed down his cheeks as he pulled her onto his lap. The woman by him scooted closer, also weeping. As he buried his face in Maia's shoulder, he freed one hand to pull all three of them together.

Gil staggered. "Mother? I don't understand."

"Your mother is the mapmaker," Shar said. "She saved all of us. Including, apparently, your father."

Zak's eyebrows shot up. Ah, that explained the strange familiarity. The shifter looked like the traitor. Abruptly, Gil sat on the ground, putting his head between his knees. His back heaved as he fought for breath. Zak felt similarly stunned. All this time, Maia had been the mapmaker but had kept her role secret. No wonder she had a place among the leaders. Without her, the fae would have wandered between the constellations until they died.

And if Gil's father had escaped their world after all, then who else had he brought with them? Shar had sent for all of Gil's family. Zak looked at the pixies at her feet, who were crying and reaching toward Miknon. Her parents, certainly. Lucky Miknon.

And Shar asked for Father. Because he thought—

Was there any chance her grandmother had survived Lord Zaidu's attempt at murder? That would explain the unfamiliar ship, at least; surely the great contriver could improve the standard design. Zak searched the new fae for someone who could be her grandmother. Several gremlins were scattered through the group, but all of them sat with someone else. Nobody was alone.

Oh, well, it was just a thought. Zak squelched her disappointment and practiced a smile for Gil and Miknon. Her friends deserved happiness, and she was glad for them. Really, she was. Her smile wavered until she firmed her lips upward.

Miknon, Ram, and Father reached the spaceship. With a bow, Shar picked up the two pixies and carried them to meet Miknon. His quiet words didn't reach Zak, but Miknon wobbled in the air and landed abruptly on his shoulder. The prince settled all three pixies on the grass, far enough from the others to offer a little privacy.

Gaby tentatively wandered closer, hands behind her back. Zak waved her onward, since the girl was one of the least alarming humans.

From the look of Gaby's blood-splattered clothes, she had been helping the healers. If they didn't need her anymore, that was a good sign.

Meanwhile, Father had been scanning the newcomers, hands clenched on the arms of his chair. His breath came in short pants, and his ears were bright green with excitement. At last, he spoke to U.N. and pointed. The boy dug in his heels and pushed the wheelchair across the grass to a couple of female gremlins.

Zak headed toward them, both eager and anxious to meet her heroic grandmother. Father slid from the wheelchair and landed between the two women. To her surprise, instead of embracing the old one, he threw an arm around each. And while he tightly hugged his presumed mother, he kissed the younger one full on the mouth. What? Why would he—

Her legs buckled, and she fell to her knees, struggling for breath. Father would kiss only one person like that.

"Zee," Father croaked, "come here."

But Zak couldn't get to her feet. She had no strength to deal with her world turning upside down. Again.

"Come on," Gaby said. "We'll help."

She drew one of Zak's arms over her shoulders, and U.N. took the other. Together, they supported Zak the short distance to the three gremlins, who were staring at her like they were starving and she was a banquet. Despite their dirty, ragged appearance, the two women raised their heads proudly. As they should, since the contriver had been the means of saving the fae.

Forcing her knees straight, Zak freed her arms and bowed slightly. "It is my pleasure to meet the contriver and…"

"My apprentice," the old woman said. "Enni."

The female apprentice the lords had left behind with the contriver. Zak dipped her head in acknowledgment, using the movement to hide her disappointment. While she was happy the other navigator had also survived, she had hoped for someone else.

"Your mother," Jadakira continued.

Then Zak had guessed correctly after all. She wobbled on her feet, and Father tugged on her hand, easily pulling her down. Now she wondered if his comments earlier had been "any," or "Enni." When

Miknon spoke of justice for those murdered or Father wished for someone with more experience, was he thinking of his wife?

Her mother — her mother! — touched Zak's cheek and smiled through her tears. "Zee, is it? You are beautiful and brave."

Shoving uselessly at her sweaty, messy hair and tugging at her rumpled t-shirt, Zak felt her ears burn. "I'm a navigator, too," she mumbled.

Her mother laughed softly. "I'm not surprised, but I am so, so proud of you." Slowly, she put a hand on Zak's arm.

Her grandmother, Jad, reached toward Zak, then pulled back.

Gulping for air, Zak closed her eyes. When she opened them, she raised her arms. "Welcome to Earth."

Enni and Jad nodded solemnly. "We are glad to be here."

Zak's arms sagged a little. She wiggled forward until her knees touched theirs. "Welcome *home*."

She raised her arms again and leaned in, unsure how to ask for what she wanted. Her arms wavered. Perhaps she was too bold.

"Oh!" Her mother laughed and reached out.

All four of them embraced in a tangle of arms and bony knees and wet cheeks. When they finally surfaced for air, they found Gil in a similar huddle with his parents and the old woman who was probably his grandmother. A few steps away in Taras's grip, his brother kept his gaze down, but his shoulders jerked in uneven sobs. Past them, Miknon had disappeared into her parents' embrace.

For the moment, Zak ignored them all in favor of her own questions. "How did you get here without a map?"

"Oh, we had a map," Grandmother said. "Ram knew the way."

Zak glanced at Gil's brother again before realizing Grandmother must mean his father, who must have learned the map from his wife. Who was the famous, mysterious mapmaker. It all made sense, but she still reeled from all the revelations.

"But how did you find us here?" She waved at the park.

"We picked up your signals to Izdu," Mother said. "We heard everything you told him as he retrieved the fleet, which allowed us to make course corrections and aim straight for here. We made as many adjustments to our contrivance as we could, based on your instructions." She shrugged. "You explained the Ki word for the fae, so we listened to every broadcast that mentioned them. And today, we picked up an unusual signal coming from this area. It seemed Fae, but not Fae, so we thought you might be involved."

Her grin was both friendly and mischievous, and Zak returned it as easily as she would have with Gaby.

Oh! Her friends. She turned and found Gaby and all four Fitches with Shar, all conspicuously not-watching the various reunions. Gaby was scrubbing her bloody hands on her pants, without much success at getting clean.

"We appreciate you arriving in time to save the king," Zak said.

"The king?" Grandmother searched the crowd. "We didn't see Arishaka."

"Arishaka died on the journey. His son rules now." Zak repeated the explanation for those who had been too far back in the ship to hear Shar introduce himself. She raised her voice. "Shar, everybody, would you like to meet my mother and grandmother?"

The five humans and the prince joined them, kneeling just outside their circle.

"Shar is the king," Zak said.

After startled glances at his casual and very human clothing, her family bowed. "Sire," they murmured.

"These are humans from my school," Zak explained, "and vital to the treaty negotiations with Ki. Gaby shares a room with me, and U.N., Alex, and Nik are the children of Helen as well as adopted siblings to Gil, son of the mapmaker."

At the skeptical looks from her new-found family, she nodded vigorously. Gil would claim his human siblings if asked.

"Welcome to Earth," U.N. said in flawless Fae.

"Greetings," Gaby said hesitantly. A faint pink spread across her cheeks.

"We are pleased to meet you," Helen said.

Alex and Nik merely nodded.

"You arrived at the perfect moment," Shar said to the newcomers. "I owe my life to you."

Grandmother sniffed. "I recognized Kishar and Zaidu and decided whomever they didn't like was probably my ally. I'm glad to see I was right."

"Is the battle over now?" Mother tightened her grip on Zak's hand. "Are you safe?"

"There's a little clean-up to do," Shar said, "but I think it's safe to say the real fighting is done. Are you ready to come home?"

"Yes." Mother pressed Father's hand to her cheek. "Oh, yes!"

Zak smiled through her tears.

"I already sent the military for more wheelchairs," Alex said. "The first bus should return soon."

"We can start without them," Nik said, "in teams, if necessary. We can probably have most of the newcomers at the road by the time the buses arrive."

Alex hopped to her feet, rolling her eyes. "I suppose you'll carry people all by yourself, you show-off."

"It's a little more efficient that way." Nik spoke solemnly, but his eyes crinkled with amusement.

"Oh, yeah?" U.N. said. "Well, I can carry *both* of Miknon's parents at once! So there!"

His siblings burst into laughter, and Nik pulled U.N. into a headlock long enough to rumple his hair.

"Excuse me, Sire." Gil approached and bowed his head, oddly formal for him.

Shar stopped smiling at the humans and rose to his feet. "What can I do for you, Gil?"

Beside Zak, her mother and grandmother choked. They had probably never heard a king offer help so freely before even hearing the request.

Gil clasped his hands behind his back and squared his shoulders. "My father offered a solution to one of our problems, but it requires your permission."

"Whatever you ask," Shar said.

Mother and Grandmother choked again.

Zak whispered, "So much to tell you," then held a finger to her lips.

"If you will allow him to claim a slave," Gil said, "he will accept

responsibility for that slave and spare you the trouble of an execution."
He glanced at his brother before fastening his gaze on Shar's face.

"I see." Shar looked at Gil's father, who raised his hands in a silent
plea, then studied the twice-traitor whose theft and return of the crown
had allowed them to end the battle and defeat the lords.

Gil fidgeted but remained silent. Poor Gil. Zak held her breath and
hoped for mercy for his sake and for his family, though she knew execution was the safer choice. Dead men betrayed no one.

"Very well," Shar said. "But there will be no more chances."

All the air gushed from Gil, and his shoulders sagged. "Thank you,
Sire." He turned toward his brother.

"Gil." Shar took a step forward. The werewolf turned back, and the
prince took another step, ending with his arms around his friend.
"Thank you," Shar said. "For everything."

Gil returned the embrace fiercely, then ran to his twin and dragged
him to meet their father and grandmother.

Wiping a tear from her cheek, Zak cleared her throat to get rid of
the lump choking her. A thought struck her. "Hey, Shar?"

"Hmm?" He was watching the reunion of Gil's family with a sad smile.

Poor Shar, who absolutely knew his father was dead. No chance of
an unexpected reunion for him.

"I was thinking," Zak admitted.

Shar grinned. "Am I to be surprised?"

She raised her eyebrows at his poor joke. "You can no longer keep
your promise to Miknon."

"Why not?"

She shrugged. "Because our families aren't dead after all, so you can't
charge the lords with murder."

The prince snorted. "How about treason and attempted regicide? Or
perhaps successful regicide, if we discover they influenced my father's
death."

"Oh." Zak nodded. "Yes, that would be enough."

Shar headed for the shifters with Nik. U.N. ran to collect the pixies,
and Alex hoisted Grandmother onto her back. Zak linked hands with
Gaby and leaned to lift Mother in the chair of their arms.

"Let's go home." Zak pressed her cheek against Mother's, heart bursting with joy.

EPILOGUE

OVER

As SHE WAITED to board a bus to the school, Gaby stared sadly at the statue of Vince. "It's too bad he couldn't be here," she said to U.N. "The war is over. Even the Greek fires have been dying since yesterday. Everybody is safe now."

U.N. grimaced. "He's not the only one who didn't make it, just the one we'll have the hardest time burying."

Though the younger boy was no longer wincing in the light, he still looked sick. That was fair; Gaby felt pretty sick herself. Even the arrival of the presumed dead family members didn't erase the horrors of the recent battle. She desperately wanted to wash the dried blood from under her fingernails.

"What do you say to another experiment?" Shar spoke from behind them, and they both jumped.

"What kind of experiment?" Gaby asked suspiciously.

"Gil," Shar raised his voice and waited until the werewolf reached him.

"Yes, Sire?" Gil's words were respectful, but his voice was weary.

"Please gather all the stonegazers of every variety." Despite the please, it was clearly a command.

"The — Yes, Sire." Gil hurried to the first bus in line.

U.N. hurried in the other direction, and Gaby awkwardly waited with Shar. The king's hair was slightly scorched in a ring around his head, and when he raised his hand to rub his eyes, she glimpsed the shallow wounds on his palm where he had let the crown taste his blood.

U.N. returned in a couple of minutes with the rest of his family, Zee, Nate, and Freya. "Miknon and Meg are staying with their families," he said.

A handful of fae gradually trickled in, including the tall gorgon who served as a school security guard. Gil was the last to arrive, escorting one of the animal-type fae who resembled a dragon with a rooster's head.

"This is everyone available," Gil said. "The others are too far away. Are we—?"

"Might as well try, don't you think?" Shar asked. "Since we have the crown now."

"Yes, Sire!" Gil directed the fae to circle around Vince, with everyone touching the statue.

Tentative hope rose in Gaby. Could they actually restore Vince? From the way they had talked, she assumed there was no cure at all. She interlocked her fingers and prayed, holding her breath.

Donning the crown again, Shar took a place in the circle. "Vettias," he commanded, voice echoing, "the war is over. Come back to us."

Nothing happened. Gaby ran out of air and gasped for more.

Freya groaned. "If you want me to zap you again, it will have to wait until tomorrow. I'm out of power."

"No, no, no," Gil muttered. He grabbed Alex and shoved her next to the statue. "Put your hands on Vince."

"Why?" Alex asked. "I have no magic."

"Just do it!" Gil grabbed her hand and pressed it against Vince.

"Vettias," Shar bellowed, "Come back."

"Come back, Vince," Gaby begged, and the others watching echoed her. "Come back."

And still nothing happened. Tears burned Gaby's eyes, and she bit her lip to hold them back. Vince had made a brave choice, knowing what would happen. He deserved to be faced with equal bravery.

Gil sighed deeply and let go of Alex. "I guess it won't work. Sorry, Vince. Thanks for trying, Shar."

The fae bowed to their prince and returned to their assigned buses. Alex shook out her arms, then pulled Gil into a hug.

"I'm sorry," she said. "I wish it had worked." She let go of Gil and kicked the statue lightly. "You should have listened, Vince. We'll miss you."

She slung one arm over Gil's shoulder and reached her other hand toward U.N. "Come on, brothers, let's go home."

They turned toward the buses, but Gaby kept watching Shar. The prince of the fae looked much younger than his eighteen-years-minus-a-day as he removed his crown and stuffed it into the back of his waistband. His shoulders slumped, and his lips quivered. He rubbed his hands across his face and turned away from the statue. Gaby quickly headed for the bus, catching up with Freya within a few steps.

From behind them came a groan. Should she try to comfort Shar, or leave him alone? Gaby cast a glance over her shoulder, but the prince had turned his back to the bus. Fists on his hips, he was looking up. Gaby followed his gaze upward and froze.

The statue was cracking.

"Gil," she croaked. "Zee."

"What—" Zee said, then she gasped. "Gil!" she shouted. "Gil, come here!"

Zee crowded next to Gaby, and more warm bodies piled behind her. Half the face fell off the statue, and where the stone had been, something moved.

Gil cackled with delight and shoved past Gaby. He threw his arms around Shar and swung him in a circle, then dropped him on his feet and kept running. At the statue, he pounded on the stone, which cracked like an eggshell. One stone foot twitched, shed rocky dandruff, and stepped forward.

"Oh, crap," Alex said in Gaby's ear before her tall presence disappeared.

Gaby couldn't stop watching the transformation as Vince turned back into flesh. It wasn't until the stone tunic crumbled that she caught up to what Alex had realized. Blushing, she jerked around to face the other way, pulling Freya and Zee with her.

Alex was already running back from the bus, an unfolded blanket held in front of her face. She hurried past Gaby, then rejoined the girls a moment later.

Gaby fanned her burning cheeks. "Good thinking."

"Not my first rodeo," Alex said, "though usually the problem is the shifters."

Dancing impatiently, they waited until Gil led Vince past them, clutching the barely adequate blanket around him with nine fingers. Shar followed, a broad smile transforming him from way too handsome to absolutely stunning. Gaby blinked and followed the boys onto the bus.

As they took their seats, Gil leaned forward and wiggled his eyebrows at Alex. "Ha, ha, it took your touch to bring back Vince. I said you were a stonegazer."

"It did not. I am not." She glared at him, hazel eyes lightening to a brilliant sage green.

He cowered in his seat, hiding his eyes behind his hands. His laugh echoed through the bus. U.N. and Nikos joined in, and Gaby covered her mouth to hide her giggles.

"Is she really?" Gaby asked Gil.

"No!" Alex said.

He shrugged. "She's not fae, but something made the difference. We'll never know."

Across the aisle, Shar whispered to Vince, and the rescued troll rumbled softly in response.

The war was ended, and relief flooded Gaby. True, there was still a lot of work to do. The lords needed to be tried and sentenced. The treaty must be finalized and signed, and all the fae needed permanent homes.

But with the war over, all those things were possible.

She sat quietly for the rest of the ride to the school, listening to the murmured voices around her. Once they arrived, exhaustion pinned her to her seat until Alex pulled her up.

The students filed wearily into the school, and the Fitches piled into their blue truck and drove away, leaving Gil and Miknon behind.

"We'll stay here with our families for tonight," Miknon explained, "and make new arrangements in the morning." She glowed a faint blue, as if she couldn't control her light.

"I'm so happy for you," Gaby said.

Miknon hugged her neck, then flew after the helper carrying her parents. Gaby and Zee staggered inside and headed for the elevator. The stairs were way too much effort right now.

"I don't even care about pajamas," Zee said wearily.

"Better shower anyway," Gaby said. "We're gross."

She wiped her filthy hands on her equally filthy jeans and immediately regretted it. The grass and dirt were bad enough, but she had helped with the injured, and red or blue or green blood all blended into a murky dried mess that screamed of pain and death.

"Ugh, yeah." Zee hit the elevator button and leaned against the wall.

"You can go first," Gaby offered. "I still have to call my parents."

Zee yawned. "Sorry, but I accept."

Gaby wrinkled her nose, wishing she could postpone the call until tomorrow. But if she didn't confess her part in the battle right away, she'd only be in more trouble when they found out.

Would they feel better if she agreed to come home now? It wasn't what she wanted, but she was no longer particularly needed at the school. Maybe Grand-mère would forgive her then. She sighed, which turned into a yawn. Someone else would have to translate for the science specialist. Her part in the fae experiment was done.

At least it would make a good story for her children someday.

Is the story really over? No!

Of course it isn't. Would I do that to you?

Then what happens next?

You can probably guess who shows up in The King of the Fae. Right? Turn the page for a sneak peek!

The King of the Fae

Being king should be easy...

The war is over. Now that Shar is officially king, the eighteen-year-old has a new council and will replace rebellious lords with ones willing to uphold his vision for the Fae. His new secretary is helping negotiate the treaty with Earth, his best inventor is trying to combine magic and human tech, and his chief linguist is working on a Fae-English dictionary to improve interspecies communication.

But reigning is a challenge.

Between high school classes, he has to complete treaty negotiations all around the world, reassure his people that they are now safe, and gather evidence to try the rebels for their crimes. If he fails, his people could lose their new home. The responsibility is crushing.

And it's about to get worse.

Heart and imagination meet in a captivating story of a young monarch who must find his way in a modern world that is nothing like his mythical origins. **The King of a Fae** *is the fifth book in the* **Return of the Fae** *series of clean YA contemporary fantasy with a dash of sci-fi & mythology, from the author of* **Unexpected Heroes**, *and is best read in order for the most enjoyment.*

Still want more? Get free stories by joining my newsletter. Every two weeks, I chat about my current writing or my life & offer book news and deals. And did I mention free stories?

Sign up at MCLeeBooks.com.

Free story #1: Spotting the Fae

Zak is considered too young to navigate the spaceship, even though he's the best among the fae.

On Earth, Gaby loves math and helping her astronomer Mama with her data.

When Mama spots a new asteroid heading toward Earth...

Everything will change.

The author of **Unexpected Heroes** *returns with a startlingly plausible blend of sci-fi, mythology, and the modern world.* **Return of the Fae** *is a clean YA contemporary fantasy series where fae from space don't match Earth's legends.*

Free Story #2: The Cat's Fortune

On another world, so long ago that truth has faded into legend, a cat and a boy seek their fortune together. You think you know the story, but do you?

Orphaned and homeless, young Aktar travels to the city of Rapata for a better life.

But it seems the rumors of gold-paved streets are false. Can he find a home and a job before he starves? Maybe with the help of a foundling kitten.

A retelling of Puss in Boots and Dick Whittington, with timeless themes of belonging, courage, and self-discovery, set on the fantasy world of Kaiatan, home of the **Unexpected Heroes**.

Please leave an honest review on any retailer or reader site. Seriously, it would really help me. :)

If you found a typo, you're welcome to report it at mcleebooks.com/report-a-typo/

Character List

Humans

Mr. Abernathy: language teacher
James Anthony: Major General
Nikolaos Antonakis: 19-year-old Greek student, semi-adopted by Fitches, "Nikos" or "Nik"
Yuri Berezin: Russian exchange student
Jinyuan Chung: Chinese-American student, "Jin"
Okoro Dambe: Nigerian refugee student
Helen Ellison (Fitch): Alex & Ian's mother
Clyde Farrell: Office of International Affairs
Alexandria Fitch: 17-year-old student, "Alex"
Ian Fitch: 14-year-old student, "U.N."
Troy Fitch: Alexandria & Ian's father
Callie Hahn: science teacher
Lt. Hays: Anthony's aide
Touji Kihara: Japanese exchange student, "Two"
Kirill Kovalenko: Ukrainian exchange student
Raquel Maxwell: Military linguist & principal

Andres Ortiz: Gaby's older twin brother, "Andy"
Armando Ortiz: Gaby's older twin brother, "Manny"
Bernardo Ortiz: Gaby's youngest brother, "Bear"
Eduardo Ortiz: Gaby's middle younger brother, "Ed"
Gabriela Ortiz: 15-year-old local student, "Gaby"
Luis Ortiz: Gaby's father
Marquez Ortiz: Gaby's next-younger brother, "Mark"
Therese Ortiz: NASA scientist & Gaby's mother
Allan Riggs: US State Dept undersecretary

Fae

Arishaka: king of the fae
Ashur: dryad, Gil's friend, "Abe"
"Freya": Zak's highborn roommate
Gil: 16-year-old wolf shifter
Izdu: gremlin, chief navigator, Zak's father, "Ike"
Kishar: fae lord, Arishaka's cousin
"Lili": gorgon security guard
Maia: wolf shifter, Gil's mother, "Meg"
Merodach: fae healer, "Miles"
Miknon: pixie, Gil's adopted sister
Nashuja: hydra, "Nate"
Nikandros: pukel, king's secretary, "Ned"
Ram: wolf shifter, Gil's twin brother, "Rafe"
Shalla: sirin, king's housekeeper, "Chantelle"
Sharrukin: 17-year-old fae prince, "Shar" or "Shaun"
Taras: naga, king's Companion (chief guard), "Tom"
Vettias: troll student, "Vince"
Wedaneus: highborn student, "Wes"
Zaidu: fae lord
Zak: 17-year-old gremlin, youngest navigator, "Zee"

Places

Ki: the intended new home of the Fae; Earth
Kunisu: the old home of the Fae
New Kunisu: the flagship of the Fae fleet

Acknowledgments

Thanks to my critique group for their usual spot-on comments: Carol Malone, Donna Gonzales, Gail Porter.

Also thank you to my fabulous alpha and beta readers: Jessica Ecklund, Lea Carter, Molly Morrison, Robin Cranney, & Virginia Cummings.

Special thanks to Jessica Ecklund for providing me with the missing link in Ian's arc.

About the Author

Marty C. Lee told stories for most of her life, but never took them seriously until her daughter asked her to write one for her. Between writing and spending time with her family, she reads, embroiders, paints-by-number, and gardens.

She has lived in five states (including Colorado), seven cities, and eleven houses so far. She knows bits of two extra languages, but some days can't even speak her native tongue fluently. She isn't any kind of athlete but does have sneaky ninja (or fairy) feet. Though not an extrovert, she does have friends besides her books. You are welcome to write to her as a new friend. :)

You can find her at MCLeeBooks.com and on Facebook and book sites.

www.ingramcontent.com/pod-product-compliance
Lightning Source LLC
Chambersburg PA
CBHW030812020726
47499CB00006B/1885